RUBBING STONES

NANCY BURKEY

ISBN: 1534989323
ISBN 13: 9781534989320
Library of Congress Control Number: 2016911159
CreateSpace Independent Publishing Platform
North Charleston, South Carolina

For Mark
Without whom this book, and my life, would not have been the same.

Chapter 1

"**First impressions. That's** what the initial psychiatric interview is about." Jane looked briefly into the eyes of each of the eight psychiatric residents. Just two weeks before, they had been mere medical students, not fully responsible for their patients' outcome—but that all changed at graduation.

She felt their eagerness, excitement, fear, resistance, self-doubt, and, *there it is*, she smiled, *there's always at least one*, cockiness. The tension of their newly realized role gets filtered through their own not yet fully examined character. Jane started to stroll back and forth in front of them again. They scribbled down notes, readjusted themselves in their seats, one cracked his neck, another his knuckles, anything to avoid the scene behind her.

"Why?" She wanted their participation, their engagement. "Bill?"

He sat in the center of the front row—a seat usually chosen to ensure being called upon.

"Your first impression begins the process of forming the diagnosis."

Jane nodded slowly. "So, one way to see my question is to think about the clinician's impression of the patient. Good. As doctors we've been taught to think about diagnosis. But why?"

"Treatments are always determined by the diagnosis, otherwise you're just covering over symptoms, like treating a fever without figuring out why it's there." He sounded confident. First-year residents arrived so influenced by their general medical training. Her job was to reshape their image of who they were in relation to their patients.

"Okay, what else?" Jane looked around the room. No one moved. "Might we need to be cognizant of the patient's first impressions of us? Could that also be important?" A young woman in the second row raised her hand. "Cathy?"

"Obviously you want the patient to like you." Cathy tapped her pen rhythmically on the arm of her chair.

"Why?"

"So they'll come back, continue in treatment."

Jane cocked her head. It was interesting how residents started with the same stereotypes of psychiatry that the rest of the world held. "I suppose that could be one goal for the first session. Any others?"

Cathy's crossed leg started to bounce. She glanced at the resident seated next to her. John, a large man with an infectious smile.

"Getting the patient to return is the primary goal if you have as many student loans as I do," John said.

Jane waited until the snickers died down. This was going to be a good group—interactive, not overly competitive. She began to stroll again in front of the class.

"So far we have diagnosis leading to treatment." Jane nodded toward to Cathy. "And the development of rapport, much like any other area of medicine. But is it the same in our field? Or is there something different in what we do?"

"Actually," Cathy said, "you can be afraid of a diagnosis. It can feel like you're being judged. It's not as clear cut as in general medicine and maybe it's a matter of opinion."

Jane watched the young woman avert her gaze. She didn't want Cathy to expose her sense of vulnerability to her fellow residents, not yet, if ever. They were colleagues, not friends.

"Very good," Jane said.

Cathy's leg stopped shaking.

Jane looked around the room. She wanted more from them. She focused on an attractive curly-haired man in his late twenties at the end of Cathy's row. He wore khaki pants, loafers, and a pin-striped shirt—casual but professional enough. He hadn't laughed at John's joke.

"Mark?" she said. "Any thoughts?"

He straightened up in his chair and looked right at Jane—focused but relaxed. "People want to know that you can be trusted."

She waited for more. None came. "That's all?"

He nodded.

"Why?" His simplicity intrigued her. Most fledgling psychiatrists got themselves in trouble by saying too much. Not this guy.

"Because they want to be able to tell someone things they can't tell anyone else, things they're ashamed of."

"So trust is the critical factor?"

"Maybe they'll like you, maybe not, but it doesn't really matter, it's irrelevant. They want to believe you can help them. They like their friends but there's limitations." He paused and took a short breath. "Patients need to know you'll handle their problems, their thoughts, their most intimate secrets carefully—with more respect than they feel for themselves."

The group sat silent. Jane glanced at the wall behind her. It was a soundproof one-way glass mirror. They were facing what looked like any other psychiatric consultation room—desk, chair, sofa, nondescript art on the walls—but with one big difference. Whoever was chosen to demonstrate the first interview would be observed by all his fellow interns and critiqued by their professor.

"You've just earned the hot seat." Jane nodded toward the door.

⅄

"So, you're trying to figure out what's wrong with your marriage. Why you're so unhappy." Mark shifted in his seat and rubbed the back of his neck. It was twenty minutes into the interview and it still wasn't clear why the woman had come in for therapy. She appeared to be in her late thirties, wore simple makeup, and had light auburn shoulder-length hair. She pulled at the white sleeve that was barely visible at the cuff of her well-tailored suit jacket— she made the ring of white perfectly even.

"Maybe I made the wrong choice from the beginning." She stared at the wall above Mark's head, unfocused. "Maybe I rushed things."

"It sounds like you feel he hasn't been there for you." Mark's tone was soft.

Jane cringed. So clichéd; maybe he'll recover.

The woman bit her upper lip and looked away. "You're probably right…it's just a feeling." She wiped her eye, dabbed it gently in order not to smear her eyeliner.

Mark held out the Kleenex box from his desk. The woman nodded her appreciation and took two tissues.

"I was so naïve—young, full of dreams. I just thought it would be different for us."

"You seemed pretty upset earlier," Mark said. "Is there something specific your husband's done? It might be hard to say, but you'll feel better if you can get it out."

Jane saw Mark sneak a glance over at the clock on the desk. His time was almost up. *Be patient, take it slow.*

"He's never home, Jim works all the time. Not his fault, I suppose. It takes a lot to support a family these days. I just thought he'd have made partner by now." She looked down at her lap. "I'm afraid he might not have what it takes."

"So if your husband didn't work so much, maybe gave up his dream to be a partner and was around more?"

"*His* dream?" John whispered to Cathy, but loud enough for the class to hear. "Take a look at those designer boots."

"We couldn't afford that. The private schools alone cost a fortune in this town. And I'm not really in a position to work myself." She looked up at Mark and smiled. "I used to be in nursing, but I've been away too long. Things change quickly and if I tried to brush up, well…" She let out a big sigh. "I wouldn't be around for the kids—soccer, volleyball, gymnastics, you name it. It might sound silly, but while they're in school I'm taking a class at the Culinary Institute, you know, in case he does go further."

"That must be interesting. And your husband…" He looked down at his notepad. "Jim, he doesn't appreciate you?"

The woman's face stiffened. "He doesn't seem to notice me."

"And that's a change?"

She nodded slowly.

"Do you have any thoughts about why?"

She shifted in her chair and adjusted the hem of her skirt. "It's not like I've lost my figure—at least some of his friends seem to notice."

Mark leaned forward and uncrossed his legs. He sat in silence for a moment, then set his pad down.

Jane took a step back from the glass. *Oh, no, don't do it.*

"Does he know you're having an affair?" Mark looked at her without blinking.

Jane closed her eyes for just a moment. When she looked back, the patient was heading out the door.

"Class, we'll take a ten-minute break and meet back here to discuss the interview."

⅄

Steve Jackson, the newest member of the faculty, held the door to the staff lounge for Jane. She walked slowly over to the coffee pot, lost in thought. How was she going to approach Mark's debacle? When a coffee mug was waved in front of her, she flinched.

"I'm sorry, how rude of me—a bit preoccupied." She smiled and held out her hand. "I'm Jane O'Neill, welcome to California."

"Thanks," he said. He took her hand briefly before searching the station for sugar and cream. "Dr. Mtubu speaks very highly of you."

"He's quite a gifted teacher himself." Jane said, pointing to the cupboard on their right.

"He seems devoted to teaching." He filled her cup, leaving just enough room to add cream if she used it. "And very charitable."

Jane nodded, then frowned. "No, he didn't."

"I'm sorry?"

"Sam didn't hit you up for his Botswana project already, did he?"

"I'm not sure it was as forceful as hitting me up," Steve said. "But yes, he did mention an opportunity to assist in some clinic he's helping build…"

"Sam means well, even if his timing's a bit off. I hope you don't take offense, I know you've got a lot to adjust to without feeling obliged to travel even further. Can't really blame him for wanting to focus on giving back to his homeland."

"No, from the sound of it they're in real need."

"Actually, I'd love to go myself, but…" Jane shook her head and sipped her coffee.

"Why not? It's bound to be an unforgettable experience." He leaned back in his chair.

"My husband's job keeps him so busy, I can't imagine getting away for that long." She straightened the pile of department announcements sitting on the table. Why was she blaming Rick? It was really the boys—charity didn't seem to hold much panache for them these days.

"So. Go without him."

Jane glanced at the gold band on his left hand.

He fidgeted a moment with his pen, then got up for a second cup of coffee. "Just a thought. So what does your husband do that keeps him so busy?"

It was refreshing to meet someone who didn't know. "He's a state legislator."

He poured the coffee slowly into his cup. "Must be interesting."

"Why? I mean, it is, but why do you think so?"

"You know, he must be…decisive. Politicians seem to be so sure of themselves, so forthright in their positions. We psychiatrists, on the other hand, are always questioning the various nuances of any topic." Steve sat back down and swirled the spoon in his cup.

"I really don't know what Rick is like at work." Decisive? Glenn had been decisive. Glenn had been strong, charismatic, like most surgeons. It had initially been so compelling. She bit the inside of her cheek. She'd married Rick, in part, for his softness.

"No, I don't suppose you would."

She could feel him watching her.

"Personally, I like ambiguity." He blew lightly over the lip of his coffee mug. Jane glanced at her watch.

He seemed to scan the staff room, taking it all in, making it his own. He didn't come off like the kind of guy who'd been persecuted in the dog-eat-dog life common in some academic institutions. He was too smart, too good-looking, too socially astute. He'd have navigated it all just fine. She glanced over at him as she stood to leave. Their eyes met and he smiled, attempting to hold her gaze.

"I think I'm going to like it here," he said.

𝄞

They stopped talking as soon as Jane entered the room. One last resident rushed in and quickly took his seat in the back. Jane looked at each one in turn—permission to speak. The two women in front responded with a sudden need to shuffle through the papers in their bags and search for an unnecessary pen. Mark sat stiffly in his chair, braced for critical feedback.

"I guess we don't need to worry about the second appointment for her," John said. It got a few giggles. Broke the tension.

Mark stirred. "I can't believe she did that. I only wanted to say what was obvious, get it out in the open, make her feel that she could trust me."

Nobody said anything. Their silence more damning than anything they might say to him.

"So, ironically," Jane said, "Mark's goal was to be accepting and gain trust, yet the patient ends up storming out. What happened?" She pulled up a chair and sat facing them.

Cathy's leg started bouncing again. "I thought he did really well."

John laughed.

"He did," Cathy said, "before she left, I mean. He seemed to have good rapport."

"I thought your intervention was right on." It was a resident from the back. "She just couldn't stand hearing the truth. You can't be fully responsible for the outcome."

"So it was the truth that alienated her?" Jane scanned the group.

A woman at the end of the front row shrugged. "She's either having an affair or thinking of having an affair. Maybe she even wants Mark to make that okay, wants his approval. Sure puts you in a tough position."

"But I don't care if she has an affair," Mark said. "I didn't *disapprove* of her having an affair."

The residents broke out in a general murmur.

"What?" Mark looked at Cathy. She held her hand over her mouth, but her bouncing shoulders gave her away.

John turned to the back wall. "Can we see that in instant replay?"

Jane spoke softly, directly to Mark. "Obviously the class thinks differently."

The young woman to his right shifted in her seat. "You sounded like you were interrogating her, whether you meant it that way or not."

"I was just trying to say it out loud—so she'd know it didn't have to be a secret, that I could handle it."

"Yeah, well, it sounded more like you were accusing her of something. I would have felt like scum if you'd said it to me that way."

Jane stood and walked over to Mark. "Tell me, why do *you* think the patient walked out when she did? Things seemed to be going well enough, then suddenly she's out of there. What do you think happened?"

He looked down at the floor. "Maybe I do have issues with infidelity. See, in my family—"

"Good point. We all bring our own histories into the room, and sometimes they get intertwined with the work in ways that sneak up on us. We think we've worked it all out, that it's behind us, then suddenly it's there, exposed. That's part of what the next four years will be about, and it's good we get to see an example of this risk early in the training. Believe me, it'll continue to come up."

"Yeah, maybe good for us, but not so good for her."

Cathy sat up straight again. "So if you'd just said it softer, not judgmental—"

"Possibly." Jane walked across the front row. "It's likely that she was already critical of herself—changing his tone might not have changed the outcome."

"She'd have felt accused, either way," the woman to Mark's right said quietly, almost to herself.

"Why?" Mark looked over at the resident. But she seemed lost in thought. He turned back to face Jane. "How?"

"We have to assume there was a breakdown, an empathic failure. She bolted because of something you did, however inadvertent and well-intended."

"But I had empathy for her. She seemed quite sweet, was being ignored at home. And however I might feel personally about what she's doing, it makes sense."

"To you." Jane smiled at Mark. "You were empathic to her story, but not her affect—not her self-hate."

"How?"

"You named something too early, it was too raw. You frightened her by exposing her before she was ready to reveal herself, in her way, at her pace—that's how she experienced you as untrustworthy. She—"

Three sharp raps at the door were followed immediately by Teresa sticking her head in.

"Dr. O'Neill? May I see you a moment?"

It was highly unusual for the clinic administrator to come to the interview room. Jane looked at her watch before stepping out.

"What's up?"

"Rick just called the front desk. He needs you to call him back right now."

Jane glanced down at her cell clipped to her pants pocket, it was on silent mode. "Thanks, I'll call him when we dismiss, just another ten minutes."

"He said it was urgent. He said the boys were in an accident, they're okay, or at least not hurt badly."

Jane turned to face her students, one hand on the door handle. "Class dismissed, see you all Thursday."

She flipped open her cell before flying down the stairwell to the underground garage.

Chapter 2

The bus jolted from side to side along the dirt road, stopping at regular intervals to let off a few schoolchildren at a time. The kids jumped down and ran from the vehicle as fast as they could to avoid the clouds of dust that would coat their blue and white uniforms if they walked at their usual dawdling pace. The rains had been particularly hard on the roads this year, providing months of work for local young men during the dry season.

Katura looked out the window at the deep potholes and smiled. Tafadzwa wouldn't be among the road workers this year. He'd finally gotten away. Other girls must have been thinking the same thing.

"So, when will your brother be back?" The voice came from several rows behind her.

Katura didn't turn around. She insisted on being addressed directly.

"Katura?" Direct, also loud and demanding.

She turned slowly to confront the girl three years her senior. Massassi was hands down the most beautiful girl in Rakops, and she knew it. Beauty commanded power.

"Which brother?" Katura asked.

"Don't do this," the girl sitting directly behind her whispered.

Massassi puffed out her cheeks and let out the air slowly. She stared at Katura, waiting.

Katura just stared back.

"Ta-fad-zwa," Massassi said.

"Oh, I thought you'd know," Katura said. "He'll be back whenever the apprenticeship is over, probably six months, maybe a year, maybe two, depends on how he does."

"Six months, then." Massassi turned back to the group of older girls sitting near her. "He could've gone straight to Chobe, could've made a lot of money there, but wanted the best training first. I'd have been scared, but…" She put her hands together to imitate the mouth of a crocodile, the Shona symbol of virility.

The other girls giggled.

"Don't let them get to you." Kagiso said. She was Katura's closest friend and they had sat together on the bus since they started school nine years ago. She tugged on Katura's long black braid. "They're just stupid."

Katura pulled her hair out of Kagiso's hand.

"Tafadzwa this, Tafadzwa that, everything is about Tafadzwa. Japera and I are nothing around here except Tafadzwa's younger brother and sister."

"Not to me, not to anyone who has a brain."

"Tafadzwa couldn't have worked in Chobe." Katura lowered her voice. "He didn't have the grades, he had to get trained back in Zimbabwe. Good looks and charm don't get you everything."

Kagiso glanced up at Massassi, who was walking down the aisle as the bus slowed for another stop.

"Not everything, but…some things."

Katura laughed louder than she meant to. Massassi turned around to glare at her before stepping off the bus.

Katura put her hands over her face, suppressing more laughter. She turned to her friend and gave her a big hug.

"What would I do around here without you?"

"Get yourself in a lot of trouble, that's what. You know, girl, one day you're going to be on your own and you'll have to watch that smart mouth of yours."

Katura sat back and crossed her arms. "Don't desert me now, you made a promise. We're going to university together, remember?"

Kagiso looked down briefly at her bag of books. "Has Japera heard anything yet?"

"Not yet. Any day now. He's got to get in. It means everything to him." Katura stood in the aisle for her stop. "I'll let you know if we hear. See you tomorrow."

⚤

Katura kept glancing over her shoulder. She was hoping Japera would come riding up on his bike and walk the final half-mile to their thatched house. It was the time of day she enjoyed most, a few moments of private talk with her older brother before they both got hit by questions from their parents about school, homework, and chores. She startled when she heard something come up quickly behind her.

"Oh, it's just you." She leaned down to beckon the skinny brown neighborhood dog closer. The dog inched in, but just as she was about to pat its head, it backed away. She laughed.

"Every day the same. Come on, we'll sit under the tree together." Katura continued her walk with the mutt trotting along a few yards behind. She looked back at him. "So, what do you think happened to Japera? Did he dump us for his friends today? You know boys. Can't trust 'em."

The dog trotted up closer to her on the familiar route and began wagging its tail. They rounded the bend and cut across her family's property to a large sprawling acacia where she dropped her book bag and plopped down in the shade. The dog circled and lay just near enough to be petted. She complied, then took out her history book and began reading. She had almost completed the assigned chapter when Japera surprised her from behind.

"Looks like you already have company." He laid his bike down and stretched out on the grass.

"Brownie here figured you were too busy for little sisters, so he volunteered to take your place." She reached over to pat the dog's matted fur. He wiggled in a little closer.

"Brownie, huh? Such a plain name for such a distinguished canine."

"He wouldn't want to seem arrogant." She crinkled her nose and stuck it into the air.

"No, not in this town." Japera's eyes scanned their house, down the street and back toward the strip that served as the town center. He let out a sigh.

Katura sat straight up and studied her brother. "Have you heard from the university?"

"Why do you ask like that?" His face gave away nothing.

"You have!" Her raised voice had the dog's ears at attention.

"Are you sure?" Japera's voice was calm. "What's your evidence?"

She sat back. "It's obvious. Every other time I've asked, you say something kind of superstitious. Like if I ask again, I'll jinx it. But today you focused on the *way* I asked—subtle, but a shift all the same."

"Very good," Japera said. His face was relaxed, but his steel-gray eyes looked intently into hers.

"Well?" she said.

"Well, what?"

"All I know is that you've heard, not what you've heard."

"Really?"

Katura jumped on her brother's long, stretched-out body and pinned his hands to the ground. She then quickly brought his left arm down to his side and wedged it under her knee as she sat on top of him, her right arm now free to do her search.

"I know the answer," she said.

He raised one eyebrow.

"You're letting me do this." He laughed as she searched each of his pockets until she withdrew a long white envelope, rolled off him, and jumped to her feet. "But I still have to see it."

He sat up and brushed the dry yellow grass off his clothes. "You still missed a clue."

"What?" She slid a letter from the envelope.

"I was late. Obviously, I went to the post office."

"Agh, I always get so close, but…" She froze. "Oh, my God." She looked up from the paper. Tears began to form in her eyes. "You're in, you're really in!" She jumped on him again, this time hugging him tightly. "I can't believe it! This is incredible!"

"Don't act so surprised. In my moment of glory I could get offended." He pulled her off him and they both laughed, staring at the paper in her hands.

"Thuto Ke Thebe," she said. "Education is a Shield."

Japera drew back, his eyes narrowed.

"It's the university's motto. See, below the emblem?" She pointed to the upper right corner of the paper.

His eyes narrowed to see the small writing. He then glanced at his sister as the corner of his mouth twitched approval. They sat quietly for several minutes.

Suddenly Katura jumped to her feet. "Come on, let's go tell Mom."

Japera smiled and grabbed his sister's arm, pulling her back down to the ground beside him. She didn't resist.

"Not so fast. We need to wait."

"For what?"

"For Dad."

"Okay." She folded up the acceptance letter and handed it back to him. "But as soon as he comes, I'm running in with you. I have to see their faces."

"No, we're not running in as soon as he gets home."

Katura sighed heavily.

"We'll let him put down his things, greet Mom and relax."

"They'll wonder where we are." Her voice was pleading, but she felt herself giving up. When he had a plan, she knew he wouldn't be swayed.

"They'll know exactly where we are," Japera said. "We're where we always are—under this acacia, talking and doing homework. They'll call us to dinner and we'll come, just like usual. Then they'll—"

"They'll ask us how our day was and you'll tell them the news and it'll be *so* exciting!"

He laughed. "No, they'll first ask you. He always asks you first. And you'll tell him."

"I can't." Katura was shaking her head. "No way, I'll squirm too much, I'll give it away and ruin it. You can't ask me to pretend like this."

"You'll do fine. And when they ask me, I'll pull out the letter and—"

"They'll both start crying. You know they will, Japera. It'll be great."

He shrugged. "Mom'll start crying. Dad will get a serious look on his face. He'll take out his glasses slowly." Japera pretended to put on reading glasses and cleared his throat. He spoke with a deep voice. "What exactly does it say here, let me see. Hmmm, well done, boy, well done." Japera slipped his imaginary spectacles back into his pocket. "Then he'll set down the letter and quietly tell mother to get dinner on the table in his usual contained and understated manner." He looked at his sister's pouting face and smiled. "They'll both cry when it's you."

"That's not true. They'll both cry, only Dad'll try to hide it."
She turned away from Japera and scratched Brownie's neck again.
She spoke softly. "We'll all cry."

⅄

Katura finished her history homework and grabbed the algebra book out of her bag. Maybe that would make time go faster. Numbers tended to hold her concentration. She glanced over at her brother, who lay on his back a few feet away from her with his eyes closed. His arms were folded over his chest and she watched the slow, deep rhythm of his breathing. She found his calm demeanor both enviable and frustrating. Tafadzwa would have made sure that everyone in their small town knew of his good news. He'd have puffed out his chest and bathed in the applause. How could their father, who was so humble himself, not find Tafadzwa's behavior distasteful? But somehow he didn't. He'd smile and watch with pride as his eldest paraded his latest accomplishment. She opened her math book and took out a few sheets of lined paper and a pencil.

"I hope I'm not like Tafadzwa." She spoke softly enough to be heard only if Japera was awake, but not loud enough to wake him. He opened one eye and turned his head slightly to put Katura into view.

"Tafadzwa's not so bad," he said.

"Oh, he's such a showoff and you know it." She put her name at the top of her paper, then added the date and page number of the assignment before setting down her pencil. "I'd rather be like you—thoughtful and modest."

"And boring. Without Tafadzwa we would've never taken our noses out of the books."

"That's not true. Anyway, he just used us as toys when his friends weren't around."

"Katura, who taught you to play futbol? Who worked with you on your skills until you made the club team? Who got us to dive head-first into the river off the north cliff before any of the other kids had ever tried? He even let us show them before he took his own turn."

She laughed. "I thought Mom was going to kill him."

Japera nodded, his eyes still closed. "You miss him, don't you?"

Katura lay back. He'd been gone longer than she expected. The house was quiet now. She looked at the large field in front of their porch. It seemed so empty since Tafadzwa left. Suddenly she turned toward her brother.

"Now that he's gone, I'm the one causing all the noise, getting into trouble. Sometimes I think there's just too much of me. I should be more like you than him."

It was several minutes before he spoke, eyes closed. "There's more ways to be than like me or Tafadzwa. You're a third way."

She knew that was all Japera would say about it, but that was enough. She returned to her homework, scribbling quickly across the page, and was halfway down the second sheet when she heard a car approach down the dirt road. She froze.

"It's Dad. Oh, no—I forgot our plan." She squeezed her eyes tightly closed. "No, I remember, I can do it, I—"

Her rapid-fire speech stopped abruptly when Japera sat up and touched her leg, a signal to be quiet. The high-pitched engine sound—not the low growl of her father's jeep—was moving slowly toward them with intermittent explosions of backfire. Their aunt's dark green sedan rounded the corner of their property, pulled up to the house, and stopped.

"Why's Aunt Maiba here?" Katura glared at Japera. "Did you tell her before me?" But Japera just stared at the car as the front door opened. "Oh, no," she said under her breath, "there wasn't time, you couldn't have."

"Shhh," Japera said. They sat far enough away that they wouldn't necessarily be seen, but voices traveled easily in the dry plain.

Katura watched her aunt get out of the car—slowly, probably painfully, because of her arthritis. Her face looked troubled. The screen door opened and Katura's mother come out onto the porch, drying her hands on her kitchen apron. She rushed to assist her husband's sister up the stairs, which had no handrails. For the first time Katura wondered if, given her father's usual attention to detail, this was really the oversight she'd assumed it to be but rather a purposeful deterrent. She turned to ask Japera, but he held his index finger to his lips. Then she heard the slam of the passenger side door. Japera's eyes squinted.

"Why's Thabani here?" Katura whispered. "I thought he was with Tafadzwa in Vic Falls."

Japera just shook his head and watched their older cousin ascend the stairs to join the women on the porch. Within seconds their mother had retreated into the house leaving the two guests on the porch in bamboo rocking chairs, moving to separate rhythms.

"It's okay," Katura said. "She's gone to make tea."

"It's not okay."

"She always makes tea." Katura was pleading with him.

"It's too quick." His low voice was slow and steady. "If it were okay, they'd sit and talk for awhile. They'd ask about each other's kids. Then she'd offer tea. Aunt Maiba would refuse, Mom would insist and go make it anyway." He took in a deep breath. "She's upset."

Katura could feel her blood rushing to her muscles. Run. Find out what this is about. Get answers. But her body was motionless, frozen, looking on with Japera.

Aunt Maiba sat silent, fumbling with the ribbon on the front bodice of her flowered pastel dress. Thabani rocked next to her with his head swung back as if examining the boards of the overhanging roof. His foot was tapping the porch in a violent cadence.

When she heard the whistle of the teapot, Katura felt relieved. At least something was going to happen. Even the mundane would be a change. But before her mother returned to the porch, they heard the sound of their father's jeep approaching. It made a great deal of noise as it bumped down the road —they used to tease their father about trying to find every pothole with his tires, just to make sure they were all still there.

The jeep slowed uncharacteristically when it rounded the corner to face the house. Their father pulled up next to his sister's car and sat with the engine idling a moment longer than necessary. Out of the back seat he pulled his briefcase stuffed with students' papers to grade and came up the stairs. Without a word, he passed his relatives and headed straight for the front door. He held it open, waiting for his sister and her son to enter his home. Whatever their business, it was not a conversation to be witnessed by the neighbors. Katura and Japera sat in silence. With nothing more to observe, she began to pack up her books and papers.

It started as a low wail, almost inaudible, then got really loud. When Katura recognized it as her mother's tortured cry, she dropped her bag and sprinted for the house as fast as she'd ever run. She could feel Japera right behind her on this path that seemed to take forever. They jumped in unison, skipping all the steps, onto the porch and into the living room. Their mother sat hunched with her hands covering her face, sobbing. Their father was standing by the rear window, looking out. Aunt Maiba watched him stiffly—a cold, defensive gaze. Thabani rubbed the arms of the couch. He kept looking up at Katura's father, then down at the floor, then back. Katura ran to her mother and stood awkwardly behind her, stroking her hair and waiting to be told what had happened.

Her father turned to face Thabani. If they were both standing, Thabani would have towered over her father's small frame, but the young man knew better than to face his elder directly. Thabani sat, head bowed, eyes intently focused on his uncle.

"I thought you were working for River Expeditions."

Thabani hesitated only a moment. "I was, sir."

"Was, meaning past tense, meaning not now." Her father left the window and paced in front of Thabani. "Did your employment end before I sent him to you?" His question was to Thabani, but he was looking at Aunt Maiba.

"She didn't know, Uncle Moyo. My mother didn't know."

Moyo stared at his sister.

Aunt Maiba dropped her gaze.

"She knew." Her father turned back to Thabani. "Now let's start telling the truth. My son is in police custody and I want some answers."

"Uncle, I told him to stay at the house, but he wouldn't listen to me. He doesn't understand the ways of Zimbabwe, but you can't tell him anything."

"You left him alone?"

"I had to find work, the tourist business is…" Thabani looked around the room as he struggled to find a word, avoiding his mother's eyes. "Complicated."

"Complicated?" her father yelled. "*Complicated?*" His eyes were wide and his hands were shaking. "Nephew, I am an educated man, tell me your complicated story and I will try very hard to follow along."

"I didn't mean—"

Aunt Maiba tried to rise, but her arthritis sent her back down into her chair. "My son is a good boy, Moyo. We are all suffering today, not just you."

Katura's mother let out a whimper, then caught herself. She reached over and patted Aunt Maiba's frail arm. Moyo turned away from the women, sat on a stool across from Thabani, and rubbed his forehead with both hands.

"Where did you see him last?"

"He was at the house. I had to go meet with an operator and told him I'd be right back, I'd only be an hour or two. But then some guys showed up. They knew Tafadzwa from before and wanted him to go to the rally. I told him not to go, but I had to leave. They were all still there when I left."

"How did they know Tafadzwa? He was a child when we left."

"He was ten, uncle. He used to brag that he still had friends back home."

Moyo stiffened. He rose and started to pace again.

"I mean in Zimbabwe," Thabani said. "He told us he still had friends there."

Katura watched her father closely. Thabani had misread him. His agitation was due to the reference to Tafadzwa's boastful character. Moyo breathed slowly. His anger could easily get him off track.

"Who were these...friends?"

"Mothudi, Kopano, Zuka..." Thabani paused, then said, "I don't know the others, there were two others that day."

Moyo turned to his wife. "You know these names, Lerato? Are they MDC?"

Katura blinked at the reference and glanced at Japera, who kept his eyes locked on their father. She tried to get her brother's attention but could see that she was being intentionally ignored. As the only Masaku born in Botswana, Katura had always been interested in her family's home country. But discussions of politics were avoided in her household and any mention of Zimbabwe's opposition party, the Movement for Democratic Change, resulted in an impenetrable silence from her father. This state of affairs was a chronic frustration to her. It didn't seem right that her knowledge came from her school studies and not from her family, who had first-hand experience.

"They were children when we left, they had no political affiliation." Lerato paused, then looked at Thabani. "Was it Zuka Sibanda?"

"Yes," Thabani said. "He's the one who was also taken, the others were released."

"You know this boy?" Moyo asked.

Lerato nodded. "He and Tafadzwa were friends when they were little." She looked down. "His father was a teacher too."

Katura's face lit up. "You know him, father? A fellow teacher?"

"No," he spoke slowly, still watching his wife. "I don't remember the name. What is it, Lerato?"

She was still staring at the floor when she spoke. "He was dismissed for refusing to join Mugabe's ZANU party."

They sat in silence, taking in the implications. Finally, Moyo said, "You went to the police?"

"Of course," Thabani said. "They wouldn't tell me a thing. They said I had to prove I was family—the names, you know. They wouldn't believe we were cousins. They just looked at the papers and said I didn't qualify to know anything. They said if I kept asking I'd be arrested too."

"So, you've come to get me?"

Thabani nodded. "No one would help me. Not even the MDC. They don't have him listed."

"Of course they don't have him listed!" Moyo was shouting again. "He's not—"

"I'll go, father." Japera stood. Moyo swung around and stared at him as if recognizing him for the first time. Japera stared back, unblinking. He stood with his legs spread apart and hands behind his back. He reminded Katura of a soldier taking orders from a general. She always thought of him as handsome and strong—not the kind of muscular build or classic face of Tafadzwa, something more interesting, more solid, but less respected by their father.

"No." Katura sprang to her feet. "Not now, you can't leave now when you're going—" Japera shook his head to silence her.

She stopped. She felt a tear roll down her face.

Moyo looked back and forth between his son and his wife. Lerato's head was in her hands and her eyes were closed. She was shaking.

"I'll bring Tafadzwa back, mother." Japera turned to Katura. "We'll both be back soon enough." Not waiting for a reply, he faced Thabani. "Let's go."

CHAPTER 3

Jane stared at the LCD screen of her cell phone. Five missed calls. Three from Jake, two from Rick. Jake? Urgent? Not hurt *badly*?

She hit the speed dial to Jake's cell phone as she headed down the row of parked cars. She hung up when his outgoing voice mail message picked up. Maybe he didn't have it with him—he was always leaving his phone somewhere. Or maybe he'd just laid it down and got to it just as it transferred to voice mail. She tried again. Still no answer. She climbed into her Acura and hit Rick's number.

"I'm sorry I had to have Teresa interrupt you," he said. "Where are you?"

She could hear noise in the background but couldn't place it. "Rick, what's going on? Are the kids okay?"

"They'll be fine. But you need to meet me at the police station. How soon can you get here?"

"The police station?"

"It's a long story—"

"Are they okay?"

"Michael's not hurt. Jake's pretty scraped up, nothing major, but I think it happened before the accident."

"What accident?" Jane started the car and backed out quickly. Her hands were shaking at the wheel. "Are you okay?"

Rick paused for a moment, then spoke softly. "I wasn't in the accident. Michael was driving."

"Michael? But he doesn't have his—"

"Michael ended up in a ditch with the Mustang—he must have found my keys in the drawer—Jake was in the back seat." He now raised his voice but she noted that the reception had been perfectly clear. The volume must not be for her benefit. "I don't think he was really running from the cops, just got startled by their lights and swerved off the road."

She took a deep breath and tried to gather her thoughts. Michael had been sneaking out a lot lately, probably more times than she knew. But to take the car and bring Jake along for whatever he was doing? She sped through a yellow light just as it was about to turn.

"Anyone else in the car?"

"Dylan, of course, and some other boy that I don't know."

"Not—"

"No, Caitlin wasn't in the car." He had lowered his voice again. "But, you know..."

She waited. Nothing. He must suspect her involvement but couldn't talk freely.

"Did anyone call Glenn?" she asked.

"Unfortunately, we can't leave him out of this one. The police call both parents."

She glanced over her left shoulder and merged onto the freeway. "I need to figure out what I want to do before he enters the scene and complicates things."

"You've probably got twenty minutes."

She pulled into the left lane. "I'll be there in fifteen."

"Drive safe. It's going to be a long night."

$$\curlywedge$$

When she turned in to the police parking lot, Jane quickly scanned for Glenn's SUV. She breathed a sigh of relief and hurried into the lobby.

"Jane, I'm so glad you're here." It was Amy Johansen at the front counter. She was talking with Rick and an officer but waved for Jane to join them. "This is Michael's mother, Dr. Jane O'Neill."

Jane cringed. She knew Amy had referenced her profession deliberately, but she didn't like other people playing cards for her. The officer glanced at her and returned to the paperwork he was filling out.

"So, Mrs. Johansen." He didn't look up. "You need to sign here to take your son. Since he's a minor, you'll be notified when he's to appear in juvenile court."

"But Dylan was just a passenger, right? It shouldn't be too bad for him."

"The beer complicates things, ma'am. I'm not sure how the judge—"

"Beer?" Jane looked at Rick. "They had beer? How'd they get that?"

Just then, the doors swung wide open and a large, muscular man wearing a sports coat that was years away from having fit him comfortably entered the lobby. He stood just inside the entrance and scanned the occupants before sauntering in slowly with a wide-based gait, his short arms swinging in tandem as he walked. Directly behind him came a middle-aged woman in high heels and a short red skirt. Amy nodded at the two of them and rolled her eyes.

"Who are *they*?" Jane whispered. Before Amy could respond, the man reached the counter just a few feet away. He rested his elbow halfway across the ledge.

"Where you got my Joey…sir?" He winked at his wife with the last word.

The woman elbowed him, mouthing "Don't." She watched the officer out of the corner of her eye as she took her husband's arm and nuzzled up next to him. When the officer looked over, she smiled.

"Tony, what a surprise," he said. He laughed to himself, then focused again on his paperwork.

"Look, Hank, I don't want no trouble from you—just here to get my boy, that's all. He done nothing wrong and you know it. Now let me sign your papers and take 'im."

"That's right, I forgot. You're very familiar with how things work around here."

"That's got nothing to do with nothing. Now let me see my boy." Tony's voice was loud, and his body started swaying back and forth.

"Actually, Tony, looks like your boy didn't do most of the damage this time, at least not directly. That kid's face was smashed up by one of the other boys."

Jane thought she saw a look of disappointment cross the man's face. Then it suddenly struck her. Michael in a fight? Not likely, it wasn't his style.

"But there's this little matter of the beer, now, Tony." The officer scribbled on a small piece of scratch paper until the ink showed up from his pen again. He finished filling out the form he was working on.

"Joey didn't take no beer."

"Tony, Tony." The officer shook his head. He got up and walked into the back room but returned immediately with more forms in his hand. He set them down at his desk and continued to write. "You're slipping. You must've forgot to tell this one about the cameras at the grocery stores?" He stood, placed another paper in front of Amy, and showed her where to sign. He then signaled for one of the younger officers in the back room to usher her through a door at the side of the lobby.

Jane realized she wasn't going to be next. Officer Hank was enjoying his conversation with this newcomer too much to follow any order of arrival.

"So, I'm guessing you're just going to pick the boy up. Is that right, Tony?" He looked up from his paperwork with eyebrows raised high. The twitch at the side of his mouth gave away his opinion.

"You got no rights to keep 'im. I'll get my lawyer in here and close this place, you try that crap on me." Tony reached over the counter and grabbed the form Hank was just finishing. He scribbled his signature at the bottom and initialed two other places.

"Course you can take him, Tony. You'll show up in court with one of your sleazy lawyers and get the boy off because a fly walked across the camera or some such nonsense. I just thought you might want to walk out that door and let him spend a night in juvie, just to know that this kind of stuff has consequences."

Tony tore off his copy of the forms and threw them at his wife. She stuffed them in her purse.

"Excuse me, ma'am." The officer turned to face Jane. "I'm going to accompany this gentleman in myself. It's best to get his business out of the way. I'll be right back." He nodded for the younger cop to go back inside. "I got it," he said. "Me and Tony are old friends."

Rick turned to Jane as they were left alone at the counter. "I don't think I've heard of that boy. Maybe he's Dylan's friend?"

"But Michael took the car," she said slowly. "Michael was the one driving without a license, with minors and stolen alcohol in the vehicle. And someone got their face smashed."

"I know, Jane." He put his arm around her and pulled her close.

She relaxed in his arms. There was something about his style, the way she fit up against his chest that she found comforting, even in the most agitating moments.

"I know you're feeling somehow responsible, but you're not. Our only responsibility now is to be there for Michael. The law will do its thing and we need to help him through it. He's probably scared to death." He looked sideways at her with an emerging smile. He whispered, "Of course, if you say I'm soft on crime you wouldn't be the first." It was a reference to his opponent's accusation in his first run for office—a predictable attack on anyone entering politics out of the public defender's office. It hadn't worked against Rick.

She swung around and faced him directly. "What happened to your speech?"

"I said I had an emergency. They assumed it's about George, and I...didn't have time to correct them." George Kettering, Rick's long-time colleague and co-author of a recent high-profile energy bill, had been hospitalized two days before for chest pain. The papers had run the article with an old picture of the two of them racing in the lap pool at their club.

"This might be one of those times it's good you and the kids don't share a last name."

"That's not what I meant. I just want time to sort this out before I get questioned about it." He looked directly into her eyes. "I'm proud to be part of your family."

The officer emerged from the back room. "Now, you know your older son's been taken care of—" he said.

"Taken care of?" Jane asked.

He looked briefly at Rick, then back at Jane. "His father called before you got here. He decided to let the boy spend a night in Juvenile Hall after I explained the options to him. We sent him over about an hour ago. But the younger boy's real anxious to see you." He looked over his shoulder and called out, "John, bring Jake Sanders out. His mom's here to get him."

⋏

It was well after midnight before she climbed the stairs. Her legs moved slowly, as if each step had to be carefully maneuvered. Rick was already in bed, sitting up with the reading light on.

"How's his leg look?" Rick continued to thumb through the legal papers he was reviewing.

"The cops actually did a pretty good job dressing it." Jane entered the walk-in closet and kicked off her shoes. "I probably should have just left their bandage on and not put him through the misery of taking off the tape."

"He needed you to see it." Rick put his papers down and watched her undress. "He probably couldn't have slept without having his mom comment on the damages."

"I'm not sure how well he'll sleep anyway. He's pretty upset about Michael."

"He's not the only one. How are you doing?"

"I just wish I could have spoken to him, found out how all this happened."

"Jake have any answers?"

"Not really, I'm not sure how much he knows, or if he just didn't want to tell his brother's story."

"So we'll have to wait until tomorrow." Rick ran his hand over the covers next to him, smoothed the wrinkles on her side. "You know, he's basically a good kid and I'm sure…"

"I'm not sure *I* did the right thing."

"You?" He put his papers down on the nightstand and closed the folder.

"Whatever's going on with Michael, jail and the other young inmates are not going to help." Jane slipped her arms into her robe and stepped back into their bedroom. "Glenn made the decision and didn't consult me. He forced me into going along with him whether I agreed or not."

"We could have gone over to juvie ourselves and insisted they release him to us."

"Maybe."

"You worried about how Glenn would react if you undermined him?"

"For me?" She stepped into her slippers. "No, I'm used to Glenn. But Michael would then be embroiled in the conflicts between his parents and it would distract him from his own problems."

"No good choices, then."

"That's what I keep coming to."

"Jane, it's not going to kill him and maybe it'll do him some good, who knows?" He reached over and turned off the reading lamp. She could still see him through the moonlight that sent a soft glow from the east window.

"You don't believe that." She smiled at his attempt to reassure her.

"I believe it won't kill him. Coming to bed?"

"I can't sleep." She reached over and stroked his face. He'd had a long week with George's illness and now with this, it wasn't going to get better quickly. He needed his sleep.

"Can I help?" He touched her fingers.

"Nah, just need to pace a little." She kissed him gently and got up.

"If you want company, wake me up." He rolled over to his edge of the bed and pulled the covers up. She watched him a moment before leaving the room.

⋏

It was 2:00 a.m. when she reached over and shook his shoulder.

"Rick? Rick, are you awake?"

He stretched his neck and grunted.

"Rick, I had a thought."

"Beginner's luck." He smiled and turned over. He pulled her close to him by slipping his hands around her waist. "I wondered when you'd come to your senses."

She pulled back gently. "No, Rick, I'm serious."

"Me too." He still sounded groggy. "I was just dreaming about this beautiful woman waking me up and—"

Jane stared at him.

Rick let her go. He leaned up on one elbow and faced her.

"Okay, what?"

"Michael needs to be exposed to something outside his little world—something more than his too-cute, fickle girlfriend, his petty soccer rivalries, his smart aleck friends, his northern California disdain."

"Juvie should do that."

"No, I mean something bigger." She looked at Rick intently. "Something that makes him feel good about himself, gives him purpose."

"We're all looking for that. And you found the answer? I'm all ears."

"Rick, stop joking. I'm worried about him."

"Sorry." He stroked her leg. "Go ahead."

"Do you remember Sam Mtubu's project in Botswana?"

He paused, waiting for her to continue.

She didn't.

"You want to take the boys to Africa to help build a clinic?" He chuckled, then saw her expression and fell back on his pillow. "Oh, Christ, you're serious."

CHAPTER 4

They'd been driving for hours by the time Japera and Thabani reached the tar road that would take them out of Botswana. They decided to stop in Kasane for lunch, but they'd have to make it quick—they needed to cross into Zimbabwe before the border closed at 6:00 p.m. Now Katura could stretch her legs and move her ankles in circles, something she'd been aching to do but was afraid they'd notice.

Japera had parked directly in front of the roadside café in order to watch the jeep. Katura knew she had to stay low in the back so she wouldn't be seen. Unfortunately, it wasn't until they were back in the front seat that she realized how stiff her neck and shoulders were also. Too late. All she could do now was try to ignore it.

"Hey, want some water?" Thabani said, after they'd been driving for an hour in silence. "I've got a jug in the back." Out of the corner of her eye she saw his hand reach around and grab the container. She held her breath. He was within inches of her shoulder. The jeep swerved suddenly—even the main roads were pocked with potholes—and for a second his fingers brushed against her.

"Whoa!"

"Sorry, didn't see it."

"Jeez, I turn around for a minute and—look out for that one." The jeep swerved to the right, and the water container rolled against Katura's side. It was cold and wet. She sucked in her stomach, hoping it would roll back the other way. It didn't.

"Slow down, the border stop is just around that turn," Thabani said. "We'll get the water when we pull over."

Katura tried to inch away from the container—silently, by imperceptible degrees. The car was slowing to a stop; she panicked and pulled away too quickly. The heavy cylinder rolled off her body and hit the bed of the jeep with a loud thump. She saw Thabani's shoulder jerk around. She winced and squeezed her eyes shut. Suddenly she heard a loud rapping on the jeep window.

"We need to see your papers." She opened her eyes to see a flashlight shining through the tinted windows on the driver's side. Someone—her brother or cousin, she couldn't tell which—was rummaging through the glove compartment. The doors flew open, the hinges creaking under the sudden strain.

"Get out now!" a raspy voice yelled.

"I was just getting our papers," Japera said. She heard him clambering out of the jeep. "No problem here, man. Our papers are in the glove compartment. All's good."

Katura took tiny breaths. She didn't want the blanket that covered her to move enough to be noticed.

"You two stand over there." The man's voice was now muffled.

It sounded like someone was emptying things from the glove compartment onto the front seat. Very slowly, she cocked her head at an angle that tented the blanket, allowing her left eye a direct view between the bucket seats. She caught the profile of a young man and recognized the faded green collar of the Botswana border patrol uniform. He leafed through papers, handing several to someone standing behind him, throwing the rest on the floor of the jeep. He climbed out to kneel down and look under the seat. He brought out an empty soda can, looked inside, then threw it, too, on the floor. She took in a deep gulp of air when the jeep door was slammed shut—not aware until that moment that she'd been holding her breath.

Suddenly the rear hatch door swung open. There was a burst of laughter as she felt someone grab her toes. It was the young officer.

"Hey, chief, check this out. We got another one." She slid backwards as he pulled her out of the jeep. She struggled, unsuccessfully, to free her legs from his grip. The water jug and Japera's bag came tumbling out with her, crashing on the ground. "And a feisty one, at that."

The older officer glanced at Katura, grabbed the bag, and searched the contents. He threw it back into the jeep.

"I'll find out why they're hiding her," he said. "You finish searching the back."

"They didn't know I was under there." Katura finally twisted her way to freedom from the young officer's grip. She started to move toward her brother but halted when the man in charge rested his hand on his weapon.

"She can't go with us." Thabani said as she approached with her imposing escort.

Her cousin turned to her. "What were you thinking, stupid girl? You were just going to sail right through the border patrol without a problem?"

"I want to make sure you don't lose another one of my brothers," she said. Japera flinched. Had she revealed too much? But the guards didn't seem to be listening to her.

Thabani laughed and spit on the ground. "We have important work to do, girl—we don't need children getting in the way." He faced the officer. "Forget the search, we're turning back."

"Important work? Right." Katura turned to the officer. "My brother and cousin think they can go see Vic Falls without me.

It's a short school break and we don't have the time to go back. I'm going."

Japera grabbed his sister's hand and pulled her close to him. "She'll be joining us. She's always wanted to see the falls and she's right, we don't have much time." He turned to the officer in charge. "Are we free to continue on, sir?"

"Not yet," the man said. "It's their turn." The officer turned toward three young men off in the distance. They wore dark navy uniforms and proceeded together, stepping over the chain that blocked the jeep on the roadway.

"You ZANU?" asked the one who approached them first.

"We're from Botswana, just visiting." Japera smiled and handed the sergeant the papers the Botswana patrolman had just given back to him. The man stared at Japera, then yelled over to the two other policemen, who'd headed for the jeep.

"I don't think he answered my question, boys, what do you think?" The two stopped walking.

"No, sir," Japera said quickly. "We have no political affiliations in your country." In the distance to her right Katura saw the Botswana police retreat inside a nearby building.

The man stared a few moments longer. He looked down at the papers, then nodded for the other two to continue. Katura thought they looked barely older than her. They opened the hatchback, threw the contents onto the road, and started feeling around the edges of the carpet. Then one of the policemen reached to the sheath on his belt and took out a long hunting knife.

"Hey, that's my father's jeep!" Katura ran over to them. "You better not rip anything."

The officer with the knife glanced briefly at her. "Don't worry, dear, I'll make it nice and neat for your daddy." He snorted and made a long jagged cut down the middle of the trunk, then slashed the carpet horizontally.

His partner was standing next to Katura, staring at her face. "Hey, she can't be MDC, they don't make them this cute." The man with the knife lifted the carpet and felt under the frame before closing it back up and turning to look at Katura.

"I don't know, Matan, maybe she is MDC, maybe we better just take her in to make sure."

Katura glanced over at Japera, who was busy reviewing the papers with the officer in charge. He hadn't noticed she had walked over to the jeep. She could call out to him, but that would raise the stakes.

Thabani walked over. He shot her a disapproving look and stubbed out the cigarette he was holding. He extended his hand to the young cop.

"Matan? Aren't you Rudo's brother?"

The cop searched Thabani's face. "Do I know you?"

"We met once on the river. Your brother and I are colleagues, work for competing companies, but you know the river. One day competitors, the next co-workers. Great rafter, Rudo." He brought his hand, unshaken, back to his side.

"And your name is…?" The cop glanced over at his partner who had finished up and was looking their way. "Which company?"

"Oh, I'm just taking some time off to spend with my family, you know." He nodded at Katura. "Your brother busy? Getting a lot of work these days?"

The cop eyed the lineup of cars that had formed behind the jeep. Someone was honking. "He's busy enough."

"You know if he's looking for a new safety?"

"How would I know?" The sergeant had finished with Japera's paperwork and was walking briskly toward them. The young cop looked nervous. "Look, you move on now, we got a lot of cars to check."

Thabani climbed into the passenger side and called out, "Hey, tell Rudo hello for me, tell him I'll come by and see if he needs some help."

The cop nodded as he headed to the next search, then turned back abruptly. "What was your name again?" But Thabani had already closed the door, and Japera was pulling out onto the road.

⋏

Katura rode for the next hour in silence, not wanting to push anything with her cousin. It was getting dark, and Thabani stared out the car window intently, as if Japera needed his eyes to help him drive. It gave Thabani an excuse for not talking to her. He might be familiar with the roads, but she wasn't sure he was useful for much else. Maybe it wasn't fair, but she pretty much blamed him for Tafadzwa's troubles anyway.

"I left Mom a note." She finally broke the silence. "She'll understand. She'd have done the same, that's what I told her."

Japera laughed. "Mom? No, Katura. You're more like Dad, bull-headed and determined. But Mom'll still understand. She'll kill you, but she'll understand."

⋏

"I'll stay with the car, you two go in," Thabani said.

Japera had just pulled into a parking space across from the police station. Japera frowned but he said nothing.

"Don't want any more trouble happening to your dad's jeep."

"People vandalize cars right outside the police station?" Katura didn't like his lame excuses. Not that she wanted Thabani to join them. She found herself distracted by him and didn't like it. She was only half interested in why he seemed to be acting so oddly. They had their own troubles; she wasn't eager to add his to the list.

He looked at her and said, "Japera can handle the details, you can try to look sweet and innocent enough to pull for their sympathies. I know it'll be a stretch, but maybe if you kept your mouth shut—"

"Let's go, Katura." Japera left the jeep, slamming the door hard behind him.

人

The anteroom was dimly lit by the flickering overhead lights. Empty chairs, mismatched small tables, and dirty ashtrays were scattered around the periphery. They walked across the tiled floor and up to the front counter. It was enclosed behind glass with a small window to one side. A thin man who looked to be in his mid-sixties, dressed in a worn navy blue uniform, sat behind the glass at the other end of the counter. He was doing paperwork and hadn't looked up when they walked in. Japera cleared his throat loudly, twice. After waiting several minutes, he rapped on the window.

"I know you're there!" the man yelled. "I'll be with you in a minute." It was at least ten minutes before he finally put down his pen and eyed them carefully. He rolled his desk chair down the counter to where the window had been cut in the barrier and opened the latch. "Yes?"

"We're here to get our brother, sir. There's been a mistake in his arrest."

"A mistake, is there?" The man laughed. "You'd be amazed at how often that happens around here." He smiled broadly and shook his head. "So often that we have an officer here just to take care of such matters." He leaned back in the swivel chair and called over his shoulder, "Sergeant, another one for you."

Katura had been standing next to her brother but took a half-step back when the sergeant in charge came out from the back room. He was much larger than the first, might even have been the largest man she'd ever seen. The muscles on his arms seemed to bulge unnaturally, and the buttons on his shirt struggled to contain his chest.

"What's the problem?" His eyes were at half-mast and his tongue moved around his mouth, as if cleaning his teeth from his last meal.

"Our brother was accidentally arrested—"

"Accidentally?" The sergeant's mouth widened into a grin. "How does a guy get arrested accidentally?" He turned to the older cop. "Listen up, this should be good."

Japera's face had stiffened. "Sir, my brother is not a member of the MDC, but he had attended a rally—"

"Not MDC but attended an MDC rally?" the sergeant said. "Sounds like he got arrested for stupidity." He stroked his chin. "Or maybe he's a spy for ZANU and we arrested one of our own? Maybe we're the stupid ones, is that what you're saying?"

The older cop laughed, got a nod of approval from the sergeant, then returned to his paperwork.

"No, sir, he's not ZANU, either. We're from Botswana. He was just visiting here to learn to raft the river from our cousin."

"So why have we not heard from the Botswana embassy, eh?"

Katura winced. As recent immigrants, her family stood on shaky ground. Japera faltered momentarily and she stepped forward.

"We didn't want to bother you with the embassy officials, sir," she said. "Not for such a small matter. You see, our brother just went down to see what all the noise was about and was confused for MDC. An easy mistake, I'm sure. We don't want to take up any more of your time, so if we could just take our brother back to Botswana, you wouldn't have to bother with him and our mother won't have to be so worried."

The sergeant looked at Katura as if aware of her presence for the first time. He grabbed a ledger book from under the counter and flipped open the cover.

"What is your brother's name, little miss?"

"Tafadzwa, sir. Tafadzwa Masaku." She stood straight, proud to be part of the negotiation. The sergeant slammed the book shut. Katura couldn't tell who spoke first. Both cops' voices soon got very loud. The older man was yelling something about a captain he seemed to think they should know. The sergeant said Tafadzwa was not supposed to have any family around. *Not supposed to?* She couldn't quite follow either one, since they both talked at the same time. Now the older cop was pointing to a framed picture of a distinguished-looking officer on the wall behind him. She noticed that under the officer's name, which she couldn't read, there were the dates of his birth and death.

"Our brother had nothing to do with your captain," Japera said, but the two cops were listening only to each other.

Finally, the sergeant grabbed the older man's shoulder. He stopped yelling but muttered something about "the finest officer this force has ever seen," before conceding to his superior and heading into the back room.

The sergeant turned to Japera, without a trace of the agitation of just moments before. He rested his large hands against the inside counter and spoke slowly.

"Tafadzwa Masaku is not only a known member of the MDC, he killed the captain of our police force at that rally. He will pay the price." His dark brown eyes bored into Japera's. "I don't know who you are, maybe a nosy journalist trying to get information, but we know he has no family here."

"You've got the wrong guy." Despite herself, Katura began to tear up. "You know Tafadzwa has family, our cousin was here last week asking about him."

The sergeant looked down at Katura, not unkindly. "No, dear, until now there has been no one looking for this man. If anyone had even asked about him, I would know." He closed the window slowly, but reopened it immediately and looked only at

Japera. "You see, if this man had family, they too would be in danger because Captain Kagona was greatly loved by his men here. So it's a lucky thing Tafadzwa Masaku," he pronounced it slowly, distinctly, "has no family."

Japera stood speechless in front of the counter for a moment. He took one step back, and the sergeant grinned.

"But wait," the sergeant said, "maybe I'm wrong. Who did you say you were? His brother?"

Katura sucked in a deep breath and was about to speak when Japera grabbed her hand.

"No," he said softly, "not family, just inquiring about the arrest."

"What was that?" The sergeant leaned his ear toward the window.

She was sure Japera's words had been heard. He repeated them louder as he continued to move backward toward the entry, gripping Katura's hand. He turned with her at the door and they darted out of the building.

"He's lying," Katura said. The tears that had just started to form in the station were now flowing freely down both cheeks.

"Mostly." Japera stood at the top of the concrete steps that led down to the street. "But not about everything." Their jeep sat unattended on the dirt lot where Thabani had parked it. Japera looked up and down the street, but their cousin was nowhere in sight.

Katura stood her ground when her brother started down the stairs.

"Katura, weren't you listening? If you go in there again you'll be arrested. That man gave us a break, but he's not giving us a second."

"A break? He's *keeping Tafadzwa*. He's got no right!"

"Are you six years old? Do have any idea why Mom and Dad left this country? He's got no right? Katura, *we* have no rights.

No one around here has rights. And that guy was real clear that if we go in there acting like we're family, we'll never leave either."

Tears were streaming down Katura's face.

"Look, we don't even know if he's in here. They could have taken him anywhere." He stepped back up to her level and reached out his hand to wipe her face.

She jerked her head back. "He's all alone and they think he's a murderer. So you're just going to leave him? That's your plan?" She was glaring at Japera. "Because you're afraid for yourself? You even denied you were his brother."

Japera stared at her, his hand still raised in the tender gesture she had recoiled from. He lowered his arm slowly but kept his eyes locked on hers.

"You're right, Katura. I don't have a plan yet." His voice was quivering. "But I will make a plan, and if that doesn't work, I will make another, and another, and another until I get Tafadzwa out."

Katura had never seen such an expression on her brother's face.

"I'm so sorry, Japera." Her voice shook. "I don't mean to put this all on you—we'll plan together, that's why I came, in case it wasn't simple. I'll—"

She stopped when they heard a loud commotion inside the station. It sounded like a half-dozen men moving quickly toward the door. Japera grabbed her hand and they flew down the stairs, rounding the corner into a narrow alley that twisted back and forth into a labyrinth of open market stalls that seemed to stretch for miles. He darted through the crowds, jerking Katura as he changed direction abruptly. She found it almost impossible to predict his moves, but it was important to do whatever it took to not be separated. She forced herself to go somewhat limp in her upper body, to be pulled along as effortlessly as possible, keeping her legs moving at his pace.

Then finally, suddenly, he stopped. They were in an alley that branched in several directions on both sides. He headed into one of the stalls and collapsed breathless on a pile of rugs. There were large hanging tapestries shielding them from the crowds.

"We'll stay here until things settle down," he said.

The shopkeeper and his wife descended upon them. They brought over one piece after the next, discarding them in a pile when Japera showed little interest. Katura admired each selection and complimented the handiwork, but her politeness was not worth their time as it become clear they weren't buying. Eventually the owners just left them alone and sat at the other end of the stall talking to each other or greeting the occasional passerby. The couple seemed to keep the shoppers away from the corner where Katura hid with her brother. She crouched below a thick rolled carpet when a middle-aged woman begun to wander toward them. The owner called to the woman. He held up a particularly well-made, but small piece, but did not move toward her. It required the shopper to change direction.

What would she say if someone approached? If questions were asked? How could her answers not lead her and Japera back to the police station?

But perhaps they weren't the first to take refuge in this particular stall. She watched the seeming ease with which the owners managed their space and the movements of others. She was baffled. Alliances were enigmatic. Maybe the stories weren't that important to these merchants who were just trying to scrape together a life here. It fit both their needs to not draw undue attention.

After an hour, the troops of police that had marched past at regular intervals began to dwindle. Katura thanked the shopkeeper's wife as she and Japera emerged. The woman looked past her and turned away, as if she'd never seen her.

They drifted from stall to stall, feigning interest in the local trinkets or food items on display, always keeping an eye down the long aisles for any sign of the police. Occasionally they got a glimpse of the men in dark blue uniforms with semi-automatic rifles slung casually over one shoulder. Katura and Japera moved deeper into the maze of shabby booths, hiding within the throng. By nightfall the thinning crowds made their situation more precarious. They needed to venture back toward the jeep.

"Stay close," Japera said, "and let me look first around the corners."

Not being familiar with the sights and sounds of Victoria Falls, they weren't alarmed by the peculiar glow they saw as they approached the area where the jeep was parked. It wasn't until they rounded the last corner, a safe two hundred feet from the police station, that they realized the glow was a fire. It was their father's jeep that was burning.

CHAPTER 5

"Knock lightly," Japera whispered.

Katura had just raised her fist to the back door of the small, unobtrusive stucco house. She hesitated and glanced around the backyard. All was dark and silent behind her, but she could hear talking inside. She knocked once, too softly, then again just a little louder. The voices inside stopped. She looked at Japera and he nodded. She knocked again. Nothing.

Japera pounded his fist on the door. Katura watched the neighbors' houses for lights. None came on despite the late-night silence of the neighborhood. All noise seemed to echo throughout the street. She scanned the houses again and now saw the changes—figures moving across the windows, closed curtains pulled back ever so slightly. Suddenly she heard movement once again inside—someone was coming. Whoever it was stopped just on the other side of the door.

"We're looking for Mr. Sibanda, Zuka's father," Japera whispered loudly at the door. "We're Tafadzwa's brother and sister."

"I can't help you," came a muffled voice. "I don't know your brother, sorry." They heard footsteps moving away.

"Wait," yelled Japera. He pounded on the door. "We can either do this quietly or all your neighbors will hear the business we have with you. Your choice."

There were muffled voices inside the house, an argument. Five minutes later the door opened four inches. A thin man in his mid-fifties with a closely cropped beard and small, round glasses peered over their shoulders, then rushed them inside. He closed the door, fastened two deadbolts, and led them into a dark, narrow room. He motioned for them to sit down and turned on the table light next to his large recliner—too large for his small frame. He stared for several minutes at Japera, then Katura.

Japera broke the silence. "We need to understand what you know about the arrest, Mr. Sibanda." He nodded his head respectfully.

The man remained silent. He stroked his face.

"We know our brother went to a rally with your son," Japera continued. "We know they've been accused of shooting the chief of police."

Katura studied the man sitting in front of her. Her mother had said he was a teacher, yet his silence was so unlike her own father's manner.

Japera stood and paced the room. It was unlike him to raise his voice, so when he turned and spoke louder than was necessary for this small living room, she startled.

"Our brother would not kill anyone," he said.

"Of course not," the man said softly. He sat back in his chair.

"Of course not? Are you mocking us?" Katura asked. "We know our brother is not a murderer, he's not involved in politics here. The only reason he would've been at that rally is because your son took him."

The man had turned toward Katura at her outburst, his face expressionless. Now he let out a quiet laugh under his breath before he spoke.

"Of course your brother didn't kill Captain Kagona."

"You said you didn't know Tafadzwa," she said. "Why are you sure?"

"Because Captain Kagona's own men killed him."

"What?" Katura and Japera spoke in unison.

"Has your car been searched a few times since you've been in this country?"

They glanced at each other.

"As I thought," he said. "The MDC doesn't have guns, we couldn't have killed him, and they know it. So even if your brother was part of our party, even if he were stupid enough to try to take out the police chief, he wouldn't have had the means."

"But why would Kagona's own men do it?" Japera sat on the edge of the sofa.

Katura shook her head and looked to her brother.

"This doesn't make sense," she said. "At the station they made it quite clear that their chief was greatly honored."

"Everyone honors the dead, there's no risk in that," Mr. Sibanda said. "He probably was liked by some, maybe even most of his men, but he'd made enemies in Harare, and that's where it counts. The government can always find a few hungry cops who'll do whatever they want for the right price."

"But—"

"Look, young lady, Kagona had been warned. The authorities were tired of these rallies outside the Kingdom."

"The—?"

"— Kingdom Hotel—it's the most elegant place in Vic Falls—too public, too much in view of international eyes. Kagona couldn't squelch the open opposition, so they'll get someone who can." He motioned to his water glass, asking without words if Katura would like something.

"What does any of this have to do with our brother?" she said.

"Or your son?" Japera asked.

Mr. Sibanda got up and went into the kitchen. When he returned, he sat down in the same slow, methodical way their father did before he gave one of his famous, poignant speeches—one in which Katura always felt she had to hang on to every word regardless of content.

"That group of boys—except your brother, of course—was known to be from MDC families. They were taken as a message, it would have happened without the shooting. It's a cat and mouse game. The cat doesn't really want to kill the mouse, because then there'd be nothing to toy with. Those boys aren't the real threats anyway. The police want to send a message to their families, to us—show that they're the ones in power and can hurt or not hurt their loved ones. But when the killing occurred there had to be a killer, and it certainly wasn't going to be one of their own."

Japera moved over to the seat next to him and leaned forward, his hands clasped in front of him.

"What I really want to know from you," he said, "is if you can help us get our brother out. As well as your son, of course."

Mr. Sibanda removed his glasses and rubbed his eyes. "I suppose you could try to get help from Senator Nyabe. He's a good man, MDC." He nodded his head, as if in agreement with himself. "He has influence and would be sympathetic, a family man himself, and—"

"Enough!" A man in his late twenties had emerged from the back room. "Nyabe won't help them."

Katura looked back and forth between the two men. Their features were the same, but the younger man was taller, well built, and much more handsome.

"Zuka!" she said. "You're out? But what about…"

Japera got up suddenly and began pacing. He stopped at the far end of the room, then turned to address the father.

"So, you got your own son out with your connections and left my brother in to take the rap?"

"Senator Nyabe could only do so much. He was beaten after he helped with Zuka's release. Right outside of the House Chamber, for God's sake." He was looking down at his hands.

"And now he's going to risk his life for my brother?" Katura raised her voice.

"He's a good man, he might still be able to—"

"—do nothing. He's weak. Powerless." Zuka stood over his father, something that would not have been tolerated in Katura's household. "It is beyond working with this system."

"We have been over this many times." Zuka's father looked up, his eyes narrowed. "It's slow, you must be patient. Yes, for one son free, ten more remain, but I could not let you sit in there, things would have happened. Martyrs get forgotten, or worse. My friends have risked so much for you, and this is the thanks I get."

"Your friends, your powerful friends. They participate in a system that gives them no voice."

"Change is possible, Zuka. It comes one vote at a time. We must work to get more of our party in—"

"They will never have a voice." As he said it, Zuka pounded his fist on the table. "The system is corrupt. You said yourself, he was beaten outside the chamber."

Father and son glared at each other.

"My brother. I am here about Tafadzwa," Japera said. "He has no value to you as another innocent martyr. You have plenty."

"Zuka would never get anyone arrested on purpose," Mr. Sibanda said. "That is not our way." He glanced at his son, who was studying Japera.

"Maybe I can help," Zuka said. "But it will be risky."

"Whatever it takes."

Zuka laughed. "You've been away, safe. You have no idea what it might take."

"When you justify the means, you become just like them, Zuka." The old man rose and came close to his son's face. "You are no different."

Zuka kept his eyes on Japera and said nothing. Mr. Sibanda motioned for Japera to sit next to him on the couch.

"Japera, where's your father? I had thought he might come."

"Father is no longer in politics. He teaches now."

Katura sat back in her seat. No longer in politics?

"And even his own son could not bring him back?" Zuka sat motionless. "I guess he is not the man of the legend."

Katura studied the two men. Is Tafadzwa being used by these men to get to her father? She glanced at the door with deadbolts. "Japera? I think—"

"We need a plan." Japera rubbed his hands together. "Let's run through all our options."

"Every road has its dangers."

"Go on," Japera said.

Katura had to get him to look at her, to signal her alarm. "We could try another MDC legislator."

Japera faced forward, intent on Zuka.

Zuka turned slowly toward Katura, his eyes narrowed and the edges of his mouth twisted.

"What?" Katura was almost yelling. "One got *you* out."

"Katura? He's trying to help us. Please?" Japera lifted his hand for her to stop. "I'll handle this."

Zuka nodded at Japera.

Like he knows me. Like he knows I'm a pest. Katura looked back and forth between her brother and Zuka. Was she reacting to being displaced as Japera's right-hand collaborator? In the moment of Tafadzwa's crisis, maybe her concerns weren't justified, maybe she was just being selfish.

She turned to Mr. Sibanda. "Could I bother you for some water?"

He seemed more than happy to accompany her to the kitchen. Four glasses sat on the counter, and he filled them from a nearby bottle. The room was neat and clean, not cluttered with vegetables, pots, and pans like the kitchen at home, which always seemed to be messy with the preparation of the next meal. These men must not be into cooking much. She handed one of the glasses to Mr. Sibanda and took the other three back into the living room. Japera and Zuka stopped talking as she entered.

Japera smiled at her and took a glass. "So, as I was saying, if the MDC had proof that the captain's death was an inside job, they'd have already gone public to discredit the ruling party." He started pacing again. "And Tafadzwa would have been shown to be innocent."

"Which is why we need to do this differently," Zuka said.

"Your different ways are too dangerous," his father said. "I can't promise you protection any longer."

"I don't need your protection, never asked for it."

"Your mother—"

"My mother lived in your world, old man—that world is over."

Mr. Sibanda stood over his chair a moment. He made no eye contact with any of them. Before Katura could get his attention, he was gone. He slammed the door behind him.

⋏

"We need to go to The Cave," Zuka said after several moments of silence.

Japera glanced over at him, then drank down his water in one gulp.

"It's a bar, a hangout for MDC. The problem is, you're not in the party, but those guys know a lot about these things and might be able to help."

"But wouldn't showing up at an MDC hangout seal our fate?" Katura scooted herself closer to her brother. "If we were seen, we wouldn't be able to deny affiliation very convincingly."

"She's right," Zuka said. "Probably a bad idea." He reached into his pocket and pulled out a flask, raised it to Japera, then poured the honey brown liquid into his empty glass.

Japera took a sip and smiled at Zuka. He then took a large gulp before turning back to his sister.

"Face the facts, Katura." His face flushed for a moment as he took in a deep breath. "Our fate, or at least Tafadzwa's, is already sealed. What other options do we have? Let him get hanged for murder? We can at least listen to these guys."

Katura's lower lip began to quiver. She looked away from him.

"Where is this place?" Japera asked.

"There's no signs or address. And they won't let you in without a known member to vouch for you." He raised the flask to his own mouth and poured.

"Tonight?"

Zuka nodded. "I'll meet you at Thabani's around nine. He needs to go with us. We may need his skills."

Japera finished his drink and signaled Katura to follow.

CHAPTER 6

Jane winced and shielded her eyes from the sudden onslaught of the bright African sun. It contrasted sharply with the past thirty-two hours she'd spent inside stuffy airplanes and crowded terminals since leaving San Francisco International. She tried to shrug off her exhaustion by inhaling deeply—the warm air was a welcome relief to her lungs after so long in an air-conditioned environment. She scanned the landscape beyond the runway.

"Wow."

"What?" Rick ducked his head under the plane's door and came up behind her on the landing. He looked out at the scene in front of him. "Oh." He wrapped his arms around her and kissed the side of her neck lightly before looking up again at the horizon.

Together they descended the metal stairs and waited at the bottom for Michael and Jake, who'd sat further back in the plane. Rick stretched his arms up and behind his back. He tilted his head left and right. Jane smiled at the sound of the familiar vertebral pop.

"Wake me up in a week and I'll be ready for action," he said.

"No such luck. Show starts tomorrow."

After Jake's tenacious negotiation, Jane had finally given in to adding a recreational piece to the beginning of their trip. She would have preferred to dive right into their work at the clinic in Botswana, and that was her plan, until Rick had approached her one afternoon: "Isn't there some river in the area we can float down and see the wildlife for a few days first? No one goes to Africa without seeing the big game." The year before Rick had missed the family's rafting trip down the American River in northern California. He'd let his work schedule get in his way. It was a decision he regretted.

Jake walked into the living room with the world atlas and looked at his step-father. "Any luck?"

"She wasn't supposed to know it was a conspiracy." Rick had the decency to look chagrined. "Anyway, you could've given me a little more time."

Jake glanced up at his mother briefly, then flipped open the book. "Mom, remember the river Piero told us about? The one in Africa where his brother works? I found it—check it out. It's not far from Rykops."

Piero Bertolli had been their rafting guide on the American River. In his mid-twenties, Piero was strong and charismatic in the way that forces prepubescent boys into idol worship. Jake had barely left his side, following all instructions explicitly and becoming quite capable on the river for his age.

"See, Mom?" Jake pointed to the map. "It's right there." She looked over his shoulder and watched Jake's finger trace the thin blue line from Zambia to the Mozambique Channel. His excitement was palpable. "He said you enter right below Victoria Falls."

Jake looked up at Michael, who'd walked in and stood leaning against the living room wall, hands in his pockets.

"What do you think?" Jake asked.

"I don't think that's what this trip is all about, Jake."

"Oh come on, we'll do the clinic right after." He was pleading with Michael to support his case. "Remember how much fun we had on the river last summer?"

Michael shrugged.

Jake set his jaw and looked away from his brother. "Anyway, Mom, we don't *all* need to be punished."

Michael stiffened, but he didn't respond.

Rick broke the silence. "Community service isn't punishment, it's—"

"Jake's right, Mom, just me." It was the first time Michael had looked her in the eye since the incident.

Rick put his arm around Michael. "It'll feel good for us to work on it together. We all could use a little refresher course on what's important and who we really are."

Michael took in a deep breath and looked at the floor. Jane knew he was struggling with that very question, but would never admit it.

"Well, I already know who I really am." Jake put the atlas on the coffee table. "I'm the guy who likes to go river rafting." He waved them all over to take a look. "First we start with a twenty-three-kilometer ride down what is known to be the best whitewater rafting river in the world. After an overnight under the stars…" He cocked his head at his mother. "The Southern Cross, Mom, think of it. Then we head out for another four days of the most amazing rapids known to mankind—Ghost Rider, Devil's Toilet Bowl, Stairway to Heaven." He pulled a webpage ad out of the pocket of his sweatshirt. "Washing Machine, Oblivion, Asleep at the Wheel, Croc Alley—"

"Persistent little brat." Michael nodded toward his younger brother.

"Michael, I want you to know—"

Michael's cell phone rang—the familiar tone that signaled Caitlin's call. He closed his eyes and bit his upper lip. It rang a second time. When he opened his eyes Jane saw the return of same dullness that had momentarily been lifted. He grabbed the phone and flipped it open.

"Hey, what's up?" His tone decidedly casual. "Oh, not much…" He had walked into his bedroom and closed the door.

Jane starred down the hall a few minutes before returning to Jake. She bent down to follow Jake's finger run the course of the river. She glanced back toward Michael's room and drew a deep breath.

"Well, maybe for a few days before." She turned to Rick. "Do you think it's safe?"

"Mom, thousands of people have done it, it's totally safe," Jake said. "And we'll be in the neighborhood. This is a chance of a lifetime."

Rick looked down at the map, his brow furrowed. He'd obviously been primed with just the general concept, not the specifics.

"But isn't that Zimbabwe? I thought—"

"Just over the border," Jake said, "not far at all, see?" He used his thumb and index finger to measure the distance on the map. "And Piero said it was the best river in the world. I don't suppose we'll be that close again."

Rick hesitated for only a moment. "Probably not."

⋀

She now stood at the bottom of the plane's ramp and looked around. She had to admit, the additional plans were a relief. Spending time on the river would give them the break they needed after the long flight before plunging into the work in Botswana. She watched Michael and Jake exit the plane. Jake seemed oblivious to his surroundings, joking as if he'd just disembarked from a three-hour trip to Denver. Michael nodded and smiled occasionally; his mind seemed elsewhere.

The lines at immigration and customs were slow and tedious. When they finally made it to one of the booths, the boys continued ahead toward the baggage claim. Jane and Rick were delayed by an officer who took his time scanning their documents. She called for the boys to wait, but they didn't hear her.

When the officer finished stamping their papers, she and Rick hurried to catch up. The arrival gate was packed, but they could spot the familiar baseball caps bobbing fifty yards in front of them. Several planes had recently landed, making passage tight despite the relatively wide terminal halls. They proceeded slowly toward the exit in a river of people all headed in the same direction.

A thin man with wire-rimmed glasses just slightly in front and to the right of him suddenly dropped a handful of change directly at Jake's feet. Michael hadn't noticed this man before. Jake stopped abruptly for the man and watched the strange coins bounce and roll in front of him. A younger man with a goatee who'd been walking quite closely behind Jake bumped him from behind. Michael grabbed Jake and pulled him out from being sandwiched between the two men.

"Hey!" Jake jerked loose from his brother's hold.

Michael turned to face the goateed man. He could feel his hot breath on his cheek. The man immediately backed away and showed his open hands to Michael before he turned and ran down the corridor.

"Oldest trick in the book," Michael said to Jake as his mother approached. "The first guy distracts you, the second one takes your wallet."

Jake felt his back pocket, still full, and watched the men scurry around the corner. "See, Mom? TV teaches you something." He punched Michael's arm. "Thanks, bro."

"We'll get the luggage, Jane," Rick said as he caught up. "You see if you can spot our driver."

Michael grabbed the last two pieces of their luggage from the carousel—the lightest two. He looked over at his younger brother, always proving himself.

"Hey, check it out." Jake had set down a suitcase nearly as big as he was and pointed to a tall man in traditional African garb with a monkey puppet on a string. The man was bouncing the puppet like a hyperactive rat around his shoulders and head. Michael watched for a few seconds, then glanced around at the rather large crowd that was forming. He was struck by the variety of colors and textures of the clothing surrounding him, then allowed himself a look at the people themselves. He didn't want to appear to be staring at people who were different from him, didn't want to appear to be gawking.

That's when he saw her—a beautiful African girl who seemed about his age– and she was staring at *him*. She immediately glanced away when Michael's eyes met hers. He startled and turned his head away as well. After all, he'd been looking around, taking it all in, a passive audience to this new world. Now he realized that he, too, was part of the stage, more than just a walk-on, he was the one that stood out, who didn't fit. He chanced a peek back toward the girl and once again their eyes met. Again they both looked away quickly.

Michael knew she wouldn't risk another look for several minutes—the self-consciousness of looking three times would likely be too much in any culture. He took advantage of this predictable reprieve and stared right at her. She seemed to be searching for someone in the opposite direction, which allowed Michael to get a good view of her profile. She had the deepest black skin he'd ever seen. Her frame was slight but solid—she looked physically strong, like really athletic girls back home. But it was the way her hips curved, the way her long, dark hair flowed over her breasts that made him catch his breath. He imagined her to be timid, not as brash as the girls he'd grown up with. He watched her grab her hair into a ponytail, then release it to glisten down her back, moving in waves as she shifted her head in her looking-with-a-purpose maneuver. She slowly began to shift her search in Michael's general direction but above his head as if peering beyond him. He knew to turn and focus on the man with the stuffed monkey. It was only fair that he give her a turn.

The puppeteer was just about to incorporate Jake into his show by having the monkey tentatively approach the boy when they heard Rick call to them. Michael turned and saw Rick pointing toward a placard with "Wagner" written in large bold letters.

"Your guide, Lorenzo, will meet you in the morning for the first river briefing," the driver was saying to his mother as Michael approached. "The others should be coming out shortly, then we'll take off for the hotel."

The man was trying to hold a second placard above the heads of the crowd. "Jenkins" was printed boldly with the number two in parentheses. Michael looked back at the first sign that had Rick's name and was now being held down at the man's side. The number four was in parentheses.

Michael glanced at Rick, who hadn't wanted to travel with strangers, but his mother had convinced him that finances dictated taking a tour. They'd counted themselves lucky that the declining tourist trade had allowed for such a small group.

"Be right back." Rick nodded toward the money exchange booth across the hall.

"Can I wait over there?" Jake was straining to see the puppet show from where they stood, but the growing crowd made it impossible. "I was in the front row."

"Just wait with us," their mother said. "I don't want to have to go find you. Michael?"

He looked over the heads of the crowd a few moments longer. "Just let him go over there. I'll watch him." He scanned the crowd, but stopped abruptly. He looked back at Jane. It had been a long trip and she looked weary. He opened his backpack.

"Hey, Jake, that guy's not so great anyway." Michael took out a hacky sack. He held it up to Jake, nodding toward the open space a few feet away, then threw it into the air. Jake scooped it up with the inside of his right foot before it hit the ground, lifting it into the air and bouncing it on his left knee back to his brother.

Several minutes later a blond, round-faced boy several inches shorter than Jake ran toward them.

This must be a Jenkins.

The driver addressed him directly. "All that energy after nineteen hours of air flight? Lorenzo will have his hands full." The boy smiled—it was interpreted as a compliment.

Michael caught the hacky sack and glanced around for the adult who must be with this kid. His eye was caught by a young African man in a wrinkled, dull green shirt and loose-fitting khaki pants leaning against a counter across from them and looking in their direction. The man turned away when he noticed Michael and concentrated on smoking a long hand-rolled cigarette. Then he was approached by two other men. One was taller and more neatly dressed than the other two, whose attention he didn't seem to really be holding despite the large sweeping gestures he made as he talked. The third man, rocking from side to side and scanning the crowd, was much bulkier. He reminded Michael of a wrestler. The men hadn't greeted each other with the hugs taking place all around them. Michael searched the long corridor of arriving passengers. They must be waiting for someone too.

"Mr. Jenkins?" the driver said. "I'm Kito, with River Expeditions. I'll be taking you to your hotel."

A stocky American man had come up to the family and was looking the group over. He turned and faced their mom directly without saying a word. He stared right into her eyes. Did he want something? Did he think Mom was here alone? Michael glanced over at the exchange kiosk. Rick looked like he was still in the middle of his transaction.

The man's silence was annoying. His face had no expression on it.

"Jane," his mother said. She extended her hand.

The man took her wrist and held it. He continued to stare into her eyes.

Michael stuck out his own hand toward this stranger—it was more of a demand than an introduction.

"Nice to meet you. I'm Michael," he said loudly.

Before letting go of her hand, the man's eyes moved down his mother's body. Michael extended his hand closer to the man, almost touching his arm. The man finally looked at Michael, shook his hand briefly, and nodded. He didn't say his name.

"I'm Tommy," the young boy said, looking from one brother to the other.

"Jake." His brother wasn't addressing anyone in particular. He was on the tips of his toes—stretching in a hopeless attempt to see the puppet show over the heads of the crowd.

"Try working out the math of over 63,500 Zimbabwe dollars to one U.S on no sleep." Rick handed a receipt to Jane.

"This is Rick." Jane touched his arm. "My husband."

Rick barely looked up but nodded at the man and child who'd joined their family. He stuffed the wads of foreign currency in his pocket.

"You are?" Jane asked.

"Paul. Paul Jenkins."

But before the pressures of small talk could begin, the tall neatly dressed man Michael had been watching earlier approached.

"Kito. Long time no see. Another river group?" He slapped their driver on the shoulder.

"Thabani?" Kito's face froze and his eyes darted beyond the man and into the crowd. There was a steady flow of arrivals moving past. Thabani stood alone. Kito smiled and threw his arms around him. "What brings you back here? I thought you were long gone from these parts."

"Ah, the river has its draw, now, doesn't it? Can't ever really stay away long." The man motioned to the other side of the room. "I'm taking my cousin and his friend down the river."

Michael now noticed that the wrestler guy had left. The first guy still stood smoking at the distant counter.

"They're picky," Thabani said. "Wanted the best guide around for their trip."

"Too bad. Lorenzo's already booked," Kito said. Thabani laughed, and a large toothy smile spread across Kito's face. Whatever had bothered him before seemed not to be a problem anymore.

"This Lorenzo's group?" Thabani said. "He's taking them down awfully young." He nodded at Jake and Tommy.

"We've no worries." Kito took Thabani's arm and started to move him away from the others.

Michael's attention suddenly shifted. The dark-haired girl he'd been watching earlier was coming toward them. Her hands were in her jacket pockets and she walked with a determined pace, as if she were on an important mission. Michael looked away and began to fidget with his backpack straps.

Kito turned to the girl. "No, thank you," he said. He motioned for her to leave them alone.

Thabani laughed. "She's not selling anything. This is my other cousin, Katura." He looked proud as he put an arm around the beautiful young girl. "Her mother sent her down with us to make sure 'the boys' didn't get into too much trouble. So we're trying to lose her as soon as we can. Any takers?" He winked at her.

She glared at him and broke away from his hold.

"I wanted to ask you about borrowing some equipment." Thabani walked with Kito a few yards away from the group.

Michael continued to fiddle with the straps of his backpack, which fit him just fine. Katura turned to him.

"I carry rubbing stones in my pockets." She took out three small, smooth stones. He looked down at them.

"You know, to relieve the anxiety when some strange girl you've been watching comes over and starts talking to you. It works better than fooling with the straps of your backpack."

"Nailed." Michael let go of the straps.

The girl placed the small stones in the palm of his hand. He stared down at them, feigning a serious inspection. He then rolled them around each other, looked up at her, and smiled.

"Now put them in your jacket pocket so nobody will know you're using them," she said. "Roll them around slowly. All your troubles will go away. It's like you've got a secret and no one knows you're worried. You can stand there calm and cool while all your fears go into those three little rocks just rolling between your fingers. It's the power of secrets."

He placed them in the left pocket of his windbreaker and rolled them around in his hand. He feigned nonchalance as he looked around.

"Wow, they really work," he said. "But I must give them back." He held the stones out to her. "You seem to have much more to worry about than I do." He nodded toward the man at the counter, who was now watching them.

"That's my brother, Japera. Don't pay much attention to him, he's just moody. I can handle him." She closed his fingers over the stones. "You might need them, might get charged by a rhino or something out there, never know."

"And these will help? Great." He stuffed them in the pocket of his jacket. "Are you from here?" He immediately regretted the question. Maybe there were obvious differences in appearance, dress, or accent that he was naïve about and he had just revealed his provincial ignorance. It was embarrassing being new.

"No, we're from across the border." She nodded to her left. He looked out the window in the direction she had nodded.

She laughed. "It's a little further than across that street."

"I knew that," he said a bit louder than he intended. He couldn't understand why this strange girl was making him so nervous. Change the subject. "So, you're going down the river, too?"

"Maybe."

"I hear it's a pretty wild river to raft. Should be great."

"I guess."

Michael could feel himself losing her attention. This was a rafting trip of a lifetime and she seemed pretty indifferent. So maybe rafting wasn't her thing. They stood in silence and watched Jake bounce the hacky sack off various parts of his body.

"He does it to practice his skills." He might as well try again. "Thinks it'll improve his soccer game."

"Looks like it might work." She was studying Jake.

"You play soccer. What position?" Then he realized his mistake. "I'm sorry, you call it football."

"That's right," she said. "Although the game is played all over the world and known by one name, your country decided to change that name."

"We already had a game called football, we had to distinguish it."

"Of course, that's right," she said. "Isn't that the game in which the players rarely touch the ball with their feet, they mostly use their hands to throw, pass, or run with it? I certainly can see why they call it football."

He watched her face light up as she spoke—she was having an awfully good time at his expense. She reached up to toss a wandering strand of hair back over her shoulder.

"And, I'm a striker."

"Figures."

She glared at him. She really was beautiful.

They watched Jake play the hacky sack in a repetitive cir-cuit: right foot, left knee, catch, and start over. Kito and Thabani moved back toward the group.

"The other man's a senator," Kito said.

Michael smiled to himself at the promotion—state legisla-ture probably didn't translate well.

Just then Jake lost control of the hacky sack and it came bounding toward Katura. She caught it like a pro, moving the small bag back and forth between various body parts before she finally glanced up at Michael. She bounced it off her right knee toward him. He caught it out of the air with his hand and held it, looking at her. He finally had her attention back.

"We're rafting down the Lower Zambezi ourselves. We'll be back in about a week. But when we're back here, we have a few days with no agenda. At least, so far." He glanced over at his mother. "Maybe we can find some locals for a pick-up game."

She looked him up and down. "Are you any good?"

"Good enough. And my brother Jake is an awesome mid-fielder."

"I'm not sure what my plans are." She glanced over at her brother for a moment, then pointed out a nearby window. "Look, there's a school with a field four blocks in that direction, there's likely to be kids playing after class. If I'm still around, maybe we can find a game." She tied her hair back with a scrunchie she pulled from her pocket. "No promises, but if I'm around, I'll be there in the afternoon." She turned and casually waved goodbye.

Jake leaned over to Michael. "Caitlin'll love to hear about this."

Kito and Thabani seemed to be wrapping up their brief conversa-tion. The adults were eager to get to the hotel, and Kito signaled for the group to follow him out the large glass doors to the van parked outside. Jane called for Michael to grab the luggage, but he stood there a moment and watched Katura join her brother. There was something about this girl that he couldn't put his finger on. It felt weird— hoping against hope to see her again.

CHAPTER 7

Lorenzo maneuvered the van through the narrow streets of Vic Falls. It was a slow crawl until they reached the road that led out of town. He was then able to pick up some speed.

"It'll be about two hours before we drop into the gorge below Devil's Cataract," he said. "That's a blind spot on the river we want to avoid."

"And the rest of the crew?" Rick asked. "Are they meeting us at the launch site?"

"Baruti and Andrew will already be there. They set it all up early so we can grab a quick lunch and take off before noon."

Lorenzo hit the brakes as he rounded a curve and approached a back-up in traffic. Jane craned her neck to see around the cars in front of them. Their van slowed to a near stop. She saw a bus broken down in the middle of the road with the ubiquitous red cross painted on the side. The bus blocked the entire lane to the point that the oncoming cars could pass only by venturing into the opposing lane of traffic.

The bus driver had jacked up the large vehicle, aided by several men who'd stopped to help, their cars now adding to the bottleneck. Jane stared out the window at the gaunt appearance of the numerous people sitting on the dirt shoulder of the road, fanning themselves in the heat. She took in a deep breath. There were mothers holding onto young children who looked wasted, cachectic.

"Is this what the clinic will be like?" Jake was frozen in his seat.

"We're working with the men, building walls, putting up a roof. Mom'll..." Michael's voice faded. He continued to stare out the window.

Jane's eyes stung as she watched an emaciated woman huddle close to a small child with huge eyes. The woman was watching the cars creep by. She bounced another infant on her lap.

"It's unbearable," Rick said to no one in particular. "Things need to change. More has to be done to help those mothers and children."

Paul turned to face him. "Does sympathy only go out to women and kids? What about that guy over there?" Paul gestured to a thin, middle-aged man who sat by himself on the dirt with his head slumped over. "He's all alone, Rick. Isn't that worse? Maybe he's already watched his own family die, or maybe he became sick and undesirable before he was even able to enjoy the creation of a family at all." Paul's voice was getting louder. "Or maybe he was rejected and thrown out by his family at the first signs of illness. Don't you realize, not all families stick together in sickness and in health?"

"I stand corrected. I'm sorry, you're right. That wasn't fair of me."

"Fair?" He turned back to his window. "Right, fair."

Jane made eye contact with Rick and leaned over. "Sounds like you touched a nerve. I wonder what that's about," she whispered. They traveled the rest of the distance to the river in silence. She let out a soft sigh when she spotted a truck with River Expeditions painted in fluorescent colors on the side. They had reached their destination and she could finally get out of the van. A simple but adequate picnic was already laid out, and soup was steaming on a propane stove set up near the riverfront.

"I was beginning to wonder about you guys," called out a man with a broad smile. He wore a dark green version of Lorenzo's blue shirt with logo.

Lorenzo stopped in his tracks. He was staring past the large black man stirring soup. Jane followed his gaze to a tall, athletic-looking young woman.

"Explain," he said.

The woman turned and pulled her shoulder length auburn hair back. She twisted it and fed the end through the hole in the back of a bright orange baseball cap.

"Andrew's sick, Lorenzo. 104 fever. Morgan couldn't get hold of you or he'd have told you himself. I'm your safety."

"Morgan knows what I'm into here. He didn't tell me because he's chickensh—"

The young woman glanced at Jane.

Lorenzo shifted his weight. "You'll guide, I'll safety." He threw off his backpack and walked down to the waterfront.

The woman shrugged and let out a deep sigh.

"Don't take it personal, Shelly," the man stirring the soup said. "The kids are young on this one and he's right, Morgan should've told him." He continued to stir. "You could've guessed he'd take safety—it took him a while to let Andrew into that spot too. It'll come, just give him time."

They loaded the boats in silence. Lorenzo then gave a quick but thorough briefing about what to do if anyone got thrown from the raft.

"Sometimes Shelly will bark out orders in very fast succession. Be ready and anticipate the changes, especially in the rapids."

Shelly reviewed the commands, which were a language all their own. She faced the new rafters throughout her spiel, smiled at the soup stirrer a few times but never once glanced at Lorenzo. She explained how the right and left side of the raft might be instructed to proceed with different strokes in order to accomplish a given move around a rock or turbulence. Other times it would be important for both sides to stroke hard and in unison in order not to change the angle of their approach.

"I'm not sure you can expect their side to keep up." Paul was grinning at Michael. "Looks to me like we've got all the strength on our side."

Tommy, who was sitting directly behind Paul, reached up high as they tapped knuckles. He then turned to Michael and nodded.

"It's not a competition, Michael," Jake said.

"That's what losers say." Tommy slapped Paul's back. "Right, dad?"

"I wouldn't diss my brother." Michael leaned over the side and dipped his bandana in the river. He tied it around his forehead allowing the cool water to drip down his face and neck.

"That's right. Jake'll make up for us." Rick turned and winked at Jake, then reached into the boat and grabbed his paddle.

"Okay." Paul nodded to Tommy to grab a paddle. "You're on. We'll race straight across this flat part and see which side dominates."

"Just make sure to keep clear of that rock on the left." Shelly launched the craft and jumped into place on the back bench. "It's got a bit of a tow on the other side. Everyone secure?"

Jane felt Jake's feet dig deeper under her seat—probably more for leverage than safety.

"Go!" Shelly yelled.

Jane grabbed her paddle tightly with both hands and focused on Rick's board in front of her. The more coordinated her stroke, the more efficient their movement would be. Her paddle glided smoothly through the water, one stroke after the next. Jake seemed to be in perfect rhythm. There was something soothing, mesmerizing about the whole thing. She looked over at Michael as she moved her paddle through the water. He seemed so concentrated, so intent on staying coordinated with Paul, plunging each stroke in unison.

The changes in Michael had been so gradual that she'd almost missed them. But now, on this river, she could see them clearly. His chest had gotten broader, his arms bulged when he forced the paddle through the water. But most striking was his profile. What had been round and soft had become chiseled, his jaw solid and square. Now concentrated on winning this race, he had a profile remarkably like his father's. Soon he—

"Keep your blade flat, Jane!" Rick yelled over the river noise. "You're falling behind our rhythm."

She startled and tried to make up speed by powering faster through the water. It was impossible. The resistance was too much for her. Her grasp slipped momentarily and the paddle popped out, ejecting the blade high above the surface. The raft began to turn left.

Rick yelled again. "We need to straighten it around! Get it back in and paddle hard."

"I'm trying." The water began to feel like a wall.

"Don't go so high above the surface. Keep it low."

"I don't mean to." The only way she could keep up with his strokes was to allow her paddle to angle slightly under water—less propelling power, but she'd appear to keep up.

"We're turning, Jane. Paddle harder."

"I know."

"Come on, we're going right into that rock."

"Rick!"

Suddenly she felt a jolt. The raft abruptly turned to the right. Jane looked around and saw that Michael had planted his paddle perpendicular to the surface of the water, which caused resistance to forward movement and turned the raft. They missed the boulder that loomed a few feet from her left knee as they passed.

"Now, straighten it out," Shelly said. "Good job. You'll all get the hang of it. No worries."

"What happened back there?" Michael whispered.

His expression was quizzical. It hadn't yet dawned on him that his strength had surpassed her. She knew he would notice soon enough. "I must have gotten distracted."

⋏

The next two days of rafting were more exhilarating than she could have imagined. Each day saw one or two of the kids dumped out into the water by the aggressive rapids, but they were quick to surface and Lorenzo immediately hoisted them back into place. Shelly was a stellar guide. She had them coordinating their strokes and responding to her commands in no time. When they finally pulled the raft onshore, Lorenzo approached the group.

"Special treat today," he said. "We came in early, still several hours of daylight. How about if we relieve you of all the duties of camp set-up and you take a trip to the market?" He turned and pointed to a small path on the far side of the beach. "It's only about two hundred meters down that trail. Just be back before dark."

"We're not much into shopping," Paul said.

"But dad—"

"Tommy, we'll help build camp then take a hike, just you and me—give these folks some time to themselves."

⋏

"What do you think you might want?" Michael stood over trinkets laid out neatly on a blanket in the dirt, organized into displays of musical instruments, carved animals, masks, and jewelry.

"Maybe a drum, or a cheetah." Jake leaned down to examine the small painted drums.

"How about a mask?"

Jake crinkled up his nose. Michael held up one darkly painted mask after another. They were at least two feet long, made of balsa wood with slits cut for the eyes, nose, and mouth, most of them painted in black and red with accents of white.

"I'll look around," Michael said to the merchant as he approached. "Got to see them all first." Jake had just picked up a small, carved animal when Michael grabbed his arm. "Let's see what they have further back in the market, there's lots of booths." He looked over at his mother. "We'll meet you in there."

"Stay together," she said.

Jake smiled apologetically at the merchant, then set down the painted lion on the blanket. They headed toward the more concentrated area of the market.

Suddenly the merchant stood directly in front of them. He'd moved faster than they expected and blocked the boys' path to the market entrance.

Michael grabbed Jake and jumped back. The man's stony face broke into a big, toothy smile.

"I think you like this one?" He held an onyx elephant up to Jake. "Or this?" It was a carved giraffe. "Maybe you like music?" He held up a wooden flute as he moved closer to Jake, who stayed behind Michael. The man blew the flute loudly, backing the boys toward his goods.

"Excuse me, mate. Mind if we get by you?" Two tall, gangly, sandy-haired young Australians walked up in khaki shorts and tattered T-shirts. Their olive green backpacks had water bottles on the sides. Sleeping bags were strapped to the bottom.

As the merchant moved out of the backpackers' way, Michael grabbed Jake and followed the young Aussies into the large market center.

"Prayer," the toothy salesman yelled after them. "Remember my name, it's Prayer. You look around, but when you buy, I give you best prices."

"Did he say Prayer?" Jake said.

"Yeah, I read somewhere that when they translate their tribal names into English, they're often names like 'gift,' or 'joy' or even boring stuff like 'born on Tuesday' or 'eighth child.' I saw one name that meant 'destined to die after birth.'"

"Ew, that's gotta hurt," Jake said. "Guess Prayer's not so bad." He turned back to take one last look at the man, who stared after them.

The entire market was a large labyrinth of blankets on the ground spread with goods, organized by category. One shop's area was not well differentiated from the next, and nearly all of them required stepping through very small dirt spaces to get to the items for sale toward the back. It was hard to tell which shopkeeper belonged to which sectioned-off area, as they stood around talking with each other until a potential customer showed up—then they'd surround the new arrival and thrust goods in their direction. The shops further back were more sturdy, open in the front, but they had three sides to them and a roof for shade. Articles were hanging from the top and sides for display.

Michael and Jake wandered past several until they saw a stall showing a variety of items that caught their attention. Michael examined the various masks' color, size, and shape but was reluctant to touch any of them. Picking up an item might imply a commitment he wasn't ready to make. He eyed the wares with caution until he spotted a long string of small, colorful stones that led to a central giraffe carved from onyx. He reached into his pocket and grabbed the local currency Rick had given him for souvenirs.

"A necklace?" Jake said. "How about that mask?" He pointed to one.

Michael shrugged.

"Which one are you getting?" His mom was looking at the dozens of masks hanging down from the walls of the stall.

"I'm not sure." Michael palmed the necklace out of his mother's sight.

"The red one might look better against your dark green bedroom wall, a good contrast. The black wouldn't show up as well," Jane said.

"See?" Jake said. It was the one he'd pointed out. Michael shot him a look.

"But whatever you want is fine, Michael," his mom said. She took Rick's arm and started toward another stall. "Keep an eye on Jake."

Rick looked up at the sky, then turned back to Michael. "I want to leave pretty soon, so don't take long."

Michael glanced up and noticed the sun was several inches above the western horizon.

Jake sighed. "We just got here," he said under his breath.

Michael turned to privately count his remaining money. Not enough for both masks and the necklace for Caitlin. He looked between the two masks, then picked up a third.

Jake stepped over a rolled-up carpet to join him. "If you want my opinion—"

"Jake, why don't you go look at those drums?" Michael pointed two booths away. "I'll be over in a minute."

"Whatever."

Michael pointed at a dark crimson mask with large lips and taunting eyes. "Sir," he called out. "I'll take this one."

The old merchant sauntered over with a large bag. Michael showed him the necklace and dropped it in. "I get your change," the man said. He took the bills Michael counted out. "Be right back."

Michael reached up and removed the hanging mask, admiring it at close range before he placed it carefully inside the bag. He didn't see the old man but could hear him rummaging around in back of the stall. He tried to see around all the hanging tapestries that blocked his view. What was this guy doing? How much change did he need, anyway? Probably didn't matter much.

He looked over at the neighboring stalls. There were some statues worth looking at. He noticed the young Australian men had drifted to the far part of the market, almost invisible with several salesmen surrounding them. One of the Aussies held some object Michael couldn't identify.

He heard someone yelling, turned and saw a crowd forming in the central open area of the market.

"You promised to buy from me!" a man shouted.

Michael squinted as he faced into the sun just barely over the horizon. He recognized the man. He struggled to see through the crowd.

"Hey, you have my change yet?" Michael called into the back. No one responded.

He turned back to the commotion and froze. A slight movement in the crowd had opened up a space through which he saw the man grab his little brother's arm and swing him around. The man was holding a drum. Jake stood facing him, looking bewildered, scared. Michael ran to the edge of the crowd and started forcing his way toward the middle.

"Leave him alone," a shopkeeper called out. "He's just a kid."

"Probably doesn't have any money anyway." It was an older woman this time, with three small children at her side.

"Prayer?" Jake said.

"See, he knows me," the man said to the crowd.

"Everybody knows you."

"He promised to buy from me." Prayer thrust the drum into Jake's hands. "Here's your drum, boy. Now pay at my store."

Prayer turned and began to walk away, leaving Jake to stare at the item in his hand as if he'd never seen a drum before.

The crowd of gawkers that had been circling Jake and Prayer parted to make an opening toward the exit of the market. Michael could see that they'd moved in close behind Jake, forcing him forward.

"I didn't promise *anything*," Jake said.

Michael could hear the terror in his brother's voice. He continued to force people out of his way.

"He's really harmless," an elderly man standing next Michael said. "Crazy, but harmless."

"But if he promised…"

Prayer loomed over Jake. "You better pay for what you have, boy."

Michael felt a sharp elbow in his side as he pushed his way forward. People were moving in both directions, some had lost interest and were getting back to their wares. Others were trying to see what was happening, forming a tighter circle. Michael shoved harder, determined to muscle his way through, but most of the bodies wouldn't budge. No one actually held him, but the restraint was just as effective. He could see his brother holding the drum as Prayer marched toward his own stall at the edge of the market. The remaining crowd was closing in on Jake.

Jake took a few steps backward when Michael heard somebody near him shout, "He's stealing!"

"I'm not stealing!" Jake screamed.

"Leave him alone," Michael yelled.

Jake turned toward Michael's voice, then ran a few steps in the direction in which Prayer had disappeared. He put down the drum in the middle of the dirt path and backed away toward Michael. The crowd closed tighter around Jake. Michael was squeezed between several young men, unable to move.

He could see a group of women talking on the other side of Jake. One of the women stepped toward him. "No problem, boy. He's not going to—"

Jake pulled away from the woman and yelled at the top of his lungs, "I'm not stealing, I didn't promise anything!"

Michael shoved one of the men in the back as hard as he could. The man fell into several others and Michael maneuvered around them. He thrust his way to the front of the crowd when he saw Rick break through the other side and into the center. Rick swooped Jake up into his arms. Jake's eyes began to fill with tears.

"It's okay, Jake." He nodded to the women. "I've got him, thanks."

"Let's just go," Jane called out. Michael could see his mother struggling to get around the crowd

"Jake didn't get anything," Michael said. He took two steps toward the men who stood in front of Jane. They moved out of his way.

"Michael—"

"If you're mad, Mom, be mad at me." He stood in front of her. "It was my fault we didn't stay together."

He saw her glance at a nearby booth.

"Give me thirty seconds." Michael grabbed a wooden lion and an onyx leopard. He held them high for Jake to see. The crowd was breaking up but Jake was still holding on to Rick. Jake glanced over and nodded.

"Both?"

Jake had already turned away. Rick and Jane were whispering, continuing to watch the crowd. They kept Jake between them.

Michael took in a quick breath. What if something had happened to Jake? What was he thinking to send him off alone? He could still feel the hold the crowd had had on him, his difficulty in breaking away to reach his brother.

Michael picked up an eight-inch drum with intricate painting on the side. The dusk light gave a slight orange cast to the objects he held.

"All three," he said to the small man standing next to him. He wadded the remaining bills from his pocket into the man's palm and ran to join his family.

CHAPTER 8

Light spilled around the edges of the window shade to reach Katura's face. She lay not yet fully awake, felt the heat on her cheek, and began her morning absorbed in the city smells. So different from home, so lacking in depth. How could the presence of cars and so many people erase what must have been there for centuries?

She sat up. It must be just about time to leave. It was sweet of Japera to let her sleep in until the last minute, but she needed to gather her things. He always underestimated how long it took her. Zuka had said they might be gone a whole week, that it would take a lot of time to make plans with the others, and she'd need to pack for the chilly nights out.

She headed to the bathroom, slapped cold water on her face, and smoothed down her long black hair. Maybe there'd be time for a shower, it could be her last for a while.

"Japera?" she called out into the hallway. "How much time do we have?" She slapped more water on her face before grabbing a towel. "Japera?" She yelled louder.

The house was awfully quiet. Could they have overslept too? After all, it had been a very late night. Still, it wasn't typical for Japera—he was so annoyingly responsible. She smiled. She was going to enjoy this.

She burst into his room. "Hey, sleepyhead—"

She stopped and stared. He wasn't there. She slammed the door and ran from room to room. No one. She looked out at the carport. Thabani's car was still there. Zuka must have picked them up. She felt her heart pounding and closed her eyes. They must've gone out for some last-minute supplies, then they'd swing back for her. That had to be it. She should have fresh coffee made for when they came in. She walked slowly into the kitchen. That's when she saw the note—Japera's handwriting. She lifted it off the counter.

Don't be mad. I guess I can't ask that of you—of course you'll be mad. But this is dangerous. You saw that last night. It's safer this way and I had to leave before you got up because I knew you wouldn't agree. Please try to understand. I'll be back as soon as I can.

I love you Katura,
Japera

She read the note a second time, crumpled it into a tight ball, and threw it in the trash. This wasn't Japera. This was Thabani's doing. Japera wouldn't have left her out like this.

She ran to her room to get dressed. She'd just have to find them before they launched—better hurry. But before she headed out the door, she stopped. Her mind was racing. What did he say? She grabbed the note from the trash and smoothed it out. *I love you Katura?* She stared at his words. He never said that. He was scared. Those were words he'd use if he wasn't sure he'd make it back. She threw down the note and raced out the door.

⋏

She stood at the shoreline of the river, winded by her run. She knew she'd missed them. A few groups of day rafters unloaded their gear, received brief instructions, and launched quickly to make room for the next group. Thabani had told her about day rafters. Short trips for the less serious tourists who wanted a taste of the great Zambezi without the commitment or talent to make it down the real rapids. For long trips he always made it his practice to get out early—it avoided the need to maneuver around them later. She scanned the groups to see if any looked like they had enough gear to be going further. She'd somehow talk her way into joining them. Maybe she could catch up.

No such luck. Each group consisted of people armed only with small daypacks, probably carrying just their lunch and a camera. She watched them for several more minutes before she turned and walked down the shoreline.

A raft with a guide, two adult passengers, a sulky teenager, and two small children passed her. The children waved, she smiled back despite herself. It was then that she noticed the raft itself. Just above the waterline she could read the logo printed boldly on the side—the same logo she'd seen many months ago on Thabani's shirt. He'd probably worn it that day to impress her father. The day they'd convinced her father to let Tafadzwa go to Zimbabwe to learn the river business. It had been quite a negotiation but in the end Tafadzwa got his way, as usual. She watched the logo appear and disappear over the waves—and then the light dawned.

Katura took off in a sprint back up the dunes toward town as fast as she could.

When she reached the storefront she was out of breath. She stood and stared at the advertisements in the window, tried to slow down her heart rate, force herself to look calm. Through the window she saw an older woman at the desk, busy with paperwork. Katura entered the store, rattling a bell, and the woman glanced up at her.

"Looking for someone?"

"No, actually, I wanted to know about your trips."

"Really?" The woman went back to her paperwork.

"Some of my father's business friends would like to take a rafting trip, they sent me down here to get some information." Katura scanned the posters on the wall. "They might even let me go."

The woman looked up and smiled at her. "Take a look at the brochures and let me know if you have any questions."

Katura sifted through the literature that sat on the far table with photos of day trips as well as longer campout adventures. They pictured guests with smiles plastered across their faces and guides maneuvering them down the rapids—

Wait a minute. In a shot of a large raft with several passengers, there—in the back—she could make out Thabani. She stared at his face. Was there a family resemblance? She glanced over at the woman, who hadn't looked up again, then stuffed the pamphlet underneath the rest.

"Need any help out here?" A younger man who'd come out from the back was speaking to the woman at the desk. Katura noticed he had broad shoulders and large hands—likely a guide who couldn't get a job down the river that day.

"Can you look at this schedule and see if you think I've got it right?" the woman said. "A second set of eyes might catch a mistake."

Katura shuffled through the rest of the stack until she found the one she was looking for. She read it quickly.

"Ah, here's what they want." She held up the pamphlet. "Mana Pools. I couldn't remember the name until I saw—"

"Oh, no, dear," the woman said. "There's much nicer places to go than there. Let me give you some brochures to take to your father's friends." She stood and picked up the pamphlets on her desk.

"No," Katura said. "They definitely want to go to this park. I'm sure this is the one they told me to look for." She smiled at the woman, who stared at her with no expression. "You know, one of the last strongholds of the black rhino," she quoted from the pamphlet in her hand.

The woman handed the brochures to the young man. "I have some work to do in the back," she said. "Can you help this young lady? Take your time. Show her all the options." She closed the back door behind her.

"No, I'm sure my friends would prefer this trip. Is there one leaving soon, because they don't have much time before—"

"Why are you asking about Mana Pools?"

"The black rhinos, they're disappearing, and these folks—"

"She's back there calling the police," he whispered. "They're just down the street. You have about three minutes."

CHAPTER 9

J ane was exhausted. Today's rapids had taken her beyond what she thought her arms could tolerate. Baruti directed the kids toward a campsite thirty yards from the beach and just on the edge of the jungle. The air was hot and dry during the daytime, relieved only by the cool breeze that swept up through the canyon, fragrant with the richness of wild African vegetation. But by night, the winds tended to pick up, and they positioned their tents to be partially sheltered by trees.

When they pulled their raft onto shore to make camp, Lorenzo turned to the adults.

"Why don't you three take a walk along the shore? You can't go very far— have to turn back at that jetty— but it's a nice walk." He pointed to the jagged rocks that were the western boundary of their beach site cove. Jane eyed the densely forested area to the south of the shore. "Oh, you can't go back there," Lorenzo said. "Even Baruti won't enter that part of the jungle."

Jane was still looking at the luscious green vegetation.

"It's extremely thick, and the wildlife is too dangerous. There's only that one overgrown trail to the left of where we'll be setting up camp, and it leads directly to an abandoned village and what's left of an old stone lodge. Used to be a tourist resort."

"Abandoned?" Jane asked.

"Destroyed by disease. AIDS hit some of the villages so hard they couldn't recover. The few survivors ended up staying in the bigger townships where they took their loved ones to die. Now they're scared to go back and there's not enough population left anyway to support a village."

"So it's still deserted." Jane tried to see down the trail, but the growth was too dense. "Sounds interesting, like finding the remnants of an ancient civilization."

"It would be, if it had been left alone. It gets taken over by poachers and other petty criminals from time to time. Anything that was interesting has been destroyed or stolen, and if you happen upon anyone, they're not the sort you want to run into."

"So if everyone knows that poachers and criminals hang out there, why don't the local authorities just go in and clear it out from time to time?"

Lorenzo shook his head. "No one wants to go near those places." He glanced at Baruti, who was tying up the gear. He lowered his voice. "They say there's angry ghosts of the sick—those who were left to die. They believe that to disturb these tortured souls would bring disaster to their own families. Anyway, the criminals won't stay there long, they have to move on to sell their goods, and the authorities figure they can pick them up somewhere else. Why risk the safety of their families for common thieves?"

"Good point." She glanced back over at the river, which turned sharply to the right up ahead. It was noisy when the wind shifted in their direction. "Ghost Rider Rapids? Is it named for these ghosts?"

"I suppose." He looked over at his comrades, who were emptying the equipment. He seemed anxious to get finished with that day's chores. "So, the beach?"

She stretched her legs and nodded. It felt like she'd been cramped in the raft forever.

"Dinner will be ready when you get back." He started to leave, then turned back to Jane. "I must've scared the bejesus out of you on that last run. But I knew the boys could do it by the way they've been handling themselves. They've done great on a really tough river."

Jane smiled. "You were worried, weren't you?"

"The age requirement used to be fifteen, but…" He leaned down and picked up the dry bag.

"But tourism's down?"

"That doesn't change the river, though, does it?" He shrugged. "These guys have done great and that's all that matters."

Jane motioned for the two men to join her on the shoreline walk. When they were away from the others, Paul turned to Rick.

"And what exactly would he have done if the kids *hadn't* seemed capable of navigating that chute? Call a cab?"

Jane shook her head. Paul might have a good point, but she was getting tired of his attitude. Her eye twitched slightly as she watched the river cascade down from the west just beyond the jetty. Two more days of serious rapids, then the rest was supposed to be a calm, scenic float. She could hardly wait.

Paul leaned over and picked up a small, smooth rock. "If I knew what this river was really like, I probably would've pulled Tommy out of here when Lorenzo first seemed nervous about the girl." He turned the stone over in his right hand a few times, then sent it skipping across the water. Jane watched it disappear into the river.

"She's doing okay." Jane felt for Shelly. It must be difficult for a young woman to break into this business, with so many men out of work these days.

"My guess is he hadn't allowed much wiggle room." Rick had his arm around Jane but was speaking to Paul. "When he got sideswiped with that change, he had to make a snap decision—either go with the flow or cancel the trip. He's probably been biting his nails the whole time and must be relieved to have reached this beach."

They arrived at the jetty and had just turned to head back when Jane startled—she could see a raft off in the distance coming toward them. They hadn't seen any others for two days, and she'd expected to be alone the rest of the trip. She'd been enjoying her fantasy of being explorers in a wild land, and these newcomers reminded her that this was a popular site for rafting.

"I guess tourist season isn't as low as we'd thought," Paul said.

Jane didn't respond, she was starring at the approaching men. Rick moved around her to get a closer view of the boat, but remained behind one of the larger boulders.

"Isn't that the guy we saw at the airport? The guy who was talking to our driver?" Rick kept his voice low.

"Yeah." Jane squinted. "And the other one was at the airport too."

"Oh, that's right," Paul said. "I remember them."

"You saw the other guy at the airport too?" Rick asked. "What was he doing? Did he come in on the arrivals?"

"How should I know?" Paul said. "He was just standing on the other side of the terminal, leaning against the counter, smoking a cigarette."

Rick stared at Jane.

"I don't think he came off a plane," she said. "He wasn't carrying any luggage. Maybe he was meeting somebody. No, wait." She thought for a moment. "The first guy said he was taking a rafting trip, with his cousin and a friend." She watched as the two men maneuvered the last small rapid before slowing down near their beach site. "I guess the friend bailed."

They watched the raft pull up to shore. The taller African, the one who'd introduced himself as Thabani, got out and pulled onto the sandbank. Shelly had been cooking about fifty yards from the shore while the tents were being assembled behind her. She put down her pan and approached the men.

Lorenzo, Baruti, and the boys had finished setting up the tents and were inside the guide's quarters. They were supposed to be arranging the rudimentary bedding, but Jane could hear noises more consistent with wrestling.

"May I help you?" Shelly called out loudly. "We've got this site, but there's another one just around the bend." She wiped her hands on her khaki pants and headed toward the shore.

"Are your guides around?" Thabani yelled.

"I'm one of the guides. Do you need something?"

"Let's keep walking," Paul said. "I need to stretch my legs and don't feel like socializing with the new campers."

Shelly was close enough to the visitors now for them to be speaking too low for Jane. But just before she was about to turn away, Jane looked back. Thabani had reached out his hand to Shelly as if to shake it, then suddenly grabbed her forearm and wheeled her around with her arm twisted behind her back. And for just a split second, Jane spotted his gun.

The younger African who had pulled their raft up onto shore reached into the boat and quickly removed a rifle he concealed under his large water poncho. She looked up toward the tents and her kids. She wasn't close enough to reach the camp before these armed men would get there.

Jane looked behind her. The low-lying sun was positioned just above the edge of the western jetty creating a glare in their direction—it might be impossible for the new arrivals to have seen her and the men, even if they'd looked this way.

Without a word, Paul nudged Rick's arm. He motioned toward the jungle trail to the south. They began sidestepping behind the scattered trees above the beach, their eyes fixed on Shelly and the two Africans.

Suddenly, a burst of laughter exploded from the guide's tent. The kids were playing, unaware of what was happening outside. Above all the voices, Jane heard Jake's boyish, high-pitched laugh. She froze.

Rick caught her eye and motioned for her to keep moving toward the jungle.

Every instinct she had told her to run to the tent, to try to escape with the boys, get them out. But it was too late. The trio was heading straight toward the tent and would get there before she could. The boys' laughter had already identified their location—even if she got the Africans' attention with some self-sacrificing ploy, it would only delay the inevitable. Jane bit her lower lip. She'd have to leave her children. She had to first get herself, Rick, and Paul out of reach from these gunmen, then she'd make a plan. Maybe they'd try to make it through the trees for help, maybe they'd split up. How could she leave the boys alone in this situation? Desperately, miserably, she kept moving toward the jungle.

"Stop right there, Senator." The thick African accent was unmistakable.

When they turned around they were blinded by the sun's glare behind a bulky black figure twenty yards down the beach. He lifted his rifle, aimed it at Rick's forehead, and took several steps toward them.

"Keep walking straight ahead, slowly, behind the tent, and don't speak or I'll shoot."

"Found some strays, Zuka?" Thabani reached the dining tent. The inhabitants had suddenly gone quiet.

Lorenzo emerged alone from the tent.

"Thabani, hey—sorry, man, this site's taken." He reached out his hand in greeting. It was then that he noticed Shelly. "Hey!" Lorenzo yelled. "What's going on? Let her go!"

That was all Baruti needed to hear—he crawled on all fours out the back of the tent. He stood up, only to face Jane and the others being held at gunpoint. Zuka had shifted his gun to point at Baruti, careful to keep an eye on the others. He marched them around to the front of the tent to join Thabani.

"Actually, Lorenzo my friend, I'm taking this site," Thabani said, "and all of you with it."

Chapter 10

With one quick move Thabani shoved Shelly toward the guide's tent. He aimed the pistol at Lorenzo.

"You're expendable now, so don't try anything stupid." There were no traces of his broad friendly smile and warm eyes. He looked at Lorenzo with the kind of stiff coldness that hints at a deep-seated rage, ready to act out at the slightest provocation. "Call Andrew out." His hand trembled. "Now."

Lorenzo squinted. His eyes darted, unfocused, back and forth on the ground. He glanced up at Thabani.

"Is this about—"

"Now." Thabani looked inside the tent flap. "Get out here."

Jane's breathing stopped while she watched Thabani's gun waving carelessly in the direction of her kids. They filed out of the tent in silence. Michael glanced at Jane and kept himself between Jake and the guns.

"Where is he?" Thabani said. He searched inside the now empty canvas room.

"We never take four on a group this size, you know that." Lorenzo stood solid. He refused to look at the gun pointed at his chest. "If it's Andrew you want, you've come a long way for nothing. He's back at Vic Falls with a fever."

Jane's focus was on the young man with steel-gray eyes who stood in the background. She remembered him vaguely from the airport. His face was expressionless except for his wrinkled forehead. His rifle, pointed at the ground, hung loosely from his grip.

Thabani laughed. "You think you know everything, don't you, Lorenzo? Well you've got this one wrong. This is much more important than—"

Zuka cleared his throat and stared without blinking at Thabani, who shifted his feet.

"I don't have to explain anything to you, Lorenzo. Now you, Baruti, and the girl get back inside the guide tent. Start walking." He didn't take his eyes—or the pistol—off Lorenzo. "Japera, tie these three up inside. Make sure they can't get loose."

"No." Zuka's voice was commanding. They all stopped and stared. "Japera, take just Lorenzo and the girl inside. Baruti stays with us. I want them split up for now. Even if the other two try to escape, they can't make it anywhere alive without Baruti. We need to keep him close—he's already shown us he'd run out on his friends if given half a chance."

Jane glanced from one to the other. Who was the leader?

A look of annoyance passed quickly over Thabani's face. He stammered as he said, "We can use him to set up the equipment before sunset. Good idea." He nodded as if congratulating himself on this fine plan. "Go ahead, Japera, take the other two." Japera and the others had already disappeared inside the tent. "We'll need to eat and get some sleep before we take off in the morning." Thabani eyed the equipment raft still loaded with supplies.

"Take off?" Paul asked.

Zuka made a clicking noise with his tongue and stepped between Thabani and the others. "Just sit here where we can watch you." His forefinger remained on the trigger of the gun. Not that it was pointed at anybody specifically, but the threat to anyone who went against his orders was clear enough.

Jane sat down immediately next to Baruti. He'd managed to fold his large body into a small compact area on the ground. His head was lowered—even his breathing was undetectable. She pulled Jake down close to her. Rick motioned for Michael to sit next to his brother. Michael hesitated a moment. He looked from Zuka to Thabani, then down at his brother. He lowered himself and sat in front of Jake.

"Move over, in a line." Thabani took a step forward. "I want to be able to see you all, no one's sneaking off."

Michael scooted over, but only an inch or two. Jake was now visible, barely. Rick sat down next to Michael, the adults book-ending the kids.

Paul continued to stand, hands on hips, eyes fixed on Zuka. Paul's stance and stocky build conveyed a picture of a man who was used to his physical presence dominating most situations.

A broad grin spread across Zuka's face. His gun shifted in his grip so that the weight rested between the side of his body and the base of his palm, his fingers caressing it slowly. Jane's attention was drawn to Tommy. The boy had moved almost unnoticed to his father's side. He looked back and forth between the two men, watched their silent standoff without calling attention to himself. When he glanced at the family of four who sat on the dirt not far from them, Jane sensed his yearning, but Tommy made no move to abandon his father. He reached up and put his hand on his father's forearm.

Paul glanced at his son and motioned for him to sit, but Tommy didn't let go of his father's arm—just stared into his eyes. The boy blinked several times, his lip quivering. Paul shrugged. He lowered himself and they sat together on the other side of Rick.

Zuka stepped back and looked at each of them in turn before he motioned for Thabani to go with him several yards away where they could talk without being heard.

Jane studied the beach to the west where they had walked earlier, before all the trouble started. There would be no way to climb quickly over that boulder-strewn jetty. Even if they could run fast enough up the beach before the gunfire started, the rocks were too big for swift ascent. The east end was bordered by a matching rock jetty with steeper cliff-like boulders that fell off precipitously into the river—even more difficult to climb than the west end, and leading nowhere.

She looked to the south and eyed the overgrown trail that she, Rick, and Paul had attempted to reach before Zuka caught them. How far was it until they could reach the deserted lodge? And then? Whatever it was, it was better than here.

Paul sighed loudly. "Now what?" he whispered.

Jane glanced at their two captors, out of earshot and engaged in their own low-toned conversation.

Rick leaned toward Jane. "What do you think this is about?"

"I don't know, but right now it doesn't matter." Jane spoke softly and kept her head facing forward. "What we need is a plan to get out."

"Probably has something to do with that Andrew guy," Michael whispered. "The tall one seemed intent on finding him."

Baruti looked up and was about to speak when Paul's foot began to shake.

"We've got to do something."

Jake's eyes lit up. "Maybe now that they know he's not here, they'll just leave us alone."

"Because life's just like that," Paul said, who was watching Zuka. "They're just about to say 'Excuse us, folks, sorry to frighten you with the guns, we'll just be on our way if you—'"

"Leave the kids alone." Jane kept her voice low but intense. "This isn't any easier on them than it is on you. In any case I don't think this has anything to do with Andrew. The younger guy didn't seem to know anything about whatever the tall one was talking about. There's something else going on."

Paul looked in every direction, paused, and stared into the jungle. He shook his head, then gazed intently across the river. "Someone has to escape."

Jane saw Michael look over his shoulder—judge the distance to get over the jetty.

"Michael, it's taller than it looks, we were just out there. And anyway…" She glanced away from him. "Maybe Rick's right, if we knew their motive, it could tell us—"

"Jane." This time Paul raised his voice loud enough for Zuka and Thabani to both look over for a moment before resuming their conversation. He lowered his voice, but the bitter edge sharpened. "We need to come up with a plan, now!"

Rick cleared his throat. "Why do you think he called me 'senator'?"

"What?" Michael glanced at Rick. "But you're not—"

"Right," Jane studied Rick a moment. "But that's what they think," she whispered. "And that's what's important. It's what the big guy said when he caught us. It must mean something." Her mind was racing. What could they want? "I just don't know if it'd be better for us if they knew the truth or not. Could make it worse." She tried to scan their faces, but her eyes kept landing on the guns. "We'll leave it alone for now."

Paul's eyes darted toward the raging river, then back to the trail.

"Even if one of us got away," Jane said, "we'd have to figure out how to get help. None of us knows our way."

"One of us does." Rick turned to Baruti.

Paul sat up. "Baruti, if you and I made it down that path, could you get us to a town?"

"Dad, how are we going to get away? They're watching our every move." Paul put his arm around his son and pulled him in tightly. Tommy's face fell, his eyes widened. "No, dad, you can't leave me here." His last words were muffled, spoken into his father's chest.

"Look, Tommy, you have to stay with Jane so I can get help. I'll be back as fast as I can, trust me on this one." He rubbed his son's head, helped him hide the tears. "Timing will be everything."

Jane glanced down the row at Rick. He was staring straight ahead. She studied the lines on his face. He looked intensely thoughtful, focused. Still, she found her own thoughts wandering to her ex-husband. Glenn was so decisive, so powerful, so ultimately bossy and overwhelming. But right now she could use some of that strength.

She followed Rick's gaze. Thabani and Zuka had walked over to Baruti's raft, which sat hoisted up several yards from the shoreline. Zuka kept his captives in his watch at all times, while Thabani looked over the equipment and removed some of the items. Then suddenly he took out his knife and slashed the air tubes of the equipment raft. Jane winced.

"They're not taking us any farther down the river."

"So we'll just have to leave before they do," Paul said.

Jane glanced over at the jungle and shook her head. "No, they may have others waiting at the other end. You could be walking right into a trap."

Paul tightened his jaw. "Got any better ideas?"

She looked over at the rocky jetties at both ends, then back at the Zambezi. "Crossing the river is the only option," she whispered.

Paul studied the river for a long moment. "I think I can get across before being drawn down near the crocs," he said finally. "How about you, Baruti?"

"No," Rick said. "I'll cross the river with Baruti."

"What?" Paul reared around so fast that he knocked Tommy over. "What makes you think—"

"I raced in college, I've been swimming three or four times a week ever since. Unless you're in better condition, I'm taking the river. We've only got one chance." He didn't wait for Paul's reply. "Can you swim, Baruti?"

Baruti hesitated. "I'll get across."

Rick studied the African for a moment, then looked back at the river. "You start as far up as possible where it's narrowest—close to the western jetty. I'll cross below you."

"Rick," Jane said, "there's—"

"I know what's in there, Jane. I'll just have to make it across fast." He looked into her eyes, then glanced at the boys. "We don't have a lot of choices."

Jane watched Thabani pull supplies out of the shredded rafts. Zuka kept his eyes on them at a distance. "You'll need a distraction," she said. "Something to pull their attention away so you can get to the river edge unnoticed."

"Hey, Baruti," Thabani called out, "get over here and help unload the food."

Baruti immediately got up and walked to the raft near the shore. Jane couldn't hear the instructions she could tell Thabani was giving him. Baruti reached into the deflated raft and pulled out two large dry bags. It was then that Jane noticed him lift his head. He studied the shoreline on the opposite side of the river, then fixed his eyes on the furthest shore before it disappeared around the river's bend. From Jane's angle, sitting several yards away, it was only a shadow, could have blended with the rocks, until it moved.

She looked at Rick but said nothing. Thabani and Zuka were too close now for her to speak. Rick winked at her. Had he seen what Baruti saw? Was he reassuring her? She searched his face. He smiled and looked away.

They sat in silence while Baruti started the propane stove and began sorting through the food supplies. Thabani checked on Lorenzo and the others.

"Lorenzo's still trying to talk himself out of this," Thabani said when he returned.

Zuka grunted.

Thabani scanned the campsite. "After we eat we better tie Baruti up for the night."

Jane watched Baruti. He kept stirring the pot, showing no reaction to what Thabani had said. He then stepped away from the stove and gathered the bowls. He was behind their captors. Baruti paused and stared directly at Paul. Neither Zuka nor Thabani were watching them. Paul raised his eyebrows. Baruti nodded toward the river.

Paul put his hand up to his face as if to scratch his cheek but with his forefinger pointed to himself, then at the river.

Baruti shook his head.

Paul paused, he still held his hand to his face. He then pointed at Baruti, who nodded. Paul glanced over toward Zuka and Thabani, now re-engaged in whispered conversation. He looked back at Baruti, staring at an area of the campground behind the large guide tent, an area that would give no direct line of sight to the shore. Paul nodded and pointed down at the ground with his eyebrows raised.

Baruti nodded again. "Yes, now," was the unmistakable answer.

"Stay with Jane," Paul whispered to Tommy, who sniffled his objection but didn't move.

Paul started to tap his right foot—it began as a slow rhythmic motion but accelerated into showy agitation. His head darted around without his eyes focusing anywhere and his breathing came in gasps. He looked down the river, up along the west end of the beach, and over at the trail. His antics caught the attention of Zuka, who nudged Thabani. Paul stood up and brushed the dirt off his shorts with quick forceful motions. He now had everyone's attention.

"Sit back down," Thabani said. "Right now, do you—"

"This is bullshit," Paul said. "This is absolute bullshit!" His voice rose even louder. "I'm not staying here, I'm out of here." He started to walk toward the trail on the backside of the guide tent.

Thabani cocked his gun. "You better think twice about that. Your little boy here looks a bit young to lose his father."

Paul turned and faced Thabani. "You're not a killer," he said. "You wouldn't murder anybody."

Thabani took a step closer.

Paul's voice rose. "I know all about you and your sad story. The girl died, but you didn't kill her. You're a rafting guide, a river rat who's down on his luck. Boo-hoo." He spit on the ground. "But you're not a criminal or a murderer. Maybe you're a terrorist wannabe, but I'm not going to help you out."

Paul backed up toward the trail as he talked. He drew them to the far side of the tent.

"You see, it's hard to take hostages. They're not all going to cooperate just because you have a gun." Paul had almost reached the trailhead. "Sometimes you have to decide if it's really worth it. Becoming a murderer is a big decision." He turned his back to Thabani and started along the trail.

The gun fired. Paul fell as Tommy let out a tortured scream.

Jane grabbed Tommy and covered his eyes, but the boy wriggled free and ran to his father. Paul lay on the ground holding his right leg. The ground became soaked with blood.

Thabani looked startled. He turned to Zuka, whose rifle had a small amount of smoke leaving the muzzle.

Jane stood up and addressed Zuka. "May I help him?"

He nodded, but after every few steps she turned around to make eye contact with Zuka, needed to reaffirm the agreement, make sure he hadn't changed his mind or misunderstood her intent. She wasn't taking anything for granted.

Paul held his leg and was clearly in serious pain. But when Tommy whimpered, Paul took in a deep breath and managed to smile at his son. Tommy grabbed his father's neck and held tight. When she reached the trailhead where the two sat, Jane ripped Paul's pant leg to expose the wound.

"I want the boy to get me some water. Would that be all right?" she called out over her shoulder.

"Okay," Zuka said. Tommy ran over to grab his water bottle.

"What the hell were you thinking?" She examined Paul's wound. "You were supposed to be a distraction, not a target." She noted that the bullet had not hit bone or any major arteries. It was a transverse wound, about two centimeters deep, and entered the back of his outer thigh midway between his buttock and knee. It was the exit wound in front that was bleeding profusely. When she wiped away the blood with her scarf, she found it to be a dime-size fairly clean hole. "And what was that about a dead girl?"

"I'm surprised at you, Jane. Didn't do all your homework, did you?" He was leaning up on one elbow and spoke through clenched teeth.

She poured the water Tommy brought over Paul's wound. He winced in agony, but the water allowed her to get a good look at the hole. It was clean. She put pressure on the wound. Paul began to hyperventilate, his arms shook violently—the initial numbing had worn off.

"Lie back down." She pulled his arm out and caught his head before it hit the ground. "Breathe slowly, like this." She pursed her lips into an oval and let out air. "I don't need you to pass out on me."

He stared straight up, not looking at her. It was the first time she had touched him, and although she assumed the most clinical stance she could without a white lab coat, she could feel his discomfort. She wrung the blood out of her bandana and tied it tightly around his leg to stop the bleeding.

"Looks like infection is going to be our biggest worry with this one," she said.

"*Our* biggest problem?"

"If you hadn't noticed, we're in this together. And if you have any more information about what might be going on, I'd appreciate it if you didn't keep it to yourself."

That's when she heard the splash. She turned and saw Baruti swimming upstream across the river, a hundred yards up. She had been so distracted by Paul's behavior that she'd almost forgotten the point of it. Rick was gone.

Zuka yelled to Thabani, "Hold them there this time." He ran down to the edge of the water and yelled over his shoulder, " and shoot if you have to."

When he reached the edge of the river, Zuka raised his rifle to his shoulder to take aim.

Jane stood and looked downstream. Rick had entered the river without a sound and was only a third of the way across. He must have waited until Baruti had started across to slip in himself. That's when she saw the ten-foot crocodile on the opposite bank slither into the water. It headed toward Rick, who now reached the halfway point. He was swimming hard toward a sharp bend to the north, around which he would be hidden from view by rocks and an outcropping of large acacias.

A shot rang out, and one of the boys screamed—a faraway noise compared to the pounding in Jane's head. Baruti went under a moment, then surfaced face down on the river's surface. His limp body drifted downstream.

Rick struggled against the current to reach the other side. Zuka reloaded and took aim. The crocodile descended under the water twenty yards from where Rick propelled himself as fast as possible across the river. Zuka steadied his weapon and focused. He paused only a moment, then shot twice.

Rick disappeared under the water, which immediately turned crimson. Jane looked away from the river and continued to adjust the bandage on Paul's leg, hands shaking, tears rolling down her cheeks.

Chapter 11

By the time Katura stopped to catch her breath, she was somewhere in an elaborate labyrinth of small residential streets. She knew Thabani's house was in this general direction but she wasn't clear exactly where. She'd dashed down little streets and alleyways to avoid being followed, but now it would take her some time to get her bearings. It didn't really matter, she needed time to think.

After she'd walked for a half-hour or so, she came to a schoolyard and stopped to rest. Children poured out of the classrooms and into the playground when the bell rang. Older kids, kids her age, headed for the rear of the school. The trees that lined the back of the field looked like the ones she could see from Thabani's back yard. She circled around the grounds and saw at a distance the edge of his property.

As she walked around the field, a group of young teenagers began to divide up into teams. One of the boys juggled a soccer ball. Maybe he was a good player—he certainly didn't seem concerned about which team chose him. He glanced her way and lost control of the ball, which sailed toward her and stopped. Katura slid her foot over the top of the ball, created a spin, and popped the ball up to bounce off her knee before she stepped up and served it out of the air back to the boy. He caught it with a solid snap down to his feet, then looked up and smiled at her. Without a word, he motioned his invitation for her to join in.

"Not today." She started to jog toward the trees. "I'm busy."

"We're here every afternoon."

⋏

There's got to be a map somewhere. Katura had gone through every drawer of Thabani's desk and was now headed for his closet. She grabbed a chair and hopped up to feel the top shelf for any papers that might be stuck between the clothes he'd thrown up there. Nothing. The bottom of the closet was a mess, so she saved it for last. She plopped herself down on the floor in front of the pile of rafting gear and started to sort through it. At the back she found a small file box and opened it. It was filled with papers, receipts from payments for rafting trips, none dated in the last two months. He must have been out of work for a while. In the back was a file folder labeled "Accident" with some newspaper clippings and a thick report. Might be something to look at later, no time now. She closed the file box.

A bright orange dry bag lay next to her on the floor. That's where she found it. In a side compartment inside the bag was a laminated map of the river, folded into a small square. Its primary purpose was to show the various twists and turns of the river with each rapid well marked. But off to the side she could make out small villages and towns on the way to Mana Pools. It was the place Zuka had mentioned the night before, where the MDC rebels had their camp—where Japera and the rest must be headed. She might be able to hitch rides or take buses and zigzag her way to that area without calling too much attention to herself.

She froze—the front door had opened and slammed shut. She stuffed the map quickly into her pocket. Within seconds a man she'd never seen before stood at Thabani's bedroom door.

"What are you looking for?" he said. He was at least twice her age, looked to be in his mid-thirties. She didn't like his tone.

"Who are you? And what are you doing in my cousin's house?" She glanced briefly around and noted that he was standing in the only exit from the room.

"Changa," he said. "I'll be staying here. I needed a place to live. Zuka told me I could crash here."

"Oh, you're a friend of Zuka's." She realized he must have gotten in with a key and relaxed her shoulders. "Why didn't you say that? You scared me." She stood up to go into the living room, but he didn't move from the doorway. "Where are you coming from?"

"Bulawayo."

"And what brings you all the way up here?"

"Business. And Zuka said I should look after you, make sure you're safe."

"Oh, that's sweet of him, but I'm fine, don't bother with me." Before the sentence was done, her mind had raced to an unsettling conclusion. Bulawayo was too far away for him to be telling the truth—the time line didn't work. The plan had only been formulated last night in the bar, and even if the guys had decided to leave her here from the start, this Changa guy couldn't have gotten word and made it in that amount of time. Katura wanted out of this room, out of this house. She took a step toward the door.

"You must be starving after such a trip, Changa. Let me find something for you in the kitchen."

"You didn't answer my question." Not a muscle moved on his body. She couldn't get past him.

"Your question?"

"What were you looking for?"

"Oh." She turned back toward the closet. "You see, I..." She bit her lip and squatted down. She searched the closet. "Oh, there it is." She reached deep into the back and pulled out a soccer ball.

"Some of the kids at the school invited me to play and I just ran home to get this. I knew Thabani would have one." She turned with the ball under her arm. "Let me make you a quick sandwich and then I'll be on my way."

"They invited you to play but didn't have a ball?" He continued to block the doorway.

"Of course they had one, it's just getting flat. May I?" She motioned beyond him.

He stared at her for a few seconds before moving back into the hallway. He followed her into the kitchen. Katura could feel his eyes watching her every move. She attempted to make light conversation, to make her movements around the kitchen seem casual. He answered her questions well enough, but there was something odd about his manner. She handed him the sandwich and excused herself to go to the bathroom.

She leaned against the inside door and let out a deep sigh. Was she reading too much into this? Hard to tell. She turned to lock the door. Great—no lock. Typical bachelor, not concerned with privacy. She took down the shower curtain and placed the rod under the door handle, secured it tightly against the vanity just opposite the door. He might still be able to force it open, but not quickly.

She scanned the room. There was a small high window that faced onto the side alley. Maybe she could open it quietly enough to not be heard. She turned the waste can over, stepped up on it, and examined the window. It was secured shut with some kind of plaster. She pushed hard on the frame to break the seal, but the window didn't budge. How long had it been there? She couldn't tell, it wasn't something she would have looked for before. But why would someone…?

When she walked out of the bathroom Changa startled her in the dark hallway.

"Everything okay?" he asked.

"I'm fine." She moved past him.

"You took an awful long time in—"

"Look, you're beginning to bug me. I appreciate that my brother and his friend want me to be safe, but I don't need a personal bodyguard, now back off." She stomped into the living room, grabbed the soccer ball, and stormed out of the house.

She'd taken about three steps down the walkway before her arm was almost jerked out of its socket.

"I'll drive you there." He pulled her over to a large van parked in the driveway and opened the door.

"It's very close, I can just cut through the backyard—"

"Get in." He didn't let go of her arm until she was in the passenger seat. He was seated beside her and had locked the doors before she had time to think. He started the engine, but before backing up, he turned to her. "Look, I just want to make sure nothing happens on my watch."

Katura was relieved to see the local kids still playing soccer when she and Changa reached them. The boy who'd invited her seemed surprised to see her but introduced her to the others and put her on his team. It was a game with kids of all ages and required the older ones not to play competitively, which was fortunate since Katura's mind wasn't on the game. When she told Changa she could walk home after the game, he'd just smiled. Now she glanced over every few minutes to see the white van on the road across from the field. As she continued to play, she felt as if something were crowding her chest, making it hard for her lungs to get enough air.

CHAPTER 12

"**G**et everyone inside." Zuka yelled over his shoulder to his comrades. Japera had come out of the guide tent just after the shots were fired. He pulled Thabani aside. They weren't listening to Zuka, but it took him a moment to notice. He watched them, then turned back to the hostages.

"Split up into two tents." He motioned with his rifle.

Jane continued wrapping Paul's leg. She stared at the leg, stared at the wrapping, tried to keep herself from thinking about Rick. She felt a tingling numbness in her fingers as she moved around Paul's thigh. *Slow down your breathing.* She counted to five and deeply inhaled, then exhaled just as slowly. She leaned over and felt the bandana that bound Paul's leg—tight enough to stop the bleeding, not so tight as to cut off circulation to his foot. She secured the knot. He was lucky no major vessel had been hit.

She bit her upper lip and closed her eyes a moment. Hit? Gunshots, how do bullets travel under water? Two shots, where'd they go? Had it hurt, was it over fast? Maybe he'd just been injured. But then there was the crocodile—she preferred bullets. She opened her eyes, which remained unfocused. She had waited ten minutes, seemed like an hour, for Rick to come up, to crawl unharmed onto the shore of the other side. Nothing. *Breathe, slowly breathe.* She forced herself to concentrate on Paul's leg. It would need to be redressed once she could get to her medical supplies, but this should be good enough for him to get up from where he lay.

Out of the corner of her eye she watched the three Africans. Who were these men? What did they want? She watched their body language but could read nothing. They were nothing more than strangers to her. Their culture, their history—she had nothing to draw upon.

"Michael, help me get Paul into the tent." It wasn't far but he shouldn't put weight on it. Paul's hefty build would be too much for her alone. "Here, lean this way on your right hand and I'll lift underneath your arm. Make sure you keep that leg stiff, no bending. Michael will hoist up the left..." Michael?

She turned to see that her son hadn't gotten up to help her. He was watching Japera and Thabani, who were whispering on the far side of the tent. He then glanced over at the one remaining raft that hadn't been shredded. It was thirty yards away, the river waves still slapping its side.

It was then that she realized that Zuka, too, was watching him. Waiting.

"Michael," she said it loud and crisp. "I need help—now."

Michael's eyes jerked up and he caught Zuka's stare. "Sorry, Mom." He got up immediately.

Paul rolled away from her and hoisted himself up. "I can walk," he said. He took a few steps before he nearly collapsed. Michael caught him just before he was about to land on Jane. She jumped up, draped his arm across her shoulder, and grabbed him by the waist.

"Just lean on me." She nodded toward the closest tent. "You and Tommy can take this one." She turned to Thabani. "I'd like to get my medical kit and bandage his leg properly, if you don't mind. Then I'll go in the other tent with my boys."

Thabani glanced at her and looked away. She took it as a yes.

Paul tried to walk on his own, but the pain was too much. Michael and Jane hobbled him toward the tents. As they neared the others, she caught the look on Jake's face. He still stood frozen where she had left him, his eyes pleading. Her usually confident boy looked terrified.

"Jake, the kit's in the bottom of my bag. Find it and bring it to me, will you?" He glanced at Paul's leg and ran for the bag.

Thabani, watching Jake from a distance, seemed on edge when he went alone into the large tent where the bags were. Jane wished she hadn't brought attention to him. He seemed so small at that moment, so young. He still had his boyish frame. Michael, on the other hand had grown a head taller in the last year. He was as tall as the Africans but not quite as bulky.

When Jake emerged with the bag she nodded for him to put it inside the tent they were moving toward. Thabani used the barrel of his rifle to open the tent and glance around before he allowed Jake in.

It was then that she saw a look of concern pass over the African's face. Jane followed Thabani's gaze. He was scanning the top of the cliff walls of the canyon that surrounded them. She searched for any movement, any sign of life that could be aware of this scene below. All was still as the sun continued to lower itself toward the horizon. Her eye moved down the canyon, drawn inevitably to the rushing water. She stared midway across the river just before it turned sharply around the bend—the last place she'd seen Rick before he disappeared under water. There was no sign of the dark crimson that had stained the water right after Zuka's shots. The river had returned to its fast-moving swirls topped with whitecaps, the flow pattern that was created by water rushing over unseen rocks below. No evidence of what had occurred.

"We'll have to eat quickly." Zuka stood several yards in front of her but was not addressing anyone in particular. "It'll be dark soon and I want everyone inside when the sun goes down. Once inside, no one comes out unless I say so."

She stared at the young man in front of her. Stared into his face. She studied the smooth black skin and dark brown eyes—so dark, in fact, that she could barely distinguish the color from the pupil. She wanted to take it all in, know it completely. This was the man who'd killed her husband—thought nothing of raising his weapon as Rick attempted to save her and her boys. He'd taken aim and fired, he'd murdered the man she loved.

Zuka opened the lid of the pot that was still steaming from Baruti's efforts. He lifted the spoon to his mouth but stopped when his eyes locked onto Jane's. Paul tugged at her arm. She didn't budge. Zuka shifted slightly in his stance. He took in a deep breath, then continued to sip from the spoon.

⅄

Jane nodded at her boys' plates, an unspoken encouragement for them to eat. It wasn't clear when they'd get their next meal. But they weren't the only ones who sat in silence and picked at the food, barely moving their flimsy camping forks. Paul and Tommy hadn't touched their plates either, and no one was talking. She found the silence deafening.

Michael looked up at her. She just shook her head—watch and wait, keep a low profile, see what opportunities present themselves. She attempted to quash her mounting rage, she knew full well that it served internally to ward off terror and grief but externally it could only make matters worse. *Keep your wits. Think forward, what's the next move? Be consciously aware of* ... She wasn't sure of what. Of anything, everything.

It was the silence that allowed her to hear it: a rustling noise in the trees. Maybe someone had heard the shots and was coming to help. She clanged her plates around to try to distract the others, but she needn't have bothered. The Africans stared at the trees bordering the west jetty.

"I'll check it out," Zuka said. He hesitated before he left the table, his eyes darting around at the campsite. "I'll take the oldest boy with me. Japera, stay inside with Lorenzo and the girl." Their two guides were still tied up inside their tent. He turned to Thabani. "Get the rest inside."

Jane grabbed Michael and pulled him to her. "No, he's staying with me."

Zuka took a step toward her and tightened the grip on his gun.

Michael reared around and took both of Jane's forearms in his. She was struck by the strength of his grip.

"Mom, I'll be fine. You stay here with Jake, and I'll be right back." She heard a slight tremor in his voice. "Trust me."

"It's not you—"

"Mom." He hadn't released her. "I've got no choice." His eyes locked onto hers. She could see the fear.

"Don't do anything to—"

"I know, Mom. I'll be right back."

Paul started to rise, then doubled over in pain, let out a groan, and grabbed his thigh.

"I'd better clean and redress his wound before it gets infected," Jane said. Michael nodded and dropped her hands to join Zuka. Jane turned to Jake.

"I need you to stay in our tent, no matter what you hear." She couldn't bear to watch Michael walk into the brush with that man. She tried to steady her voice. "I'll be right in when Paul's cleaned up." Jake looked up at her, his eyes hollow. "I'll be quick, promise." She waited until he nodded. "Tommy, grab a couple of water bottles and come with us."

When they were inside, Paul let go of her support and hopped on one leg over to his cot. He'd kept his injured leg as stiff as possible, but now that he was required to navigate this small room, movement was necessary. His breathing was strained and his teeth clenched against the pain by the time he reached the cot to sit. Jane lifted his leg slowly. He let out a soft low moan. When he finally lay flat, she turned away and busied herself with the medical kit. He needed time to regain his dignity.

Once his breathing returned to a regular rhythm, Jane ripped Paul's pant leg, just above the wound. With the small scissors from the kit, she cut the removed piece of cloth into a three-inch-wide strip on the diagonal of the fabric in order to form one long, sturdy bandage. Tommy stood motionless in the corner of the tent.

"I need a helper, Tommy."

He moved toward her—but only two steps—then stopped. She pulled the second cot closer to where Paul lay and patted it for Tommy to sit next to her. He didn't look directly at his father's leg. Jane gave him the first-aid bag.

"I need you to hand me things while I clean up your dad's leg. You see," she whispered with a wink at Tommy, "that guy out there thinks he's really hurt your dad, but we know better. It's important that we let them think your dad is bad off. You can even act all worried. That would help. It's our secret that this is no big deal, okay?"

Tommy snuck a peek over her shoulder at the wound.

"Can you check in the bag for a cotton pad to clean up this blood? We need to—"

"Don't touch my blood." Paul jerked his leg away from her. He grimaced and then fell silent.

Jane's mind was racing. She looked down at his wound, then back at him.

"Tommy," she said, "could you look around the tent to see if there's an extra blanket somewhere? Maybe over in that far corner under the bags? Dig around, I'm sure you'll find something."

She glared at Paul, who was offering no explanation for his sudden outburst. When Tommy was out of earshot, she whispered, "Look, you and I haven't exactly gotten along swimmingly, that's no secret, but you need this wound cleaned and if you have some blood-borne disease it's time to fess up. You've got about fifteen seconds before your son returns, so start talking."

He sat staring at the roof of the tent.

"I don't have a lot of patience, Paul. My husband's been killed, my youngest boy is frightened to death in a tent all alone, and my teenager is out wandering the forest with an armed killer." She tried not to feel the impact of her own words. She focused on her irritation with Paul.

He exhaled a heavy sigh. "Hep C."

Jane studied his face. His shame was worse than his disease.

"Tommy," she said loudly, "did you find that blanket yet?"

"Is this good enough?" He held up a light thermal throw that must have been provided for sitting out in the evenings.

"Perfect, now put it gently over your father's good leg so he doesn't get chilled while we work." She glanced over the first-aid supplies as Tommy placed the blanket.

"Now, Tommy." She turned and faced him. "Any time you work with someone who's been bleeding, you have to wear gloves. It's called Universal Precautions. No matter who it is. Got it?"

He nodded.

"So we're going to practice that here. There should be a couple of surgical gloves in the kit. Get them out so we can get started."

⋏

They had just finished securing the final exterior bandage when she heard muffled voices outside. Jane stood up and put her right index finger to her lips. Tommy immediately stopped chattering.

She inched toward the opening in the door, tried to recognize the voices, the words.

"It was nothing," Zuka said, "just a croc. But I think we should move out tonight."

"Tonight? But…"

Jane couldn't hear the rest. They must have moved further away from her.

"Mind if I go and get my mom? Take her over to our tent?" Michael's tone was obsequious.

Jane let out the deep breath she hadn't been aware of holding. Her shoulders relaxed.

"I'll get her," Zuka said. "You and your brother start breaking down camp. And move fast. Take only what you can carry on your backs. Toss everything else, including the tents, behind those trees and out of view from the river."

Jane ducked back behind the mosquito net opening. She grabbed her medical bag and was just about to close it up when she stopped. The glistening steel of the scalpel handle caught her eye. She quickly dug around and found the small flat cardboard squares that held the blades. She slipped the handle and blades into her pants pocket, then closed up the kit. Just in time—the door of the tent burst open.

"Get out here." Zuka looked around the tent, then held the door for her to exit. He grabbed the medical bag out of her hand. "I'll keep this."

Chapter 13

"That was stupid." Jake lay on the far bed and stared at the ceiling. He looked exhausted but seemed wide awake.

Michael moved a dresser frame out from the wall, the drawers and hardware had already been removed. He moved his foot along the dirt floor searching for anything loose. "This place has been totally cleaned out." He looked under Jake's bed.

"I can't believe we left the beach because of a crocodile," Jake said. "There're much worse animals in that jungle."

Jane glanced over at her youngest—maybe contempt was better than fear.

"Especially after dark." He shook his head.

They'd walked all night, and Jane was spent by the time they reached the deserted resort. It had been nearly impossible to see, the path lit only by the occasional moonlight that worked its way through the dense canopy. Paul had tried to do most of the hike without leaning on her, but he had groaned frequently, twisting and turning his ankle on the uneven terrain. Their slow pace put Jane and Paul behind the others, yet they still had to travel faster than Paul should have been moving. Zuka had taken up the rear, and they didn't like him getting too close, so had to keep pushing themselves. By the time they reached the huts, Paul's left thigh was red and swollen, and his wound was oozing a thick yellow substance Jane knew was a precursor to pus.

Tommy had already collapsed on his cot and appeared to be out for hours. Jane cleaned and redressed Paul's wound again, then left so he could get some rest with his leg elevated. She'd told the boys to stay up and wait in their hut. She needed their help for her next move.

"It wasn't about the crocodile." Michael stuck his head into the adjoining bathroom and looked around. "Besides, I don't think they're real concerned about our safety."

Jane looked out the front window. She scanned the open picnic area all the huts faced—tried to imagine the line of sight in every direction. The guest huts formed a semicircle around the large main stone structure that still supported its colorful hand-painted sign for the Zambezi Safari Lodge. With its grand entrance and massive open-beam construction, this building must have once served as the dining hall and gathering place when this was an active jungle resort for tourists. She could see remnants of its previously luxurious incarnation—not that it would ever have been glamorous in a western way, but its thatched roofs and high ceilings still gave the appearance of grandeur. The architecture appeared to have been designed to blend with the surrounding African vegetation when well kept. Now that same vegetation was about to take it over.

On the other side of the kitchen's loading dock, facing away from the guest huts, stood rudimentary accommodations with canvas sides. These must have served as the workers' quarters—near the kitchen and much less attractive than the guest huts that dotted the grounds. Jane studied them before she focused back on the barbecue area where Japera sat on one of the outdoor tables, rifle at his side.

Jake leaned on one elbow and faced his brother. "But Zuka said you guys found a crocodile."

"Oh, we found a croc, all right. But it was already dead, just washed up on shore." He glanced over at Jane. "Mom, what's the plan?"

She took in a deep breath. "I need your help, both of you."

Jake sat up and bit his upper lip.

"I need to get to Lorenzo. They have him tied up in the back of the workers' hut. Japera's keeping guard while the other two get some sleep." She paced a moment, then sat down on the bed and leaned forward toward Michael. "I need you to go out there. Talk with him, keep him busy, make sure he faces away while I go in through the back."

Michael combed his fingers through his hair and looked away from her.

"He has the first watch. I helped him build the fire and make some coffee. It gave me a chance to casually talk with the guy. He's kind of quiet, not as jumpy as the others, not as angry." She looked down at her hands in her lap. "But Michael, if you don't think…"

"It's safe?" He came out with a choked laughed. "Nothing here is safe, Mom." He peered out the window for several minutes before he spoke. "It's okay, I can do it."

She watched him study the angles, judge the distances. She waited for his shoulders to relax before she spoke again. "I'll have to sneak behind those huts on the far left and the lodge. There's at least four spots where he could see me, and the gap between that last hut and the lodge is huge."

"I'll look for that. I'll make sure he doesn't see you."

Jake got up from his cot. "But Mom, if they catch you—"

"Jake, you need to stay in here…" She walked over to her youngest.

"What do I—"

"…and wait. If Michael sees anything go wrong, if he needs me to know there's a problem, he'll call out to you. Loudly,

Michael, not obvious, but loud enough for me to hear you. Call for Jake to join you, say you want to show him something, the stars, the moon, whatever. That'll be our signal."

Michael stood silent and stared out the window.

"Michael, I need you to be loud enough—"

"Don't worry, Mom." His eyes were watery as he turned away from her. "You'll hear me."

⊀

The bathroom window was covered with a fine mesh screen. The warm African breeze kept the room a constant temperature, and permanent windows wouldn't have been necessary at this resort even in its prime. Jane popped the screen out and lowered herself to the ground behind their room. It was only a short distance to the area behind the workers' quarters, but it took her over ten minutes to reach Lorenzo's hut. The twigs and branches in her path required her to move with the utmost care—the moonlight was bright enough to make her passage behind buildings highly visible were Japera to look in her direction. But Michael's conversation was engrossing enough to keep Japera's attention. When he chose, Michael could be quite the conversationalist.

She knelt down on the ground below the canvas wall and took out her scalpel. She popped the blade in place, then heard movement inside the hut. Her head jerked up—silence. She could feel her heart pounding, took in a deep breath and let it out slowly. She steadied her hand as she approached the bottom of the canvas. Suddenly she heard it again. This time it was unmistakable. She listened for words—there were none. But there was definitely movement, maybe a chair scraping on the floor, someone walking, she couldn't tell. She waited and listened. Should she abort the plan? If someone had entered the front of the hut Michael would have seen it, he would have warned her, unless he couldn't. But the noise wasn't enough to be a scuffle with Michael. It seemed to come from inside the hut.

"Really?" She heard Michael's voice, muffled by the distance. He was still in the picnic area. "Wow, that's amazing."

The blade was sharp enough to enter the canvas without difficulty, but the sound of the fabric slicing forced her to cut slowly. Zuka and Thabani were in the hut just on the other side and hadn't been there long enough to be in deep sleep. Finally she had a slice about eighteen inches long. She went back to the corner. Moving up would be louder—it was against the grain of the fabric.

She was about to extend the slit vertically from the corner when the toe of a boot appeared in the hole she'd created. She jumped back and held the scalpel tight. The boot disappeared back inside. She waited—nothing.

"Lorenzo?" she whispered through the opening.

"Shhh."

She opened the slit further, making the opening just large enough to allow her to wiggle her way into the small structure. She gave her eyes a few moments to adjust to the darkness, then focused on Shelly. She was tied to a small cot in the corner, sat halfway up with her legs stretched straight but appeared to be asleep. A thick rope passed through her mouth and was secured around the back of her head.

"We don't have much time," Lorenzo whispered. The bandana tied around his mouth was soaked in saliva. He'd worked it down his face with his teeth. "I've almost got my hands free. Help me out."

Jane took her scalpel to the back of his chair. He'd already loosened the knot with his movements, and it took only a few quick slices to free him completely. He reached down to untie his feet.

"Here, this'll be faster." She sliced through the rope that bound his ankles.

He stood and stretched. He glanced over at Shelly, and Jane moved to untie her.

"Jane, hold on a minute." They could hear talking outside. He knelt down and peered out the opening, then went to the west window and attempted to see around the corner where Japera stood watch.

"Michael's with Japera, keeping him distracted."

"He's a good boy, Jane. Solid kid. This is just all too much for those boys, shouldn't be happening to them." He stared out the window.

"If you and Shelly can get to someone, contact the American Embassy—"

"No, I'm doing this alone. It's too dangerous out there. Carnivores, remember?" He smiled at Shelly. "And she'll just slow me down." He sat on Shelly's cot and rubbed her leg gently.

She stirred.

"We talked, decided that if one of us could get loose I'd be the one to run. I know my way around." He got up and moved toward the opening. "Japera will be making the rounds soon and it's better if it looks like she's not in on this, like I was acting alone and no one's messed with her ropes. Keeps her safer."

He examined the two slashes Jane had made in the canvas.

"We've got to make this look like it was done from the in-side—make sure they don't think you're involved either." He searched around the floor of the hut. "Here, help me out. Take the sharp edge of this rock and rough up the edges of the slash."

"Go straight to Harare, to the U.S. Embassy," Jane said. "Don't talk to anyone in Vic Falls or anywhere else, we don't know who's in on this." She'd just about finished working on the edge of the hole when she heard Michael's voice.

"Jake, I know you're not sleeping. Come out here, just for a minute."

Jane grabbed Lorenzo's arm. "That's the signal, something's happening." She glanced over at Shelly—their eyes met for a moment. She was moving her legs, seemed to be twisting in the bed, and then the shadows shifted and Jane couldn't see her well.

Lorenzo stuffed the cut rope into his jacket pocket.

"Jake, get out here. I want to show you something." Michael's voice was louder.

"Go now, Jane, I'll be right after you. Shelly…" He was at her bedside in seconds. "I'll bring help, I'll be back as fast as I can. Just tell them you woke up and I was gone."

Jane slipped out of the hut and felt Lorenzo's body wiggle out right after her. "Be safe," she said.

"No worries." He hugged her, then took off into the brush. Jane ducked around the back corner just as she heard Zuka going up the stairs to enter Shelly's hut.

⋏

Jane put her hands in the basin of water that sat on the bathroom counter. She looked in the faded mirror. She'd barely slept all night wondering how far Lorenzo had gotten. How long would it take him to get to the embassy? Even after he made it back to Vic Falls it would be at least a full day to Harare, and he wouldn't trust the phones. He'd need to go in person. She tried to visualize the map but couldn't quite picture the scale. Whatever it was, her task now was to keep her family safe just until help arrived.

She'd lain awake thinking about what the reaction would be to Lorenzo's escape. How would this change her captors' plans? Maybe they'd move to another location. That would be hard on Paul, but at least someone would be searching for them. In the wee hours her mind had wandered to obscure details. Glenn was listed as the emergency contact for the kids. Would they notify him? Would he fly out? She slapped cold water on her face. Why was she thinking about her ex now? Some crazy fantasy that in her most desperate moment he'd finally come through for her? She shook her head, dunked it under water, and let her hair be fully submerged. She was wringing out the excess water when she heard the boys begin to stir in the next room. She walked out of the bathroom.

"I'm going over to check on Paul's leg."

"Anything you can do about all this light, Mom? I can't sleep." The sun shone brightly through the front window that faced east. Michael pulled the top of his sleeping bag over his head.

It was then that it struck her. She was squinting. She backed up into the bathroom. The contrast was unmistakable. She looked over at the bathroom window. The screen was gone and there was a wooden door standing upright against the opening—the same window she'd exited from the night before. She pushed on the door, which rocked slightly but held secure.

ᛉ

"Did they block off your bathroom window too?" she asked. Paul's room was a mirror image of her own. "Mine's got an old door wedged up against it with a huge boulder on the outside."

Tommy came out of the bathroom and wrung the water out of a white cloth.

She noticed his hand was quivering.

"He feels kind of hot."

"I'll take it from here, sweetie."

Tommy handed her the cloth.

Paul stirred as she felt his skin, damp and very warm. His lids opened halfway at her continued touch.

"I'm okay, just need to sleep."

"Michael." It was Japera outside the huts. "Help me unload this."

She glanced out the front window and saw a dark van coming down the road. From the looks of it, Japera was expecting it, probably supplies. At least for now they must be planning to stay a while.

She unfolded Tommy's rag—it was a pair of boy's white briefs. She smiled at Tommy.

"It was all I could find." He looked away. "Dad must've dropped your rag on the hike last night."

"This'll work just fine." She laid the briefs across Paul's forehead. "Maybe this will all be over soon."

Paul snorted and sat up slightly. "So you found a phone and called in the cavalry?"

She unzipped his sleeping bag and exposed his leg. She felt the outside of his bandage. It was still dry.

"Don't worry, Tommy, he can't be too feverish if he can still make fun of me." She looked at Paul. "We should leave this on for now, but you need to start antibiotics. I'll have to get them from the medical kit somehow." That was unfortunate—she'd hoped to avoid much contact with their captors.

"What makes you think it might be over soon?"

She looked at the swelling around his ankle, compared it to the left. She let out a sigh and whispered, "Lorenzo's going for help."

"What?" He raised his voice and hoisted himself up further.

"He's going to try to make it to the embassy in Harare." She felt relief in saying it out loud. "I helped him escape just before dawn."

"Are you nuts?"

"*Thanks* might be more appropriate. You've got two-plus edema in the ankle—it's not draining well. Wiggle your toes."

"Two out of how many?" He complied with her directions. "And how do you know he's going to the embassy? How do you know he's not in on this?"

She touched the top of his foot. It was warm. She felt for a pedal pulse.

"Two out of four—maybe we won't have to amputate if you keep your foot elevated." She stuffed a sweatshirt under his foot and threw the top of the sleeping bag back over his legs. "You're paranoid, or maybe it's the fever talking. Is hope just not part of your emotional repertoire?"

"You think those guys got all that rafting equipment from our driver? They'd need someone with a little more clout than the guy who takes people from the airport to the hotel, don't you think?"

"But Lorenzo—"

"Remember how Lorenzo reacted to Shelly?" His voice was getting louder.

"Yes, but we talked about that and—"

"Maybe we had it all wrong." He looked over at Tommy. "Maybe it wasn't just concern over the kids after all. Maybe there was something else about that other guy being here that was important to their plan."

She watched a drop of perspiration work its way down the side of Paul's face before she glanced out the window. No one was currently within earshot, but they were moving supplies and would pass near enough to hear him if the breeze was right, especially if he kept talking louder.

She looked back and cocked her head. "Go ahead," she whispered. "But keep it down."

He stopped and stared at her. Then he wiped the back of his neck with the rag and sat back. He closed his eyes and said nothing for several minutes. When he opened them again he looked for a moment at his son before he focused on her.

"Yeah, I'm not big on hope. And maybe you're right, maybe it doesn't make sense that they're both in on this. When they reach the embassy and tell them about Rick, about us still being here—"

"They? I said I helped Lorenzo escape. Shelly's not with him."

"But Shelly *was* with him, wasn't she?"

"He'll be faster alone."

Paul hesitated a moment. "That okay with her?"

"She didn't object."

Jane glanced at the bathroom, light streaming through the window. Why had her window been barred? They would know that Lorenzo was gone by now, but did they know she was part of his escape? Did Lorenzo really think Shelly would be safer here, or…? She looked back outside. She had to talk to Shelly. Michael, Japera, and the driver carried another load from the truck into the main lodge. When they all disappeared inside, she made her move.

CHAPTER 14

"That doesn't make sense. Why would they keep him tied up?" Jane loosened Shelly's hands. She didn't want to cut the rope, she'd need it later.

"From what I can gather, they need to have a lot of people on the inside. You hear about it, but I never really believed it—until now."

"Inside?"

Shelly glanced at the door. "In different commercial businesses, people who are sympathetic to their cause—will come through on favors when they need it."

"The rafts?"

"Exactly." Shelly slipped her hands out and rubbed her wrists. "They don't want to blow Lorenzo's cover. They may need him again in the future, so they make him look like an innocent victim of this mess. You know, a mole."

Jane shook her head. Shelly's explanation didn't jibe with her experience of Lorenzo, especially at the end—the way he'd hugged her, his reassurances seemed genuine.

"I don't know, Shelly, he's not from Zimbabwe, didn't seem interested in their politics—more like a river guide who's just as likely to be here as South America, or anywhere else where the water flows fast." Jane peered out the side window as Japera came out of the front of the lodge, stood on the porch. She held her hand up to silence Shelly until he'd turned and gone back inside.

Shelly smiled. "Good cover, isn't it?"

"But why?"

Shelly shrugged. "Business has been really bad and people get desperate—some people even end up taking money from both sides. I can't really blame them." She pulled at the rope that bound her feet to the bed. "But it seems awfully risky."

Shelly's ties had been loosened since last night and she no longer had the gag in her mouth. She said they'd questioned her about Lorenzo's escape—part of the plan to make it look like he wasn't with them.

"You didn't tell them that I—"

"Of course not."

Jane watched her closely. "Then why is my window blocked?"

"He must've told them. Look, Jane, it's not your fault, there's no way you could have known about him." Shelly stretched her neck to look out the window just above her bed. "He certainly fooled me. Any thoughts about what we should do now?"

Jane noted the quick change in subject. She watched Michael unload another bag from the truck, he didn't close the back so there must be more. She still had a little time.

"So where will he go now?" Jane searched the girl's face. Was it safe to trust her? To help her escape?

"He'll probably just hide out until all of this blows over, then come out of the woods like he got lost. It's quite believable, especially since he's not a native. I wouldn't want to be out there alone."

"What? You're not—"

"They need us all now for the negotiation." Shelly bit the side of her mouth and looked away. "It was clear from what they were saying—no more losses, that's what they called Zuka's craziness. Anyway. . ." She took in a deep breath and rubbed her ankles. "I'd never make it across the basin alive."

"But you weren't on their list, they don't need you. Someone has to go for help and you—"

"They do now. If Andrew had been here it'd have been a different story. Thabani has it out for him. But now they want me alive, just in case the American government is less motivated without Rick. They think working with two governments will be to their advantage." She stopped and looked down at her hands. "I'm so sorry about Rick."

"Thanks." Jane got up and paced the room. She wasn't going to share her mourning with this girl, not here, not now anyway. She needed to keep on track. "I just think it's too dangerous for you to stay here. You never know what those three are going to do." She paused a moment. "Especially Zuka."

Shelly wasn't young enough to be Jane's daughter, yet she found herself feeling maternal toward her—young, pretty, it wasn't safe. Shelly looked around the room, she seemed to be struggling with her options. When her eyes finally rested on Jane's, they were pleading. Gone was the confidence Jane had been impressed with on the river. It was clear that what lay in the wilderness frightened her more than whatever these men could do. Everything Jane read had warned her never to wander away from a trained native guide who knew the terrain. *But compared to what?* Travel books weren't exactly weighing that risk against being held by men with guns. She studied the soft features of this young Australian girl. There was something about having her here that added an extra burden on Jane's shoulders.

"Okay." She sat at the foot of Shelly's cot. "I need to get into one of their heads, make them question what they're doing, break up their solidarity."

Shelly sat back, her eyebrows furrowed. "How?"

"I'm not sure yet. It depends. The first question is who."

Shelly was silent for a moment. "Japera seems the nicest, the softest of the three."

"He's not the leader. He won't have enough sway with them." Jane 's stomach clenched. What would it be like to try to get close to Rick's murderer? She squeezed Shelly's fingers. "Zuka. I've got to—"

"No." Shelly sat up, her face emphatic. "Not him, Thabani."

"It's okay, Shelly, I can do this. It's for my kids." Jane was clear the tables had turned, now it was her responsibility to keep everyone safe, not this young girl's. "Rick would want me to do whatever it took."

Shelly drew her hands away. "He's not their leader, Thabani is. Zuka's just the muscle, like the hired help."

"I'm not so sure. He doesn't seem to be taking orders from anyone."

"He's gotten quite a bit out of hand, but they're reining him in now. Thabani promised that. Lorenzo was really upset—hopping mad—about the shootings, I guess they must've promised him no one would get hurt."

So there's already dissension in the ranks. Jane walked over to peer out the window.

"You think he's upset enough to go to the authorities? If it's just about money, how committed could he be?"

Shelly paused for several minutes before she spoke. She was holding something back.

"Jane, no matter how he feels, Lorenzo won't be able do that—he can't betray them. They've got too many men out there…everywhere." It seemed to pain Shelly to have to say it, to dash Jane's hopes.

"But—"

"Anyone who's gotten themselves in this deep can't back out." Her eyes began to water. "Not now, not with the murders." She swiped at her eyes to get rid of the tears.

"But if you know all this—if they've said it in front of you—doesn't that mean they don't expect you to make it out alive?"

Shelly laughed with no trace of amusement. "They thought I was asleep. Thabani'd come in here and whisper to Lorenzo. They'd have long conversations while they thought I was out cold. That's how I knew about him."

She was like a child who's pulled one over on her parents.

She smiled at Jane. "I was the youngest of four girls, we shared one bedroom, which required me to fake sleep like a corpse to hear the conversations of my older sisters. It was the only way I'd ever know what was going on. You can't lie too still, it's a dead giveaway—sighs, occasional turning, and periodic leg twitches are the key." She licked her fingers and rubbed her face, removing the last remnants of her tears.

Suddenly Jane heard the tailgate shut. Time's up.

"Don't," Shelly said, "don't make me stay here alone. You have no idea how awful it is."

"I'll be back as soon as I can." She looked directly into Shelly's eyes. "Trust me, I'll be back."

Shelly nodded. She scooted back on her cot and spread her arms.

Jane grabbed the rope and began tying Shelly back up. "Tell me everything you know about Thabani. Quickly."

⋏

Jane rounded the back corner of her hut and climbed up the stairs to the porch. She stopped at the sound of her sons arguing inside.

"What's your problem, anyway?"

She stood still in the silence, waiting.

"Come on, out with it, Jake. You might as well tell me what the problem is." Michael's voice had softened to a coaxing tone.

"You know."

"No, say it."

"It's just…" Jane heard the crack in Jake's voice. "If we weren't here—"

"You're blaming me for getting us captured?"

"No! I just wish we didn't have to come to Africa."

"You wanted to come as much as—"

There was a thud, something had been thrown down on the floor.

"You think it's my fault we came?" Michael's voice was getting louder.

"If Mom hadn't been so worried about—"

"That's right, Jake, it's my fault. And I fired Zuka's gun for him too, right?" Michael lowered his voice when he mentioned Zuka's name.

"I'm just saying, if Caitlin hadn't been such a jerk, that whole thing wouldn't have happened."

As far as she knew, it was the first time Michael's girlfriend had been mentioned in relation to his arrest. Jane had always suspected Caitlin was involved. She took a few steps closer to the door.

"Caitlin didn't hit that guy or buy the beer—"

"Dylan bought the beer. You didn't have to take the rap for everything, Michael. Not to mention making Mom think you're on your way to a life of crime."

"At least you got a trip to Africa out of it. I guess that's why you never told her yourself." They were quiet for a minute.

"It's your story to tell," Jake said. There it was—the brother's code, in place since they were young, a byproduct of the divorce.

Michael walked out the door. He glanced at Jane, then brushed by her.

She let the screen close softly. Jake was shuffling through his bag. He found his paperback and plopped onto his cot. Through the screened window she saw Michael walk over to Japera and sit across from him on a picnic bench.

"He's seems quite sure of himself."

"Not really." Jake spoke into his book and turned a page.

She looked again out the window. She couldn't make out what they were saying, but they looked, for all the world, like friends talking. Japera had been on guard for several hours and probably was glad to have company.

After Rick was shot, Michael would stand by her bed or next to her chair fidgeting, trying to come up with words to soothe her. She'd let him comfort her, but only for his sake, unable to truly allow his empathy to touch her. The role reversal made her uncomfortable. After all, he was only fifteen—too young to be comforting his mother. Widowed mother? Widow. A lonely word labeled what she was now. She put her head in her hands.

⅄

When Thabani came out of the hut he shared with his cousin, he went right to the stove and stirred the fire under the pot. Jane had hoped Zuka would take the shift after Japera and she could get some rest. But with Zuka asleep, this was the moment to make her move. She turned back to Jake, deep in an Orson Scott Card book, probably his second reading.

"Stay in here," she said and turned to leave.

"Mom?" He put his book aside and looked at her.

She sighed and sat back down next to him. "Listen carefully."

⅄

Jane made a noisy approach as she walked to where Thabani was stirring the leftovers. She knew better than to surprise him. He looked up at her, then over at the other two. Everyone should have been asleep for his shift.

"I just wasn't hungry earlier," she said. "Is there enough for me to have a small portion?"

"Yeah."

She glanced back and saw that Japera was focused on Michael, as planned.

There was something about these two cousins that struck her, a side of them that was in contrast to their current situation. At meals Japera always served her first and made sure the boys had enough. When they walked through the jungle, Thabani accompanied her into a secluded area if she had to go to the bathroom. He kept his distance and turned away. Good breeding, her mother would have said.

"Whoa, that's plenty." Thabani had dished up more than half of the leftover stew. She sat down at the far end of the table.

Michael and Japera got up to go to their respective huts.

"I'll be done in a few minutes," she called to Michael. He nodded and headed in.

Suddenly Paul's door swung open. The noise he made descending the porch stairs seemed absurdly loud. Tommy had found a thick sturdy branch for his father to use as a walking cane.

"Heard some voices out here, thought I might join the party," Paul said.

They all stared at him. Jane wasn't sure what it was—his manner? His tone? Whatever it was, the tension was palpable. It would be just like him to spoil this opportunity.

"What's the matter?" Paul glanced at Thabani. "Am I interrupting something?" An accusing tone, and directed at her. Out of the corner of her eye she saw Japera in the shadows.

"No party, Paul," Thabani said. "You should go back inside and get some sleep."

Paul approached them slowly, leaning heavily on the stick. "I'm glad I'm not intruding, I've got some questions and thought you might be of some help."

Thabani moved a few steps toward his rifle, by the stove.

Michael was instantly at Paul's side. He put an arm around his shoulder.

"Why don't you save those for the morning? Everyone's tired here, and—"

"Don't patronize me, Michael." Paul pulled away with too much force and lost his balance for a moment. He grabbed onto the branch with both hands and steadied himself, his face distorted into a grimace, then turned to face Thabani.

"I want to know exactly what it is that you're trying to get out of this." He shook his head, closed his eyes. He took in several labored breaths and put his hand over his right thigh. "I'm getting off on the wrong foot."

He snorted at his own joke.

"The thing is, maybe if I understood what was happening here, what it is you want, I might be able to help. There might be a better way." Paul glanced down at Thabani's rifle, still leaning against the stove.

"You need to get back inside, Paul," Thabani said. They were both several feet away from the gun.

"I just thought that maybe—" Paul leapt toward the gun. But his injured leg didn't allow for the kind of swift movement he was attempting. Thabani got there first.

Twenty feet away they heard a rifle cock. Paul froze.

"You've been asked twice to go back into your tent." Japera's voice boomed across the yard. "This is the last time. Go back into your tent."

"Dad!" Tommy called from the doorway in a shaky voice. "I need some help with my sleeping bag. The zipper's stuck." Paul hesitated, then limped back up the stairs.

Jane began to eat her stew, determined not to look up.

"Good night, Mom," Michael called on his way back to their hut.

Thabani turned to his cousin. "Get some sleep, I've got it."

As soon as Paul was inside, Japera disappeared into his own hut. Thabani ate his soup sitting across from Jane.

She'd read somewhere about a group of people—the Vietnamese, or were they somewhere in the Middle East? The guards weren't allowed to eat with the prisoners—eating meals together broke down barriers, formed unconscious bonds.

"It's such a different sky," she said after a long but not uncomfortable silence. The moon had disappeared over the canyon's edge, now the thousands of stars were all the more brilliant. "It's like there's too many stars to tell which ones are constellations."

Thabani picked at the food in his bowl. He wasn't watching her directly, but she could tell he was aware of her movements.

"They blend together in one big mass of light. I can't see how you tell—"

"It's over there," he said, pointing to a small cluster of stars. "The Southern Cross? It's what everyone from the north wants to see."

She pointed her index finger in the general direction he showed her, but there were a lot of groups.

"I can't quite—"

"See that really bright star? That's Acrux, the bottom of the cross."

"Got it," she said. "Thanks." She held her finger on the star, attempted to follow it to form the entire cross.

Thabani came around the table and sat next to her. She held her breath.

He grabbed her finger.

She froze.

"No, that's Alpha Centauri, the brightest star in the southern hemisphere, part of Centaurus. Move over just a little to the right, to that other bright one." He guided her finger, his head close to hers, and followed her line of sight. Jane remembered what Shelly had said. Before the incident, he was known as an excellent guide who enjoyed the outdoors and pampered his guests.

"Now I've got it," she said. "But it's so…"

"Small," he said and laughed. "Guides expect that. Everyone wants to see it, then they're disappointed when it doesn't span half the sky."

He let go of her hand and scooted away. It must be painful to remember.

She stood up and gathered the plates. "I'll get some rest. Hope your night's not too dull." She turned back to him. "Actually, I hope it is."

CHAPTER 15

"Coffee?" Katura asked.

She laid her book on the table and got up from the couch. She'd spent the whole morning trying to act casual about having this guy essentially glued to her side. She made a big breakfast and chatted with him, staying away from any topics that might show concern about her brothers. He seemed relaxed, but now it was show time.

"I'll make a fresh pot before I take off." She started filling the pot with water.

"Katura, you know I can't let you go out by yourself."

"Have it your way, but I have a scrimmage and it's likely to last for two hours. Hey, you want to go? Should be a good game." She stuck her head around the corner and raised her eyebrows.

He looked at his watch. "That's not going to work. I need some things from the market, you'll have to go with me."

"But I promised I'd be there." She gave it her best rendition of a teenage whine.

"I'm sure they'll manage without you." He picked up the newspaper and began reading the front page.

"I'm sure they can." She banged pots around the kitchen. He read his paper without looking up. She took the pot off the burner and poured the boiling water over the coffee in the filter.

"I'm actually not that much of an asset, it's just that...well, you know, I think one of the boys kind of likes me."

Changa grunted and turned the page of the paper.

"He'll probably come over to find out why I'm not there —"

Changa jerked the newspaper down to stare at her. "You told them where you live?"

She poured the coffee slowly into a fresh cup. "You can see the top of the house from the field, and some of the kids asked about me. They don't seem to get a lot of newcomers."

"Who are these guys?"

"Don't worry. I'm not interested in him, not really. Milk or sugar? Oh, right, you take it black."

"I don't want anyone over here."

"I'm sure they'll just go away if I'm not home. It's not like they'd break in. I mean, I don't really know these guys, but they don't seem like criminals or anything." She handed him the coffee and went back into the kitchen. It was several minutes before he said anything.

"No, you'll play in that game. We'll go to the market afterwards."

"It's really not that important."

"I said, you'll play."

"Suit yourself, but then we'll have to go to the market tomorrow. It closes at four and there won't be time." She opened a cupboard. "Looks like we have enough here to wait another day—"

"No."

Changa stood and walked to the back window. He stared in the direction of the school. Katura held her breath.

"I'll drop you off, but you better be there when I come back at five."

He sat in the van a good ten minutes before he started the engine back up. She heard it loud and clear but restrained herself from looking. Just play the game. Dribble, pass, run into open space, call for the ball.

Out of the corner of her eye she saw the van turn the far corner. She waited. Sure enough, he circled the block, disappeared for a few minutes, then came back around. The third interval was longer, but finally, she was sure he was gone.

Chapter 16

"Thabani!"

Jane heard Japera call out from the picnic table where he was looking over Michael's shoulder. The kids were up early, couldn't sleep once the sun rose. Jake had found his small travel chess set in the bottom of his backpack. He set it up to play his brother before breakfast.

"Thabani, Changa's here."

Zuka came barreling out of the hut. "I'll take care of it. Let Thabani sleep."

Japera turned around. "He specifically said—"

"I can handle it."

"Of course." Japera walked toward Thabani's hut. "But I promised him I'd get him, so I'll just—"

"I said, let him sleep."

Japera stared at the hand gripping his arm.

Zuka released him.

Japera walked up to the door of Thabani's hut and opened it slowly. He stood for a few minutes before he closed it.

Zuka was already in the van.

Jane stood up and stirred the kindling on the fire. "It's still a bit chilly this morning, don't you think, Jake?"

"I'm fine." Jake looked up at Michael. "It's your move."

Michael stared at him without blinking, then moved his eyes toward his mother without turning his head.

Jake looked at his mom. "Actually, Mom," he said, "I'm kind of cold. Need help getting wood?"

"No, you two keep playing, I've got it." She picked up the small pieces of wood near the open fire pit, then moved toward Zuka and the driver. They were sitting on the back of the van, the open doors blocking their view of her.

"You know how to play this game?" Michael asked Japera and picked up his pawn. She knew he'd keep Japera distracted from her movements.

"It shouldn't change things," she heard Zuka say. "No one needs to know he's dead."

"Unless the body turns up downriver," Changa said. "Then we've got trouble." He threw a rock into a bush twenty yards away. A flock of small birds burst into the air.

"We still have the family," Zuka said.

"They'll assume they're dead too. Or they'll say they're dead to justify not doing anything. If we had the senator—"

"We don't." The van rocked.

Jane froze.

"The plan stays as it is, no changes," Zuka said.

Her shoulders relaxed. One of the men must have just changed position.

"Yeah, well, I've got to get back before the girl wakes up—"

"And if the body shows up I'll go public with one of his kids, the youngest one," Zuka said. "We'll do a picture with me, the kid, and that day's paper. Whatever it takes, we'll eventually get their attention."

Jane held her breath. Jake? She took a step back. Her foot slipped, crunching small sticks on the ground. The van door swung closed and Zuka stood staring at her. He raised his arm, but Japera grabbed her and pulled her back in time to avoid a blow.

"My fault, Zuka. I've got her."

Jane picked up a few sticks off the ground. "I was just getting—"

"Right." Japera led her over to the bench where Michael and Jake played chess. She heard the van doors slam and watched the two men walk further away from camp.

Jake moved his knight. "Checkmate."

"What?" Michael said.

"Looks like he's got you." Japera put his hand on Michael's shoulder.

Michael turned to face him. "I bet you beat your older brother all the time. You were rooting for Jake the whole game, weren't you? Sit down, I'll take you on."

Jane got up and stirred the fire. She felt Japera's eyes on her.

"I'm going back to the hut," she said. He glanced over at the men walking in the opposite direction and nodded to her. Now she could get some sleep before Thabani awoke again. Whatever alliance her boys were forming with this young man, it was more likely to happen without her around.

⋏

"It's time, Mom." Michael shook her shoulder.

"Already?" She got up and grabbed her sweatshirt. It was her third shift with Thabani. "Is he alone?"

"Has been for about a half-hour. I waited to make sure the others weren't coming back."

"Any news on your end?" But she knew if there were, he'd have woken her up right away.

"Zuka was with Japera the whole time—I couldn't even get close. Then when Thabani came out they both decided to get some sleep. Zuka's going to take over in about four hours."

"Why so soon?"

"I think they're expecting another delivery. Zuka seems to want to be around for those." Michael handed her a bowl of luke-warm grilled vegetables.

She ate and watched out the window. "And the others?"

Michael laughed. "Paul tried to convince them that he needed to exercise his leg."

She stopped mid-bite.

"He tried to circle camp, see where we are. It was pretty obvi-ous he's planning his great escape."

"What did Zuka and Japera do?"

"That was the funny thing. They kept an eye on him but let him wander—don't think they're too worried about anyone making a mad dash into the wilderness. And by the time he came back he was really limping. He went in to elevate his leg."

She thought of Shelly, her fears of leaving camp.

"Mom?"

"What?"

"Did he say a name?"

"Who?" Jane was looking out the window. Thabani sat look-ing at the stars, rifle in hand.

"The driver. Changa. I couldn't hear well, too far away. But it sounded like he said he had to get back before the girl woke up. Did he say her name?"

"Not that I remember. Why?"

"Oh, nothing."

"You think he was talking about the girl you met in the air-port? It might make sense—she's Japera's sister, right?"

"Yeah, I guess."

"You'd be disappointed if she were in on it, wouldn't you? What was her name?"

"Katura. It doesn't matter, Mom. I just feel stupid."

"It's a different world out here, Michael."

Michael picked up his paperback and turned over. Jane went back to looking out the window.

⊼

Thabani was about to make his camp rounds but stood and looked toward her hut. He glanced up expectantly when she came out the door.

Jane slowed her pace as they rounded the backside of Shelly's hut. She noted the enormous variety of flowering plants, luscious ferns, and fig trees.

"There must be some underground water in this area," she said loud enough for Shelly to hear her. She knew Shelly was still in there, but she'd had no chance to slip away and check on her.

Thabani held his index finger over his mouth. She rounded the bend and saw why—two small antelope were foraging under nearby trees. They glanced at the interlopers, then calmly resumed eating. Jane took in the white spots on their strong hindquarters and necks, the stripes on their backs and sides over coats of chestnut brown. They stood just under three feet high and had foot-long straight horns with a distinct twist.

"Bushbuck," Thabani whispered. "As usual, grazing at dusk."

Just then a large male warthog walked within ten yards from where she stood and stopped. Although it was smaller than the antelope, its large head with prominent tusks and wart-like skin below each eye made her stiffen as it came closer. She reached over and grabbed Thabani's arm.

"Careful, not all the natives are friendly," he whispered. They moved backward together. It must be a line he used when guiding. Now so out of place.

"You mean not as friendly as the ones carrying guns?"

He didn't respond.

The bushbuck had lifted their heads at the sound of her voice and bounded off in the opposite direction, out of sight of the path. The warthog stared for a moment before letting out a low, sustained grunt.

Jane and Thabani didn't move.

It stood for a minute longer before it turned and trotted off with its tail straight up like an antenna.

"Want to follow him?" Thabani asked.

She shook her head.

"Too bad, he's an amusing fellow."

Amusing? Her heart racing.

"If we followed him to his burrow we'd get to see him enter butt-first. He has to do it that way in order to keep his tusks facing out—in case we try to attack. It's a smart way to do it but it looks pretty funny. Quite entertaining, actually."

"I'll take your word for it." She smiled at him—she wasn't moving any closer toward that swine.

"Those guys can get pretty rough if they've a mind to." He reached down and picked up some nearby branches, long enough to poke at any small wildlife that approached. They circled the north side of the resort and headed toward the more forested area, away from the structures. They walked for at least ten minutes in silence.

"You must have been quite a guide," she said finally.

"I was fair."

"You enjoyed it, didn't you?"

"I suppose."

She stepped over a fallen tree trunk. "I mean, until that accident, it must have been fun to—"

"Look, I don't want to talk about that." There was something in his tone, something softer than his usual signal to stop. "It's over, okay?"

"That's good." She sat down on a boulder a few feet away. "Because often it's not over."

"No, it's over. Definitely over."

"That's good. Because, you know, for some people a thing like that just goes on and on—in their heads, I mean. The scene just flashes in front of you, again and again, like it's still happening. Can't get rid of it." She pointed to her temple. "In here, I mean."

He was very still but didn't say anything.

She waited, then picked up a stick and started drawing in the dirt. "Sometimes the scene changes, different outcomes…"

"Different outcomes?" He shook his head. "No," he said quietly.

She nodded, but didn't look up at him. She waited in silence.

"It's always the same—her face, pleading, staring at me. It's like I can hear her words calling to me."

Jane continued drawing a labyrinth in the dirt.

"The dreams are the worst, like she's whispering from underwater, her hair swirling in front of her face. . . I can almost make out her words." Thabani shook his head. "It's stupid. You can't hear people underwater."

He suddenly threw a stone across the path, squarely hitting an acacia trunk thirty yards away.

"It all fell apart because of Andrew's report."

Jane reached down and removed a couple of twigs from the middle of her drawing, smoothed over the dirt and began sketching again.

"It's not that what he said was so damning—a few things here or there, but nothing of consequence. No, he's more clever than that. He saw his opportunity. He just took his time for the report, and that's all it takes. First an incident, then nothing for weeks to clear my name? After that, it didn't really matter what the report said."

"Her words?" she asked softly. "What does she say?"

Thabani looked confused.

"In your dreams, you said the girl spoke to you under water."

149

"I said I could almost make out her words. I can't really…"

He took in a deep breath. He squatted, picked up a small stick, and started following the trail of her dirt labyrinth. It was several minutes before he spoke.

"She's begging me, like I'm not trying hard enough. Like she knows something. . . knows I won't get to her fast enough."

Jane continued drawing. His eyes followed her lines as they became more detailed. He had stopped drawing himself.

"When they found her body they said she hit her head on a rock. They said she died instantly."

"Does that help—to know she didn't suffer?"

"Not really. The bottom line is, she died on my watch. I was the safety. And that's not at all how I remember it. For me, it's like slow motion. I'm always seeing the same face." He looked directly at Jane for the first time. "I'm not even sure it's hers. She's white, with blond hair. That's all I really remember. I see her everywhere. Every time I see a young white woman I see her." He looked away from Jane. "Even in your face. But she was younger than you."

"And not very forgiving."

"I didn't know her that well."

"No, at this point you've invented her. And you've made her awfully cruel."

"I haven't made her anything."

"The girl in your head expects you to reach her when she was out of reach. I'm just saying, maybe that's not what she's like at all. You're right, you don't know her. Maybe she'd understand that you tried and that it was impossible to save her. I don't know her either, but maybe."

Thabani sat motionless for a minute or two, looking down at the ground. He stood up when Jane did, and they started walking toward camp.

"Maybe," she heard him whisper.

CHAPTER 17

"**S**helly, how're you holding up?" The girl didn't react when Jane came in—odd, she'd been so desperate before. "I'm sorry it's taken me so long, they've been watching us pretty close."

"I'm sure you tried." Shelly's voice was flat.

"We have a few minutes, they're circling camp." She looked closer—Shelly wasn't tied up. Jane grabbed her own wrist and held it up. "Hey, you're free."

Shelly turned slowly to look at the ropes that still hung from the ends of her cot, as if seeing them for the first time.

"Yeah, for now, who knows when these guys'll change their minds again. I try to leave the hut, I get shot. Don't really need ropes when you've got guns." She turned away.

"Shelly, what's going on?"

"I can't do it, Jane. I can't be in here alone day and night. I'm going—"

"Do they say why you can't come out with us?"

A long pause.

"They think I'll plan an escape, that as a guide I'm the most likely to be able to go for help." She swallowed hard. "I mean, since Baruti..."

She sat on the cot and put her arm around Shelly. The girl broke into tears. She laid her head against Jane and began to rock back and forth. From the beginning Jane had noticed that Shelly was close to Baruti, that he'd been supportive to her. She'd had no one to console her about his death. And the isolation was killing her.

"He seemed like such a good man, Shelly."

"The best." She began to rock again. "There was something so special about him. He was trying to help, to do good, that's all he ever wanted."

"He obviously thought the world of you."

She laughed, tears still running down her cheeks. "You know, he'd sneak over and in that low voice of his he'd give me hints, little pointers on how to survive working under Lorenzo. Invaluable really. He didn't have to do that, just going that extra mile—always thinking about the other guy."

"You must miss him terribly."

"It's just not fair—why him?" Shelly suddenly pulled away from Jane and faced her. "Oh my God, Jane. I'm sorry, I'm being so insensitive."

Jane glanced toward the window, tried not to think of her own loss. Her grief was private.

"Look, maybe I should just run, make a break for it and see what happens. It doesn't matter now, I might as well make myself useful, maybe I'll even get out."

"No, Shelly."

"How the hell else are we ever going to get away from here?" Shelly looked over at the slit in the canvas Jane had come through. "We have to try something. You wanted me to go before. Well, now I'm ready."

Ready? Shelly's skin was pale and she'd lost weight. Her willingness to take the risk gave away her hopelessness. A third loss on their side was more than Jane was willing to contemplate.

"Look at me, Shelly." Jane took hold of her hands. "Our plan is working. You need to stay here. I'll try to be back as soon as I can, but you have to hold tight."

"Thabani? What's he going to do?"

"He's coming along, I just need a little more time."

"But what's—"

"I know this is hard, but be patient. We'll be out of here soon." Through the window she saw Japera round the corner of Paul's hut. He'd be heading for the center of camp in another minute. "I've got to go now."

Shelly reached out, but Jane had already moved to her exit in the tent.

"I'll be back. Don't worry, it won't be long."

Chapter 18

By the time she found the right doorway, Katura knew she didn't have much time. It hadn't been easy to find the bar despite having been there just two nights ago. It had been dark and there weren't any identifying signs. Zuka said that was because it was a secret meeting place for the MDC. They called it The Cave, and it had been chosen because it blended so well into the neighborhood. Too well. She was hoping it would be less intimidating in the light of day. She had to find a way to Mana Pools, and someone in there had to know how to get there.

She knocked and waited. No one came. She knocked louder. Maybe they didn't open this early. She was about to pound again when she heard the latch inside slide open.

"Who's there?" It was a low male voice, but she couldn't see its owner. Beyond the crack of the door it was pitch black. The windows must be covered from the inside.

"I need to talk to someone."

"And who would that be?"

"I'm not exactly sure—"

The door closed to about six inches wide as the man yelled back into the room. "Anyone here waiting for a girl?"

Someone said something she couldn't make out, then there was an outburst of laughter.

"No, honey, I think you've knocked on the wrong door." He started to shut it, but she grabbed his arm.

"Please, I need some help." Her eyes had adjusted. The man at the door looked to be in his late twenties.

"What exactly do you need?" He said it softly, but she shivered. Before she could think what to say next, he grabbed her around the waist and pulled her next to him. "I'm sure I can help you with whatever it is." She pulled Thabani's river map out of her jacket pocket and tried to squirm away but his grip was too strong.

"I need to know how to get to Mana Pools. I thought someone here might be able—"

He twisted her around to face him, holding her tightly by her forearms. She could barely move. He looked up and down the street behind her. "What makes you think we know about that place?"

"Hey, I remember that girl." It was a woman, at a table several feet from the entrance. "She's the one who came in the other night with Zuka and those other guys."

The man let go of her, and Katura moved into the bar. She recognized the woman immediately.

Two nights before Japera had followed Zuka to a large round table in the back. He'd left Katura standing with Thabani at the bar. She had clearly not been invited to Zuka's private meeting and she stood around awkwardly—watched from a distance as her brother was introduced to a group of young men. The light was too dim for her to make out the men at his table. Had Changa been one of them? She bit her lip and stared at the now empty table. Her memory of details was good, but never as good as her memory of her feelings. It was the details she needed to recall now. *Think, Katura.*

"Can a guy get a beer around here?" Thabani had said as he stood next to her. Her cousin's nonchalance had bugged her.

She remembered the bartender glancing up for a second but continuing his whispered conversation with two men and a large, androgynous woman in a dark green suit—the same woman who now sat in front of her. But at the time it was the men who held Katura's attention. The man with a full beard and thin lips kept his eyes on Thabani. After some moments he finally signaled to the bartender.

"Yeah?" The bartender turned only his head—he kept his outstretched arms firmly planted on the bar in front of the trio. "What can I get you?"

Thabani had looked at the bottles lined up on the wall. "I'll take a Carling."

"One?" He still hadn't moved.

Thabani had glanced at Katura. "Just one—" Suddenly Thabani was slapped hard on the back of his left shoulder. "What the…?" He turned to face a young man with bad skin and a bright smile. "Rudo!" Thabani grabbed the man's hand, shook it, knocked knuckles, and stamped the top of his fist. He turned to the bartender. "Make it two."

"Good to see you're back in town," Rudo said. "You working?"

Thabani waited for the bartender to open the bottles and hand them across the counter, then flipped him a large tip in addition to the price of the beer.

"Let's talk." He looked around for a place to sit.

Katura had waited to ask for a glass of water from the bartender before she joined Thabani and his friend—not that she felt welcome, but there was something about this place that made her uncomfortable standing alone for long. The bartender leaned over the counter and talked quietly to the older man at the bar, with the bearded man and woman in green listening in. Katura was thirsty, but after a few awkward minutes it seemed impossible to get his attention. As she began to weave her way through the crowded room, she squeezed past the trio. The man with the beard had suddenly jumped up and grabbed her right forearm.

"You seem to have a purpose," he said.

"Do I?" Katura tried to pull away from his grip. She glanced over her shoulder toward the back of the room, but there were too many people in the way for her to see her brother or cousin. The man laughed and tightened his hold on her. The older man just sipped his beer and watched.

"Such a young serious girl." The man holding her turned to the others. "What do you think she could be doing here?" He turned back to Katura, pulled her in closer, and sat back on his stool. "Seems like an odd place to look for your schoolmates or find a new boyfriend. But maybe that's exactly what you're do-ing." He'd pulled her next to him and ran his fingers down the nape of her neck.

"Let her go," the woman in green had said. "She came in with Zuka, or didn't you notice?"

"I noticed." He shot a quick glance toward Zuka's table, then back at the older, silent man to his left. "But he doesn't seem too concerned about her."

Nonetheless, he had relaxed his grip ever so slightly at the mention of Zuka's name, and Katura twisted to break his hold. She couldn't get free—just squirmed in place—but her movement caused the man's jacket to gape open, revealing a large revolver on his left hip. He moved forward to maintain his hold on Katura and at the same time tried to tug his jacket back into place.

The woman laughed and exchanged glances with the older man.

Katura stepped back and almost pulled the man off his stool, but she was instantly free. She stood facing them, angry at having been grabbed but mostly angry at her own naiveté. How could she possibly not have known that the MDC were armed? What else had Zuka's father lied about?

"Look, dear," the woman had said, "this isn't a place for you." She spoke quietly, tenderly, her manner at odds with her severe appearance. "Why would they drag you along?"

"They didn't. I'm here because I want to be."

"Oh," the woman said, "and what is it you want to do for us? We might be able use your kind of spunk."

Katura sighed. "I'm not here for your cause. I have my own." She turned to leave.

"Interesting."

Katura didn't like her condescending tone.

"Then maybe we could help you."

"I don't think so. It's your cause that has my brother in jail, and your party does nothing to stop it. You know full well that the ZANU killed that police chief, and yet my brother—Tafadzwa, his name is Tafadzwa—is dragged in to take the rap so—"

"Look, girl, you can't talk to her like that," the bearded man said. "This is political, not personal. It's too bad about your brother, but we have a lot more important fires to put out than your family problems. There's a whole country here that—"

He stopped when the older man raised his hand, palm out. Everybody waited for him to speak.

"It's always personal," he said. "At least, it starts out that way. When we forget that part—the part about her brother, your sister, someone else's mother—that's when we forget why we're here. You keep it personal, young lady, because that's all that really matters."

Katura shifted from one foot to the other. She looked at the woman, who smiled but made no attempt to break the silence. The old man lifted his head and stared into Katura's eyes.

"Good luck with your brother."

Katura had wanted to hear more from this man. She wanted to know what could be done, if her brother was safe, if he would be released. This man seemed to know so much more than he said. But it was clear that he'd finished with her, that she'd been dismissed. Low conversations sprang up around her. The group had returned to their own business and closed her out.

Now she looked around for the old man, didn't see him.

"I hope I wasn't rude the other night," she said. The woman smiled.

"Not rude, just outspoken. But I'll tell you again, this is no place for a young girl to be. This is the second time I've had to save you from one of these bastards."

"And I appreciate it." She reached out her hand. "I'm Katura." The woman shook it and nodded. No name given.

"It's the least I could do. Now, why do you want directions to Mana Pools?"

"It's where they've gone, to plan how to get my oldest brother released. I need to be there. Japera needs—"

"You can't go there. It's too dangerous. Anyway, I'm sure you won't find them there." The woman looked down at the table and took in a deep breath.

"I'll find them. I have to. Thabani might mess up again, might get Japera in trouble. I have to…" She stopped, the woman was starring at her.

"You don't know." The woman scooted her seat back and got up. "You need to see something." She walked over to the bar and whispered to the bartender. He glanced Katura's way, then handed the woman a newspaper from behind the bar.

"It's all working out so far."

She recognized the voice and turned slowly in its direction. *No sudden, attention-grabbing moves.* Changa was seated just a few feet away. He was facing away from her, drinking a beer.

"But I've got to get back now, work to do." He scooted back his chair.

Katura rose. He would pass right by her table on his way out. She moved quickly to the bar, stood so that the woman blocked Changa's view of her.

"Just don't let Zuka see this again. He's upset enough about his friends." The woman opened the paper and handed it to Katura—then sat on a stool. She was now in full view.

Suddenly there was a commotion in the back. Two guys were standing at a table and yelling.

"Hey, knock it off back there," the bartender called out.

The man who had let Katura in and several others started moving toward the back. They blocked Changa's exit, but only for a moment.

Katura grabbed the paper and nodded toward a small hallway behind the bar. "Be right back. She ducked into the women's bathroom, relieved to find the window open. She popped out the screen, jumped down into the alleyway below, and ran.

She was almost back to the field when she stopped to catch her breath. She pulled the newspaper out of her pocket and slipped into the doorway of a closed shop. A sentence into the article she realized it wasn't about the arrest at all. The story described a government raid on rebels—traitors, it called them—at Mana Pools. A massacre of more than three hundred. No one got out alive.

She stood perfectly still for a few seconds. She staggered onto the street, then found herself running, running desperately back toward the field as fast as she could move. Tears were flowing down her cheeks. Japera and Thabani dead? She let out a moan as she rounded the corner, then stopped. Why go back? Who was Changa, anyway? She had no idea now what side he was on or what his real purpose was. Her mind was racing, trying to put things together.

She sat down under the trees near the field. She could hear the kids playing. She lay down in the grass. *Think. You're missing something.* Suddenly she sat up. This didn't make sense, the timing was off—the woman had said Zuka was upset about his friends. She must have meant these friends, the MDC. Katura pulled the paper back out of her pocket and looked at the date. The raid had been three days before she even got to Victoria Falls. Japera was still alive, or in any case wasn't at the massacre. The plan had been to unite with the rebels at Mana Pools—at least, that's what Zuka had said. He said they'd be able to help. But the massacre had already happened and Zuka knew about it.

A soccer ball came rolling into the trees just as a white van rounded the corner and stopped across the street. She hopped up, grabbed the ball and came running toward the field.

"My throw in!" She tossed it in to the feet of the player nearest her.

"Hey, what the—"

"Sorry, guys, my ride's here. Gotta go."

Chapter 19

Jane finished going through her bag for the second time. She wasn't sure what she was looking for, just anything that might be useful. Coming up empty, she stuffed the bag under her cot as Michael burst through the door, startling both her and Jake.

"It's a hostage exchange." His energy was palpable. "Japera says they're close, real close. This should all be over soon." He threw his jacket on the bed, grabbed the last piece of bread on Jake's nightstand, and stuffed it into his mouth.

Jake stared at his brother. Michael looked from him to his mother and back.

"This is great news. Didn't you hear me? It's almost over. How come you guys aren't more excited?"

"Tell me everything he told you." She knew Japera had gone into his hut and Thabani was just finishing up rounds before getting Zuka for the next shift. She'd kept her conversation with Thabani light tonight, not wanting him to back away from her after having been so vulnerable the day before. She didn't want to scare him off before her next move.

Michael sat down across from them and let out a sigh. "It's simple. They're making the U.S. embassy negotiate with the police. They're going to exchange us for Japera's brother."

"Where's his brother?" Jake asked.

"In some jail."

"No big surprise," Jake said. "These guys aren't exactly boy scouts."

"No, Jake, you don't get it. His brother's totally innocent but he's being blamed for killing some police officer. It's dangerous in their jails, he might not make it out. Japera's really worried about him."

"The guy out there with a gun is a devoted family man? Mom, help me out here, Michael's—-"

"You'd do the same for me, wouldn't you, Jake? If I—"

"If you killed a cop? Would I take people hostage and risk their lives?" Jake slapped his forehead. "Oh, no, I got that wrong. Lives aren't just at *risk*. Or did you forget? Baruti and—"

"Japera didn't shoot anybody, Jake."

"Yet."

"Boys, stop. We need to focus." Jane started to pace but kept an eye on the window. "Michael, what makes Japera think the embassy will go along with this?"

"He thought Rick was a U.S. senator, that the embassy will want to help them out for a trade."

"So that's why they took us." Jake seemed to relax.

"Thought?" Jane turned to face him. "What's he think now?" Jake sat up. "You told him Rick wasn't—"

"No, of course not." Michael said without looking at him. "I mean, I started to. I don't know what I was thinking. But he didn't really get it."

"What exactly did you tell him?" Jane shot Jake a look to quiet him. If Michael felt defensive he might distort his report.

Jake glared at his brother but kept silent.

"We were just talking—like regular talking, just about our families. I started to explain the difference between the U.S. Senate and the state legislature and right in the middle of it I realized…" He lifted a water bottle to his mouth.

"Michael." Jane sat down across from him. "What was Japera's reaction?"

Michael took a long swig and swallowed, he took his time to answer. "He got worried, I mean the look on his face—"

"Great, he figured out we weren't important enough to get his brother out of jail." Jake slammed his book down on the nightstand. "Now we're totally f— "

"Jake." She glared at him, then turned back to Michael.

"No, not like that, Mom." He spoke softly. "Like he was worried about us, about me."

Jane put her hand up to stop Jake's next comment. "You said he didn't get it."

"I back-tracked fast. Told him they were really basically the same thing, that Rick's an important government politician." Michael glanced up at the ceiling. "I mean, was."

"And then what, Michael?"

"I told him it wouldn't matter to the embassy. Anyway, it doesn't seem to. That guy that delivers supplies? Changa? He's like their middleman. He told Zuka everything is going well. Japera says the exchange is about to happen."

"So why's Zuka involved?"

"I don't know." He sat back a moment. "He was the one who brought Japera's brother to the rally where the cop got shot. I guess he feels like it's his fault the brother was in the wrong place at the wrong time and the whole mistaken identity thing happened. He probably feels guilty."

She nodded. But Zuka sure didn't act like a guy who felt guilty. In fact, just the opposite. She patted Michael on the knee.

"Good work, honey."

Jane continued to go sequentially through their bags. She knew she should move quickly through Rick's—she had work to do— but despite her intentions, she brought his shirt up to her face, the one on top, the one he'd worn the day before they were taken. She rubbed the fabric over her cheek. His scent, so familiar, so comforting and alive, still permeated the cloth. With a deep breath she took it in, let herself remember just for a second his touch, his essence. She looked around, making sure the boys hadn't seen her. She folded the shirt back up neatly and replaced it in the bag.

She felt the corners of Rick's bag and found the keys to their Acura, presumably still parked in a long-term lot at San Francisco Airport. She dropped them in the side pouch of her own bag. *Always room for optimism.* She pulled out the shaving kit and searched its contents. No luck. With post 9/11 airport security, he must have left his Swiss Army knife at home. She took out Rick's anti-malarial pills and added them to the boys' supply and moved on to the boys' bags. Near the bottom of Michael's duffle she found a small package.

"Hey, that's private." Michael grabbed the package out of her hand.

"Michael?"

He shrugged his shoulders and opened the small box, taking out a necklace with a carved onyx jaguar in the center. He turned to block his brother's view of the gift.

"Probably for Caitlin." Jake didn't look up from his book. "He just doesn't learn."

Michael closed up the duffle. "There's nothing in there that's of help, Mom—just clothes and my toothbrush."

She was about to insist on checking for herself when they heard a soft rap on the door. She signaled for the boys to be quiet and walked over to the window. Thabani stood alone. She looked at her watch. Zuka should have relieved him over an hour ago.

"Paul's leg looks bad," he said. "Can you take a look?"

⋏

Jane slowly descended the wooden stairs of Paul's hut and wiped her hands dry on her jeans. She gazed at the stars for a few minutes before she realized that Thabani sat alone on the picnic table just a few yards from her. It was now hours after he should have awakened Zuka.

"I need different medicine."

He stared at her without responding.

"The Keflex isn't holding him."

"Then clean the wound better." He turned away and scanned the periphery of their camp.

"Look, you saw his leg." She tried to keep the anger out of her voice. "The skin's inflamed and swollen a good six inches from the wound, it's tight and hot. He's developing a raging cellulitis and it's going to become systemic soon if we don't take care of it quickly."

He continued to stare off.

"Thabani, you have to listen to me." She walked around to face him directly. "The medicine I have isn't good enough. At home he'd be on IV antibiotics. Maybe if you can get me a few things we can turn this around, but—"

"I heard you." He took in a deep breath and let it out slowly as he stared into her eyes before he looked away again.

She waited for more.

Nothing.

She sat down across from him. "What about that guy who brings food—Changa, I think? If I make a list, could you give it to him? I'll list several choices of medicine. I don't know what he can find around here. I also need clean bandages and sterile saline."

Silence.

"It's clean water."

"I know what it is, Jane."

She bit her lower lip. "Sorry."

"I just don't know what I can do."

She searched his face closely. He looked pained by his words.

"I'm sure you'll do what you can."

They sat in silence for several minutes. He made no move to get Zuka, just stared out into the distance. He seemed on the verge of saying something. She waited.

"Thabani?" she said finally.

He didn't respond, didn't look at her.

"Thabani, what if the embassy doesn't care? What'll happen to us?"

Nothing.

She rubbed the back of her neck. "I'm just not sure how much the embassy or the State Department is going to risk. It's complicated, even for a senator."

Thabani turned his head slowly and stared at her.

"Oh, God." She closed her eyes and held her breath. "Japera?"

He nodded.

"Does Zuka know?"

No response.

"It's not too late. You could turn this around."

He laughed. "Murder's not well tolerated in this country. Unless it's done by the government."

"But it wasn't you, Thabani." The light from her hut let her see the side of his face. His jaw muscles were tightening, grinding his back teeth. "You never fired your gun."

She watched him look over toward Paul's hut, now dark. She knew Paul was making himself the most expendable of the group, but if she guessed right, another death would be one too many for Thabani. She watched his face. That was it—Paul's worsening condition was the last straw for him. He knew exactly what was at risk.

Thabani turned to face her.

"I'd make sure you got out," she said, "you and your cousin. I'd tell them the truth, what role you played. I'd make sure they understood."

"But why?"

She smiled and nodded toward her hut. "You're not that much older than my boys, not even ten years older. I bet you've got a mother worried about you somewhere, family worried about that boy in jail. My boys would do the same thing if they were in your shoes. Look, I know your intentions were good, but things didn't go as planned and it's only getting worse. Let me help you out of this."

She heard a distant motor. The truck was approaching. She reached into her pants leg pocket and took out a pen and scrap of paper. She wrote down the supplies she needed and handed it to him.

"Give this to Changa, we'll figure out the rest after he's gone."

He stared at the list, then stuffed it in his shirt pocket. He looked over at the hut where his cousin slept.

"Japera, too," she said. "I don't know what will happen to Zuka. After all, he's committed—"

"Of course."

"But you and Japera are different. We need to focus on getting everyone out safe. You and I can figure it out, Thabani, we can make it happen." She waited until he was looking at her again. "You can trust me on this."

He looked steadily into her eyes, then nodded slowly.

"I know."

✦

"Where's Zuka?" Changa jumped down from the cab and headed for the back of the truck.

"Sleeping." Thabani grabbed a bag of supplies and set them on the steps of the lodge.

Changa turned his watch to catch the light.

"I thought…not that it matters." He continued to unload the truck.

"How are things going?" Thabani asked.

"On schedule."

"Any news about Tafadzwa?"

"Who?" Changa set the last bag down and started to walk toward Zuka's hut.

Thabani got in front of him. "My cousin, Tafadzwa. What's happening with him?"

Changa shook his head. "Never heard of him. A local guy?"

Just then Zuka came down his stairs. "You early?" He turned to Thabani. "Why didn't you wake me?"

"He doesn't know Tafadzwa."

"No worries, man. That's stage two." He smiled at Thabani. "First we get their attention, then we negotiate for prisoners."

"Prisoners?" Thabani said. "We're not here for prisoners, we're here for Tafadzwa. One innocent guy that you got involved—"

"It's bigger than that now." He turned to Changa. "On task?"

Changa nodded and climbed back into the cab. Zuka waved him on.

Jane wanted to stop him, to give him the list Thabani had in his pocket before he left. But Thabani was pacing now, agitated. She tried to put herself in his line of sight, closer to Zuka. There was still time to give Changa the list. Thabani glanced over at her—he looked right through her.

"Sorry, Zuka, this is a family issue. We'll solve it within the family." He turned to walk toward Japera's hut, but Zuka stood in front of him.

"A family issue? Really, Thabani?" Zuka smiled. "Is that what you've led Japera to think?"

For the first time Jane thought Thabani seemed confident. Thabani was watching Zuka closely, not faltering.

"This is my country." Zuka raised his voice. "And it was yours too before you and your family ran out on it. We can't let the world sit by and watch while some madman destroys everything it stands for."

Thabani just stared at him. He seemed deep in thought. Contemplating his options? Zuka took a step toward him.

"It's just a river for you, isn't it? A place to make money and if that dries up you'll move to another."

"We never should've gotten you involved," Thabani said.

"Bit late for that." Zuka blocked Thabani from getting around him. "I *am* involved now. And I'm sure as hell not taking orders from a rafting guide."

"Sorry, Zuka." Thabani adjusted the rifle that hung from his shoulder, made it more accessible. "You're not going to bully your way with us any more. You screwed up, not us, and now we have to figure a way out of this mess."

Zuka laughed and took a few more steps forward. Thabani moved sideways, pulling Zuka further away from where Jane stood, his hands on his rifle.

"I screwed up, is that how you see it?" Zuka said. "Aren't you rewriting history a bit?"

"What are you talking about? You killed those two men. One a native of your beloved country and the other our only real bargaining chip. Brilliant move, Zuka."

"No, Thabani, you killed them. You didn't make sure they stayed where they were supposed to like I told you to. You gave me no choice. The blood's on your hands. Two more innocent people die on your watch."

Jane saw Thabani's face and wanted to interrupt, to intervene somehow. Maybe if the widow spoke, said something clarifying—

Zuka slapped Thabani across the face. Thabani fell back, losing his balance momentarily.

"You really think you can get out of this that easily? These people are just going to forget who you and Japera are after being held hostage for five days?" He snorted, an ugly sound. "I have a mission here and it isn't over, it's just beginning." He started to turn away.

"No, Zuka, it's not—"

"We're done talking about this. You're not ruining the plan." Zuka turned toward the stove, grabbed his rifle, and headed for the coffee.

"Zuka." Thabani was standing up straight again. "You don't get it. It's over."

Zuka stopped in his tracks. He turned back slowly, calmly, rifle in hand. "I don't get it?" He raised the rifle.

"That's not necessary," Thabani said. "Look, we need to—"

The shot was loud, echoing through the canyon for what seemed like minutes, hours, days. She watched Thabani fall to the ground, the blood trickle slowly over his lips, his eyes stared blindly ahead. His right arm jerked once, maybe twice, then relaxed. Was that the way to describe a dead body? Relaxed? Behind her she heard the muffled sound of a child crying. Was it one of hers? She didn't move, couldn't turn. She just stared at Thabani, the blood now pooling under his mouth.

Chapter 20

"He wants to talk to you." Jake spoke softly as they walked back and forth across the grounds.

"What's he want?" Michael picked up the pace. He'd been avoiding Paul since his attempt to grab Thabani's gun. He didn't trust him. Paul was impulsive or, worse, sloppy.

"He says he has a plan," Jake said.

"And?"

"I don't know. All I know is, he wants to talk to you." They rounded the corner of the main lodge and completed their second lap. "What else are we going to do? Now?"

Michael looked at his brother, who didn't elaborate. "Scared?" Silly question—who wouldn't be? Michael kicked a rock on the path, sending it into the bushes. "Mom's going to be okay."

"I know." Jake answered too quickly.

"I just need time to think, figure out our next move. I just don't think Paul's going to be much help."

"Right." Jake looked down at the ground, his breathing heavy. Jake had been spending more time with Tommy lately, been around Paul. He'd know Paul was a loose cannon. "But—"

"You don't think I can handle this." After all that's happened, why should he? Still, it was disappointing. They'd always stuck by each other. "You're just like dad," he said. He regretted it immediately.

Jake stopped in his tracks. "Michael, this isn't a race." He waited until Michael stopped too. "What's your problem? Dad's not even here. Paul's got some plan he wants to talk to you about and it won't hurt you to listen. That's all I'm saying. You got something better?"

Michael looked around. They'd stopped far enough away from the huts so that no one could hear them.

"Why don't you just tell me his plan?" Michael had been busy over the last two days taking care of their mother and had been glad Jake wasn't around, but now he wasn't so sure. "What's he saying about Mom anyway? What'd you tell him?"

"Nothing and nothing. Just hear him out, will you? It can't hurt."

His little brother could be incredibly stubborn—he wasn't likely to get any more out of him. Michael scanned the empty horizon. He'd made a habit of searching for movement, anything to signal that someone might be out there. The brothers watched a large crane pass overhead on its way toward the river.

"And you're totally wrong about Dad," Jake said. "That's not why he left you there."

Michael studied Jake's face. They'd never talked about this. "But he said——"

"I know what he said—to you." He glanced up at Michael and shrugged. "He didn't leave you in juvie to make you tough, he left you there because he knew you could handle it. He thinks you're strong—stronger than any of us. He just didn't want Mom bailing you out again and giving you the idea you were soft."

"Again?" Michael raised his voice.

Jake shrugged.

"His words?"

"Yeah."

Michael bit his lip and looked away. He watched a second crane follow the same route toward the river. He wished he had his younger brother's calm—the calm that comes from not feeling primarily responsible for what happens.

"Really? Dad said strong?" It was risky to ask for reassurance from Jake, but he couldn't stop himself. "He used that word?"

"Hey, it's not what I think. I think you're a wuss."

Michael laughed and punched Jake in the arm.

"Let's just see what Paul wants. It can't hurt."

Michael continued to circle the grounds with his brother at his side. They walked behind the lodge, unused except for food storage. It was the coolest building in the resort. They turned around and headed back before they reached Shelly's hut, didn't want anything they did to be misinterpreted.

"Well?" Jake said.

Paul wasn't someone Michael wanted to join up with—still, it wasn't like Jake to nag.

"I suppose it's just a consultation, just information." He smiled at Jake, an inside joke—it was a line their mom used when she was trying to get them to consider something they didn't want to do. It doesn't necessarily require agreement or action, she'd say, just an ear.

Michael started walking toward Paul's hut. But that hadn't been his experience—somehow these consultations had a way of taking over.

⅄

"Jake will distract him," Paul said. "He'll wait until after Zuka's made his rounds, when he's back sitting on the picnic table. We take our places, then Jake comes toward him from the front. He starts yelling from a distance as he approaches, so Zuka doesn't hear us coming. Jake falls down, captures his attention."

"And you think he's just going to sit there while we jump him?"

Paul took his time to answer. "He can't shoot in three directions at once, Michael. We'll have to be fast. As soon as Jake has his attention, we both move in together."

Michael looked down at his hands. He was picturing the scene. "Why's Jake in front? Doesn't that make him most likely to get shot?"

"I don't think so. It's unlikely he'll see Jake as a threat."

"Great, so he'll turn and shoot which ever of us he hears first."

"As I said, we have to move together. And fast. We have to get to him before he has time to aim at either of us."

"Time to aim. You should have seen how fast he shot Thabani. I don't think he even took aim at all."

Michael stared at the man in front of him, studied his face. Paul's right eye twitched before he looked away. Michael's heart was racing. He hated Paul at that moment, he wasn't sure why.

"Hey, if you don't trust me…" Paul shook his head.

Why should he? All Paul has to do is hang back for a few seconds. Michael gets shot while Paul wrests away the rifle and saves the day. Michael glanced over at Jake. *Beware of anyone who demands trust without earning it*—one of their father's favorite sayings. Jake's head jerked up and his eyes locked onto Michael's. He nodded ever so slightly. Michael turned back to Paul.

"And Tommy? What's his job?" But Michael knew the answer. Paul had no problem putting him and Jake at risk, but his own boy would be kept inside while they tried to ambush Zuka.

Paul just stared at him. Michael nodded, not breaking eye contact. He didn't really expect a response.

"So you're just going to walk over to the stove, but I have to somehow get myself behind that tree without Zuka noticing? Why?"

"He's not going to let us surround him from three sides," Paul said. "He'll get up, move somewhere else so he has us all in view. You're more agile than I am, we need you to do the trickier part. I think you can handle it."

Michael stiffened.

Paul stretched his right leg, bent his knee, and rotated the ankle. It was a sharp contrast to the injured leg propped immobile under a blanket. His eyes darted around the hut.

"Look, Michael, I've thought this all out, gone through all the different options and this is the best one. Now, are you up for it or not?"

Michael hated this guy more than ever. The way he put it, if Michael thought this plan was ridiculous, he was a coward.

"Maybe you think you can come up with something better." Paul crossed his arms. "Let's hear it."

"How about if I go over by the tree, but in plain sight. He knows I'm there but it's for something, I don't know, something that wouldn't alarm him. Like I left my sweatshirt over there, or something. Then Jake screams, maybe he's been bit by a snake—"

"Ouch." Jake grabbed his calf.

Michael grinned. It was just like Jake to prefer a snakebite to falling down. "Then I'll come running toward Zuka, which would make sense because he's in between where I'm standing and Jake's screaming. You surprise him from behind right when I'd be passing by, except I don't. I turn and grab the gun while you grab him." Michael raised his eyebrows to his younger brother, who nodded. It made a better scene for Jake.

Paul shook his head. "Won't work. You'd still have to get the sweatshirt there without him seeing it. And that brings you back to the same problem."

Michael saw the ends of Paul's lips curl upwards. He was happy because he thought Michael's idea wouldn't work? He wanted to hit him.

"No, listen." Michael's voice was getting louder. Paul was glaring at him. Not good. He needed to work with this guy, to come up with a plan, but Paul was really pissing him off. "Let's say Jake goes over there, like he's going to climb the tree, and drops my sweatshirt—"

"No, you listen to me, young man. You're making it too complicated. Zuka's not going to let Jake climb the tree to get high enough that he might figure out how to get out of here."

"But it's also too risky for me to be sneaking around the other side of camp for no good reason in front of Mr. Trigger-Happy sitting there with a loaded gun." He was nearly yelling now. "We need a better plan." He stopped and glanced outside again. Japera was rounding the lodge toward the center of camp. He needed to keep his voice down.

Michael closed his eyes and rubbed his head. He needed to work this out. Maybe Paul was right, maybe the only way to turn things around was to get the gun away from Zuka, and the only way to do that was a mass effort.

"I've got an idea."

"Oh, this should be good."

Michael's jaw tightened. He stood and walked to the far end of the hut before he continued.

"Tommy and Jake will be playing around, like they usually do. I'll come out of my hut just as Tommy tags Jake and runs toward the tree. I'll take off after Tommy, but suddenly, just as we reach the tree, Jake screams that he's been bit. I run toward Jake, or it'll look that way, but when I reach Zuka, you jump him and I grab the gun."

"Tommy's not going out there."

"Dad, I can—"

"All he has to do is stay at the tree, he won't be involved in the action."

"I said, he's not going out there." Paul kept his eyes on Michael, ignoring Tommy. And now, for some reason, he was smiling. "How's your mom feeling?"

"Fine," Michael said quickly. "She'll be fine. Why?"

His mom had barely moved since he'd carried her to their hut when she collapsed on the ground right after Thabani's murder two days ago. He'd even thought for a moment that she too had been hit, but there was no wound. Michael brought her water, which she sipped, but she wasn't talking or eating.

"Just haven't seen her out for meals and wondered...Tommy," Paul nodded his head toward the back of their hut, "hand me two of those new pills."

"New ones?" When had supplies come into the camp?

Jake brushed by him and glanced out behind the side curtain. "We might not have a lot of time, we don't know how long Japera's shift is." He turned to Michael. "Maybe we should figure out if there's even a way to get to your spot without being seen, a trial run."

Michael glanced down at him. Jake shrugged.

"We could at least see if it's even possible."

Paul took a sip of water and cleared his throat. "I'll be standing by the stove on the left—warming my hands, making coffee, something like that."

Michael looked out the window. He could feel his heart pounding in his chest, his breath shallow. He scanned the camp. Finally he looked back and forth between the tree, the huts, and the stove. He was trying to figure out the angles.

"Zuka will keep his eye on me until Jake distracts him," Paul said.

"If not, talk to him, get him to look in your direction."

"No, I've tested this. He doesn't trust me, he keeps his eye on me when I'm silent, but if I talk he goes back to scanning the area, he knows where I am if I speak."

Michael raised his eyebrows at Jake. Paul had this worked out better than he'd thought.

"Anyway, you need to get behind him and to the right, behind the big tree that shades the picnic area during the day. You know the one?"

Michael nodded. It was on the far side of his hut. Still, he'd have to go twenty yards in open view without being seen. "If it's impossible, we're going with my plan."

"If he's facing either my direction or straight ahead toward the huts, you can get there without being noticed—won't be easy, but you can do it. The moon will have dropped toward the horizon by then, so you'll be in the shadows. You'll have to sneak around behind both huts to get there. Make sure he doesn't hear you. When Jake comes out, he'll turn this way. Soon as Jake has his attention, he'll twist his ankle and start screaming. Or pretend he's been bitten, whatever. It'll be our signal that it's time to move in. Move fast and don't stop until you have your hands on his gun."

Michael swallowed hard. He tried to picture himself wrestling the rifle out of Zuka's hands.

"Our goal is to separate him from the weapon. I'm bulkier than you, so I'll pin him down. If I'm struggling, hand the gun off to Jake and help me. Or better yet, shoot him."

Michael turned away. He pictured the two men fighting, rolling on the ground, trying to distinguish the two in the scope.

"Just keep shooting, Michael."

He looked out the window over Jake's shoulder. Japera sat where Zuka would be in a less than an hour.

Michael turned to his brother. "I'm going out to talk with Japera. Give me about ten minutes, then come out. I want to see what he sees, how sound travels, where the worst parts are. Say you're looking for something you think you dropped, make something up. Then go over to that tree and back to our room. Go behind the huts, like you're searching. Go as quietly as you can.

"Got it."

Paul let out a deep sigh. "Come in and wake me when the change of shift happens. Tell them you're checking on my leg. Then go back to your hut and wait for me to get to the stove before you move in. I'll be walking very slowly, painfully. Don't let it fool you, it's part of the show. And Michael..." He waited until Michael had turned back to face him. "If you can't figure out how to get there, there's no other plan."

Chapter 21

Katura stood stirring the pot of vegetable soup. It needed to cook down some but had turned out pretty well considering the limited ingredients she had to work with. She'd found a few spices Thabani must have brought in after visiting his mother. She took another sip and set down the ladle. She turned to wait in the living room, then jumped.

"Don't sneak up on me like that!"

Changa stood leaning against the far wall with his arms crossed, chewing on a stick.

"Want to try some?" She dipped the ladle. "It's not quite ready, probably another half-hour."

"That might just be enough time."

"Time?"

He smiled.

Her heart started beating faster. "You know, it's great you're back early. I have a load of laundry and I can take it down while the soup—"

He grabbed her around her waist and spit out the stick. "You're not going anywhere."

She squirmed but couldn't get out of his grip. He was moving her down the hall toward the bedroom. She could smell beer on him—a strong smell, like it was coming out of his pores. He grabbed both her arms and clenched her wrists together, holding them in one hand behind her back. She didn't like the way it forced her breasts out. She hunched her shoulders forward. He pushed her onto the bed, still holding her arms. She began to kick, but he flung one of his legs over her and pinned her down.

"You like it rough? Well, I've got news for you. I like it rough, too. So we should do just fine."

She forced herself to relax—made it feel like gravity was just pulling her down through the bed, every muscle limp. Then she turned and looked at him.

"Actually, you're not so rough—not compared to Zuka."

"What? You're not Zuka's."

She smiled. "Ask him yourself."

He released her and staggered off the bed. "Look, he doesn't need to know about this. I was only playing, wouldn't have touched you. You know that, right?"

He was out the door before she could respond.

Chapter 22

Michael cupped his hands to his mouth and called across the yard. "We'll find it in the morning, when it's light out."

"Hope so," Jake called back. He searched the porch outside their hut one last time before turning in.

Japera barely acknowledged Michael's presence several feet away, even though they sat on the same table, facing the huts. Michael looked at the gap between his hut and Paul's. Jake had dashed across, as quickly and quietly as possible. But the movement was eye-catching. There was no way he could sneak between the two structures and not be seen by Zuka, who would be sitting where he now sat. Wouldn't work.

There had to be alternatives. If he could sneak farther back behind his own hut, somehow forging through the brush before cutting across to the west and reemerging on the other side. . . But that meant entering what he referred to as no-man's land. If Zuka happened to get up and walk around the back, there were no trees—no cover of any kind. Nor was Zuka the only threat. Wildlife came out at night, some of it predatory.

What if Jake went into Tommy's hut first, came from that direction and pulled Zuka's attention more toward the northwest? With the moon in the east, it was darker on that side of camp.

Zuka would have to strain to see Jake and might naturally turn his body away from the gap between the huts.

Michael let out a deep sigh. It was hard to predict. Zuka's characteristic nonchalance could result in his barely turning his head toward Jake. Yet lately, since Thabani's death, Zuka seemed a little jumpier, not like he startled easily, just more vigilant, more focused.

How about the other direction? If Jake could find an excuse to come toward Zuka from the east, the bright moon in his eyes might keep him from seeing movement to his left. Of course, if a cloud moved across the sky, blocking the moon's light...

Michael rubbed the back of his neck. His head hurt. He glanced over at Japera. Lost in thought too? Or suspicious of Michael's silence.

"Nice night," Michael said.

Japera nodded, letting out a barely audible grunt. He glanced up at the moon, then went back to just staring off into space. They hadn't spoken since Thabani's death. Michael struggled with what to say, how to approach him. Even if this mission were successful in getting his brother released, what would it mean for Japera to return to his family now that his cousin was dead?

"I'm sorry about Thabani," Michael said.

Japera kept his head straight and the muscles in his neck tightened, but Michael could see his eyes were darting about, not focused on anything specific, almost frantic. Then the darting stopped, and he nodded.

"Thanks."

Michael waited for more. It was the middle of the night, quiet except for the occasional sounds of some animal scavenging in the distance. Out of the corner of his eye he watched Japera, probably not more than four years older than himself. He sat guarding. Guarding what? People too injured or lost to go anywhere anyway? Waiting for something from the outside to happen? They had no information about what was going on or when they were likely to know—both acutely aware that within their small camp it was getting increasingly dangerous, for both of them. Yet Japera held a gun. It lay across his lap, the barrel resting away from Michael. Would this guy really ever pull the trigger? It was incomprehensible to Michael. He'd sat many a night talking with him, about school, family, siblings, the usual stuff. He liked hearing about Botswana, about Japera's hopes for his future, not unlike his own. At times he forgot all about the rifle.

"Were you close?" It seemed like a lame question, but he couldn't think of a better entry. They shared a common experience. Zuka had killed Michael's stepfather and now Japera's cousin. Didn't that make them partly on the same side?

He looked at Japera with renewed hope. This was it. His father's words were never more applicable. Trust can't be demanded, only earned. Paul's job had been to distract their captors, to keep them away from the river for Rick and Baruti's escape. Sure, he'd pulled their attention initially but he hadn't finished the job, and the ultimate result spoke for itself. Why should he put his faith in Paul? Let alone trust him with his and Jake's lives.

"Japera." Michael got up and started to pace. "I was thinking about Thabani—"

"I don't want to talk about him." Japera wouldn't look at Michael.

"I understand, I really do." He tried to think ahead, to explain his plan. Where was he going with this? What he really wanted was Japera's help, but that seemed ludicrous. "I mean, it wasn't really about Thabani. Not directly. I just thought that if we—"

"No, Michael."

"No?" Michael moved in front of Japera, trying to force eye contact. "No? You haven't even heard what I have to say. I just thought that we—"

"No. There is no *we*, Michael. *We* are not the same. *We* doesn't exist." Japera stared at him now, stared directly into his eyes, but he didn't feel seen.

Michael stepped back, the whole scene seemed out of focus, unreal. Something about Japera, the way he looked at him. Like he was already dead. Was that it? Japera's seen his cousin killed, Rick, Baruti, none of it matters? He doesn't expect any of us to make it? No, this doesn't make sense.

"But it could." Michael looked down at the rifle.

"It's not that simple." Japera's hands shifted on the gun. "You'd better get inside." It was the first time Japera had ever spoken to him like a hostage. The first time he'd pulled rank. Michael didn't move.

"Why not? He's nothing to you. And what makes you think he's going to do anything to help your brother?"

"It's not safe." Japera stood up. He held the rifle loosely at his side. "Get inside, Michael. We're not having this discussion."

He heard a noise from the workers' hut. Zuka was awake. Michael backed up slowly. He turned to face Paul's hut, stood staring at it for a moment. He took in a deep breath.

"I'm checking on Paul, see how his leg's doing." He started across the grounds, then remembered Jake. He needed to re-route his course, to draw Zuka away from being able to see him head for the tree later.

"No, I'll check with Jake first, make sure he's asleep. Then I'll check in on Paul." This wasn't sounding right. The pounding in his head was getting worse. He was messing up. He turned back to Japera, who seemed to be watching him intently.

Michael stared down at the ground several minutes before he looked up. He shook his head. "You're just not who I thought you were, Japera. My mistake."

"Michael—"

Zuka came down the steps. Michael didn't take his eyes off Japera, who just stood without moving or saying anything.

"Yeah, my mistake." Michael turned and walked slowly up the stairs to his hut.

⋏

"Think about it," Michael said, "the guy hasn't gotten much sleep. He'll be easily distracted."

"I don't know, it sounds really dangerous." Jake was sitting up in his bunk, legs stretched out under the covers. "I'll have no way of signaling you if it's safe to cross. He's totally trigger-happy and if he sees you sneaking around…"

"Hey, this was your idea in the first place."

"It was Paul's idea." Jake was always a stickler for details.

"You agreed with him."

"I changed my mind. It's obviously not going to work. I was in plain view and you're bigger than I am."

"You stumbled. I won't."

"You saw me before I stumbled."

Michael glanced over at his mother, who had barely stirred when he walked in. Her eyes were closed, but she didn't seem to be asleep.

"All you have to do is get him to look anywhere but toward that gap."

"Then after you've crossed—and, by the way, I'll have no way of knowing when that is—I have to get him to look precisely in that same direction. No problem." Jake's jaw was set. He wasn't budging. "Are you nuts?"

Michael scooted up onto Jake's bunk and leaned against the wall. "Okay, let's figure out a signal, certain words you can say that'll mean it's clear or not."

"Like a script, because I'm so good at that and anyway, what could go wrong? If there's a problem, the only thing that could happen is—oh, I don't know, my brother gets killed?"

"Come on, help me out here." He tucked his legs under the covers, and his feet touched Jake's for a moment. "Jesus, you're hot. You catch something from Paul?" Maybe it was the light, but Jake looked pale. He leaned over to feel his forehead. Jake pulled away.

"I'm not up on germ theory, Michael, but I don't think wounds are contagious. I just feel a little sick to my stomach—probably too much of that mushy stuff, sadza or whatever it is." His eyes looked unfocused, glossed over.

"Are you going to throw up?" Michael hopped off the bunk and grabbed the plastic bag they'd used for dirty laundry. He dumped the clothes out on the floor.

"Don't talk about it, I'll be fine. I have a splitting headache."

"Jake, if you're going to puke, take this—"

"I said, don't talk about it." He held his head. Just then his stomach made a spastic motion. He grabbed the bag. Michael put one hand on his back, the other on his forehead.

"Get as much out as you can." He shot a glance at his mother. She hadn't moved. "Maybe those anti-malarial pills are making you sick."

Jake shook his head, his face still in the bag.

"It could be a delayed reaction."

Jake picked up one of the dirty shirts and wiped his mouth. "I'm not taking them."

"What?"

"I've been giving them to Paul for his infection. Can't hurt."

Michael wanted to slap him. Anti-malarials weren't going to do anything for whatever bug was eating Paul's leg.

"Jake, you idiot—"

Jake threw up a second time, this time with more force.

Jane was out of bed and at his side. Michael moved out of her way. She felt Jake's head.

"What else hurts?"

Jake just stared at her, then looked at Michael.

"Have you been coughing?" she said.

He shook his head, then groaned. His eyes stayed fixed ahead.

"Joint pain?"

He nodded.

Michael shifted on the bunk. "Mom, I've laid out his pills every day. I just assumed he took them."

"It's probably not malaria—something else. Get him water, a lot."

"But—"

"Every hour. Jake, I don't care if you have to get up every twenty minutes to pee, you're going to drink constantly."

"But it hurts to walk, I'm sore..." His voice faded under her stare.

She turned to Michael. "And I want it boiled, which means you're going to have to have water on the stove almost all the time. Keep it coming. Make sure he takes three of my adult dose anti-malarials every day for three days, then he can return to his usual dose." She walked over to the window and moved the curtain slightly to look out front.

"But I thought you said it wasn't—"

"In case I'm wrong." She closed the curtain and walked into the bathroom. They heard the water running for quite a while but were afraid to speak, afraid anything they did might put her back into her previous state. When she reemerged she looked different. Her hair was combed out and fell neatly over her shoulders. It was longer than she usually kept it, flowed in waves down her back. She'd changed into clean clothes, a white tank top and khaki shorts. The boys exchanged glances.

"I was going to get Paul and—"

"Let him sleep." She peered out the window again.

"But we had a plan."

She turned and glared at him.

"Right." He nodded. "You have your own plan."

It was then that he noticed what it was about her. What struck him as different, as if she weren't his mother, the woman he had known all his life. It was her eyes. They were stone cold. They were missing the life, the joy, the spontaneity he'd always taken for granted. Her face was hard granite. He didn't know the woman who walked out of their hut.

CHAPTER 23

Zuka slammed his fist down on the table next to her. "What are you trying to get at?"

Jane smiled—she finally had his attention. "You know exactly what I'm saying." She spoke calmly, conversationally, as if her comments were not meant to be provocative, just factual. "You know this is nuts. There's no way it's going to work."

The water started to boil. She glanced over at the stove and stood up slowly, shaking her head.

"You think you know so much." He turned away from her.

She could lose him again. He was getting agitated, his eyes darting around the empty camp. She couldn't play tug-of-war alone—it was crucial that he not lay down his end of the rope and walk away. She caught his eye and smiled. He glared back at her.

"Your government will respond."

She was clearly annoying him, but he couldn't resist.

"Really? These things actually work out, do they?" She stared straight into his eyes and laughed.

He was silent, eyes shooting daggers from only a few feet away.

"That's what I thought. You're good, you know, it was almost believable." She poured a small amount of boiling water into a bottle, secured the lid, and shook it before pouring out the contents on the ground. It was the best she could do at steriliza-tion. When she glanced back up he was looking toward Japera's hut. "Oh, don't worry, he's got a lot of reasons not to figure this out. He needs it to be this way."

"I didn't say I was worried." He leaned back, gazed at her with his eyelids at half-mast, as if he weren't trying to see her clearly.

But she knew better, she could feel the tension of his focus, the purposefulness behind his feigned nonchalance. She forced herself to tune in to him, to gauge his uncertainty. It required that she ignore everything she felt about him. She compartmen-talized her gaze.

It was his hands that finally freed her thinking, brought her to another place, a more dangerous place. They were smaller, looked softer than she would have imagined. As he spoke his fin-gers caressed his neck. She watched as they moved gently across his smooth dark skin, pulling her in. When Zuka noticed her watching, he froze, then he looked away.

"You know how I figured it out?" She waited for his return. It took a moment, but when he looked back at her his eyes were on her body. "I was thinking, you just don't see a lot of governments roll-ing over under threat of hurting a few of their citizens who venture off to foreign countries. If that's all it took, this kind of thing would happen a lot more often, right? And that's when it struck me."

She turned and poured the rest of the water into the bottle before replacing the lid. She took her time, allowed him to watch her on his own terms. "Either you're really stupid. . ." She cocked her head back, licked her bottom lip slowly, and smiled. "Or this is about something else."

Zuka drummed the fingers of his right hand on the table. She watched his movements carefully and then allowed her eyes to move up to his arms, his chiseled biceps. They seemed to tighten ever so slightly with each respiration, making the definition of each muscle more pronounced. Her gaze moved across his chest, broader than a young man's. He was older than she'd originally thought.

"So it stands to reason that this is a long shot. And if it actually works, great—you get your friends out in a prisoner exchange and you're a hero. But if not, then what? It's certainly not going to just go away easily, not for you or for them. No, it'll be a battle until the end, won't it? You get taken prisoner, or killed, but either way"— she dismissed the difference with an airy wave—"you get the attention of the international press, and that's the point. You may even be a heroic martyr to boot."

Zuka stood up. Jane avoided looking at his face. She chose to watch his arms, his chest now moving rhythmically with his quickened breaths.

"I'm not interested in being a hero," he said. "I'm not doing this for myself."

"No, of course not." She stepped back. "I suppose you're just desperate."

He was on her before she knew it. "Who says I'm desperate?" He tightly gripped her arm, pulled her body in.

He was braced for a struggle, had clearly expected her to pull away, to resist. She forced herself to relax, let her body stand effortless next to his. She glanced down at his hand wrapped completely around her upper arm, his fingers resting inadvertently against her breast, then looked up and into his eyes. She could taste his breath.

Zuka let go and stepped back.

Jane laughed. She turned toward the stove, where she'd left Jake's water bottle. She might as well take it to him. She'd planted a seed, accomplished as much as she could for now, and—

Zuka grabbed her again. He twirled her around to face him, clutched her by both arms, and pulled her against him. His tongue entered her mouth.

It took her a minute to realize that she was being guided toward his hut. He stopped to kick the door where Japera slept.

"Your shift!" he yelled. He held her until they could hear movement inside, a grunt of acknowledgment. Then he nodded toward his own hut. She pulled him close and kept his attention away from her awkward gait. As they mounted the stairs to his hut she could feel the scalpel that lay just inside the sole of her right shoe.

人

"Michael, come out here."

He popped his head out from inside his sleeping bag, scowling. The nerve of this guy. Japera banged on the door with something solid.

"Michael?" He waited a few minutes before opening the door. Japera stuck his head in and glanced around. "I need some help gathering wood."

"Too bad." Michael slipped back into the sleeping bag. He could hear Japera walk into the hut and stand over him. He waited. Nothing. Finally he reemerged. "What are you going to do? Shoot me?"

Japera's brow furrowed. "No."

"Why not? You're the one with the gun." He stared at Japera's rifle.

Japera looked down at his side as if seeing the gun for the first time. He looked back at Michael.

Michael watched the sadness move across Japera's face. He didn't care. They had been friends—sort of, or so he thought. It all seemed crazy now. What could he have been thinking? He hated Japera for letting him think any such thing, hated himself more for believing it.

Japera glanced around the room. He seemed startled by Jake, who lay facing away from them on his bunk, curled up and holding his forehead with both hands.

Michael sat up. "Leave him alone."

Japera walked over and sat on Jake's bunk. Michael could see the perspiration on the back of Jake's neck. Japera pulled down the top of his sleeping bag and grabbed the bottom of Jake's shirt.

"I said, leave him alone." Michael jumped up and stood in front of Japera. "Don't you dare touch—"

Michael gasped when he saw Jake's back. Japera had lifted his shirt to reveal a blotchy red rash extending all the way to Jake's waist. Japera ran out of the room before Michael could stop him. He returned a minute later with Jake's water bottle.

"Drink all of it."

"It all just comes back up."

"So take in twice as much as comes out." Japera waited until Jake had finished half the bottle, then turned to leave. "I'll boil more water," he said. "But I've got to get wood first." He started out the door.

"Japera?"

Japera stopped and waited, not facing him. Michael took a deep breath. He hated needing anything from Japera.

"Do you know…what's wrong with him?"

"It's dengue." There was no uncertainty in his voice.

"What?"

"Dengue fever."

"You know, the last time I saw dengue fever in San Francisco was—oh, I remember now—never. Because we don't have these damn diseases that—"

"Michael." Japera looked down at the ground before he spoke. "I'm sorry I can't do what you want. I can't help you."

"Can't? Can't? Don't you mean won't? Your brother's in jail and now mine's going to die. How does that get either of us anywhere?" He was near tears and knew it. He sucked in a deep breath and held it. He didn't want Japera to see him cry.

"He won't die."

"You know that?"

"He needs lots of water, clean water. We…" Japera swallowed hard. "I need to boil water."

He reached for the door but didn't open it. They both stood just a few feet away from each other, not speaking. Finally Michael turned to Jake.

"I'll be right back. I'm going to get wood for the fire."

⅄

Michael kept his distance, almost daring Japera to rein him in. He welcomed the confrontation that didn't happen. On his second trip to the wilderness area outside camp, he leapt across a small creek and found a good supply of wood. He gathered a load into his arms and was about to head back when he spotted something—no, someone. No, a *dead* someone, lying just yards from where he stood. Curled up, half buried in leaves, was a body. Michael jumped back and dropped the wood.

It took only a few seconds before he recognized the clothes. He walked slowly forward and gagged. Lorenzo's corpse lay at his feet. Michael looked quickly around. As far as he could tell, he was alone. He stood still, not moving, listening. He heard nothing. He backed away from the body and began picking up the wood he'd dropped.

He looked again at Lorenzo. The scarf—why did he have their mother's scarf draped over his face? Her bandana, the one she'd used back at the beach to wrap Paul's leg. The last time Michael had seen it was when they were hiking through the woods to the Safari Lodge. Had he seen it recently? He wracked his brain, couldn't remember. If Paul had dropped it, Lorenzo couldn't have picked it up. He was in front with Thabani for the entire distance. Zuka had taken up the rear, but it didn't make sense that he would have picked it up and given it to Lorenzo.

He walked up to Lorenzo's body, knelt down on one knee. The bandana was placed carefully across Lorenzo's face. It was an act of respect, not likely to have been done by whoever killed him. Michael looked around the forest again, still silent.

Chapter 24

Jane reached over the side of the bed, swept the floor with her fingers, back and forth. She kept her breathing slow and steady, but Zuka sighed loudly next to her. She waited a few seconds before resuming her search, moving her arm methodically in the pattern of an imaginary grid. Where were her shoes? She'd placed them precisely within reach only hours ago.

Had Zuka inadvertently kicked them under the bed? She scooted her body to the edge and leaned over to look under it.

Just then Zuka sat up.

"Sorry, I didn't mean to wake you, I was just going to the bathroom." She tried to calm the tremor in her voice.

He stared at her a moment, then at the door that would be her exit to the bathroom in the main lodge. He leaned down and picked up her sneakers from his side of the bed.

"You'll need these."

Could he feel the difference in weight of the left one? A faint smile crept across his face. Or was it a smile? It certainly wasn't infectious, not the kind that pulls you in as if there's a bond between two people. No, this was more evaluative, like he knows something he's not sharing—stop it. She was reading too much into it.

"Sorry, I tried to be quiet."

"I have to get up anyway." He pulled on his pants quickly and was out the door.

Jane lay back, acutely aware of the nakedness of her body that lay on top of the open sleeping bag. It was as if it were not her own, something just used for a purpose. By him? No, by her. And the risk to herself? She didn't want to think about it, not now. Later. She closed her eyes. Now what? Had he figured out her plan and thwarted it? Doubtful. She took the scalpel out of the shoe. He wouldn't knowingly have given it back to her. She looked at the blade. Could she really slit someone's throat?

Not someone's. *His.* She stared up at the ceiling, pictured Zuka that day on the beach, pictured him running on the sand to the western jetty after shooting Baruti, saw him raise his rifle as Rick tried to cross the river. That was the man she had to kill— not the man she'd had sex with last night.

She looked around the room, bare except for the clothes thrown in a pile in the corner—her own mixed with his. How quickly the repartee, the disdain, the contempt had turned around. At first it had been a challenge to play the part of the seductress to this man she so loathed. She'd had to deny so much, take herself out of her own reality. She had to see him as passionate rather than brutal, intriguing rather than terrifying. This role called for her to match his strength, his power, his forcefulness.

But it was herself, not Zuka, she'd found most confusing. With him she had been something different—her own performance so foreign, so dissociated from her sense of self. Maybe even exotic at times. She shuddered. Nobody had ever used 'exotic' to describe Jane. Balanced, capable, bright, maybe. But never exotic.

A slight breeze entered the cracked window, mixing the fresh jungle aromas with his smell, their smell. She took in a deep breath before stopping herself—what was she doing? She pulled the sleeping bag over her body and put her hands over her face.

This man was a murderer. He'd killed Rick and now held her and her sons hostage. Had she let herself get so swept up by whatever Zuka stirred in her to have forgotten why she was there? Or worse, had she delayed too long, allowed him to wake up before she carried out her plan? No. She was trying to find the shoes when he sat up...She clawed at her scalp.

She turned, grabbed the blade, and brought her thumb sideways down the edge so as to assess the sharpness without cutting. She pictured the act, forced herself to walk through it one more time in her head. The incision would need to be deep. Cutting the jugular vein would be easier, the carotid artery more decisive. Zuka's obvious ability to overpower her if given the smallest chance required her to be quick and thorough, no room for hesitation. It had to be over immediately.

She focused on the last moments. In the time it took for him to bleed out, his hands would be on her, his grip struggling for his life, or at least struggling to end hers. She looked back at the blade. Was it sharp enough to penetrate the trachea? Hard to tell, it was a short blade.

She flashed on the instruction she'd received as a med student. Palpate the trachea, feel for the soft spaces between those hard, impenetrable bands, and stab quickly for a life-saving tracheotomy. The casing of a ballpoint pen could do it, or so the story went. She never knew anyone who'd actually tried. It didn't matter. She wouldn't have time to palpate his throat. If the blade didn't glide through his trachea with one quick movement as she passed through the artery, she'd need to reenter the other side of his throat to get the second carotid—and by that time he'd have her.

Maybe one would be enough.

She slipped the scalpel back inside her shoe and began to get dressed. She tried to reassure herself that she hadn't blown her best opportunity. It was a hard sell. Returning had not been part of her plan, but—

The door swung open. Zuka stood poised to enter, which he did not. He watched. Jane instinctively turned away to button her blouse. He laughed. She turned to face him, glaring. It was not her intention to challenge his right to be there, his right to take whatever he wanted at any time—after all, it wasn't his anger she was pulling for.

But she had to work at it. The moment he saw her as easy or sleazy, if he thought she wanted him, that was the moment he'd lose interest. Her role was clear—strong, challenging, and slightly defiant. She needed him to want her again, and soon.

Zuka tilted his head back, standing with one leg up on the threshold, his rifle slung over one shoulder. In the cat and mouse game of sexual interest, he clearly saw himself as the catch. Given his physique and natural poise, it was likely a role he was used to.

She tried not to see beyond this as she slipped on her shoes—tried to ignore all the other thoughts about him that had occupied her mind before that night. The sun was coming over the eastern horizon, and the others would be out soon. There was something about their unspoken pledge of secrecy that heightened the tension and, she hoped, the desire.

He brushed past her to the one remaining piece of furniture in the room other than the bed. It was a nightstand with a single drawer and large open space underneath. He took out matches to start the morning fire in the stove. It was then that she noticed her medical bag, barely visible in the back of the nightstand.

Zuka motioned for her to walk out in front of him, not so much from politeness as necessity given the tight quarters. She stepped back out of his way and allowed him to pass instead. He frowned. Quickly she reached under her shirt as if to readjust her bra before venturing outside. He hesitated a moment, then took the hint.

As soon as he was gone she knelt next to the nightstand and riffled quickly through the bag. It took her a few moments to find the bottle she needed.

ᛟ

Jane wiped down Jake's forehead with a damp rag. He didn't have any energy. He had a relentless fever and hadn't been out of bed all day. She smiled at him, his eyes weren't completely glazed over.

"Here, just a little more." She lifted the spoon.

He shook his head and lay back down.

"You're keeping it down better today," she said. He'd told her he still felt nauseated, that his head still pounded, but at least he hadn't thrown up.

Jake whispered something inaudible and turned over.

"Japera says it's dengue fever," Michael said. Jane hadn't seen him come in. "But he's not a doctor, what does he know?"

She nodded. Maybe. The Africans would have seen a lot of it. She got up and sat over on Michael's bed. She decided to leave Jake alone, let him get some rest.

"I know you're angry with him, but you need to stay close. Pick up any information."

Michael shrugged. He sat down next to her. "Mom, whatever happened to that blue bandana of yours?"

She glanced over at her bag, then remembered. "I used it on Paul's leg back at the beach. If he still has it, it's probably all bloody. If you want a bandana, I've got two others in my bag. One's red, one's yellow. Take your pick."

"If he had dropped it on the hike to here, would Lorenzo have picked it up? Could he have it?"

Jane got up, rummaged through her bag, held up the yellow bandana. "Just take this one."

He took it but seemed reluctant.

Why on earth? Michael had never cared much about style or color. If he closed his eyes ten minutes after dressing, he probably couldn't tell you what he was wearing. Jake, on the other hand—

"Thanks, Mom. But if Paul dropped it, the blue one—wasn't Lorenzo in front of us the whole time? And he had no more contact with Paul, right? He stayed in that hut until he escaped."

"Right." She'd decided not to tell the boys what Shelly had said about Lorenzo. It was better that they hold on to the hope that he might bring help. "I'm not sure how long it will take him—"

"I was thinking about that. Thought we'd better keep working on things here." Michael got up to leave, then turned back. "Mom, I think you should stay away from Zuka."

She swallowed hard—some decisions aren't made by committee. "Michael, I have to—"

"Not with him." He wouldn't look at her. "We have to come up with a better plan. If you don't, I will." He was out the door.

Jane watched him walk up to Japera. They sat on the picnic table talking for a few minutes before Japera got up to make his rounds of the periphery. Michael shook his head and motioned toward Paul's hut. He rose and walked in that direction, but as soon as Japera was out of sight, Michael turned back to the stove. He kicked at the smoldering embers, bringing on a sudden flare of sparks. Then he picked up a stack of wood and ran with it behind Paul's hut. He came back for more, reducing the pile to less than a quarter of what it had been.

Strange. She'd ask him about it later.

CHAPTER 25

Katura retreated to her room. She told Changa she had some read-ing to do. The truth was she found it hard to think while he was around. She shut the door and flopped on the bed. If Japera wasn't trying to enlist help at the Mana Pools hideout, then where was he? Zuka obviously knew they weren't going there, but did Japera? He had seemed willing to follow that guy anywhere.

A week ago all she knew of Zuka Sibanda was that he'd been arrested with Tafadzwa. In fact, she and Japera had thought he was still locked up with their brother when they went to find Zuka's father for help. Everything changed after that.

That's it. She grabbed her soccer ball, but was jolted by the loud sound of drilling. She listened for a few minutes, then opened the top drawer of her dresser—

Where was it?

She emptied her clothes from each drawer onto her bed—useless, she knew she'd stuffed the money Japera had left her in the top drawer, but it gave her time to think. She replaced the clothes neatly, then ventured out into the living room. Changa sat in the entry with the front door open. He'd removed the door latch and was installing another.

"New lock? Good idea," she said. "Can't be too careful these days." She watched him closely. He scooted back on the floor, effectively blocking her ability to leave.

"I have to go out later," he said.

She made herself wait, knowing he would tell her more when he was ready. Sure enough, after a few minutes he said, "My mother's sick." He picked up several sizes of screws to measure their length against the depth of the door. "I won't be gone long today, but tomorrow…" He made his selection and continued to drill into the door. "Need to make sure you're safe, might be away a few days."

"I'm sorry to hear it." She reached down and picked up the new lock. "About your mother. Hope it's not serious." Sick mom, right. How lame an excuse was that? But then she'd been working hard to convince him she was naïve enough to believe just about anything.

The lock looked weird. She turned the hardware around in her hand, then realized why—he'd altered the locking mechanism. It could be latched from the outside with a key but not opened from inside. He was planning on locking her in tomorrow when he left for several days.

Changa grabbed the lock out of her hand, then glanced down at the soccer ball next to him.

"Remember I have another practice today? I told you about it last night." He never seemed to listen to her chatter anyway, maybe he'd miss the lie. "Big game in the morning."

He glared at her, unblinking. She shifted her feet.

"Did I forget to tell you? Sorry."

He placed the lock in the newly created hole.

"The guys wanted to come over and meet you."

Changa stopped turning the screwdriver.

She waited a moment. Let it sink in. "But don't worry, I told them you were shy and I'd meet them at the field. In fact, I better get going or they'll be right over to get me."

He didn't move for a long moment. Then he slowly shifted out of her way. Katura moved past him onto the walkway, then turned back.

"Oh, what time will you be back? So I can have dinner ready."

He continued working and didn't respond. She hadn't expected him to. She wasn't planning on returning anyway. She crossed over the front lawn and was just about to round the corner where she'd double back away from the field when she heard his booming voice behind her.

"Katura, what are you doing?"

She froze. From the sound, she knew he was too close for her to be able to run and get away from him. How had she blown it? She turned around slowly.

"Aren't you forgetting something?" He held up her soccer ball.

"Gee, thanks, but we're using one of the other kid's. They think mine's gone a bit flat."

Changa squeezed the ball between his two large hands and shrugged. He turned and headed back toward the house. She heard the front door close.

Chapter 26

"Hey!" Zuka yelled out his door. "Coffee."

"I'm not your—"

The door slammed, and he was back inside his hut.

Apparently I am. She searched the bags that had arrived last night, no coffee. She pounded on the door, then tried the latch.

"Your delivery boy only brought tea."

He was sitting up in bed reading a newspaper. Changa must be bringing them in with his deliveries. Zuka quickly folded up the paper and looked up at her, his face unreadable. She hesitated, then walked in and set the cup down on the bed stand.

"I found it in the bags. I don't know the brand, but Japera said it was good." She took a sip of her own cup. "He's right."

Zuka motioned toward the bed, scooting over to allow enough room for her to sit without touching him. She took another sip of her tea. He seemed to be studying her.

"How's your boy doing?" he said.

She stiffened. In here she wasn't a mother, didn't have a family, wasn't a wife or—worse—a widow. Here it was different, had to be different. She stared at her tea, then moved the cup slowly up to her mouth. It was important he not see her anger.

Zuka picked up his cup, looked at the tea, took a tiny sip, swirled it around. Would he be able to discern the bitter taste of morphine? She'd been careful not to put in too much but couldn't risk testing it herself.

"Too hot." He set down the cup.

She shrugged. "Thought you could handle it."

Zuka suddenly grabbed her, pulled her down on the bed and flipped her around. She held her breath and clenched her fists. It wasn't just the suddenness that startled her. It was his strength.

Then there was a shift. He laid his hands softly on her thighs—moved them down her legs, touching her skin lightly, almost imperceptibly. When he reached her toes he rolled his fingers over them one at a time, both hands gently massaging the curves of her foot. He took each toe, caressing as if it were the only body part he cared about, as if each toe required his total concentration. She sat up on her elbows, watched him. He locked onto her eyes, his face motionless as he continued to slowly, methodically work each muscle.

She lay back, tried to focus on her feet. For now, she needed to be out of her head, away from her thoughts, her plans—pretend she was his lover. She forced herself to focus on his touch, on each finger he moved across her skin, the palm of his hands as they alternated between deep massage and gentle caress. He needed to feel her yield everything to him. She took in a deep breath and pictured his hands moving across her, pictured herself giving every inch that he touched over to his fingers, closed her eyes and pictured Rick. He moved the palm of his hand down the bottom of her feet, pushing deeply into the soles. She squirmed. The pressure was not exactly painful, but she was aware that it could be, that he was precise in the depths of his touch.

Her thoughts suddenly went to the tea. He hadn't had any. Was there a way to make that happen?

She felt her left foot being lifted, his right hand under her calf. His tongue moved between her toes, sucking ever so slightly, then down the sole of her foot. She swallowed hard—a tingling sensation moved throughout her body, her breaths became shallow. The back of his fingers moved up her calves to her inner thighs. He stopped and moved back down, retreating to her ankles. He crossed her feet, nudged her flank, motioned for her to turn over. She obliged and lay on her stomach.

He moved his hands up her legs and around her hips, slowly lifted her shirt. He straddled her waist as he smoothed his hands over her shoulders and down her back. His left hand massaged deeply into her back muscles while his right softly caressed her neck, his fingers moving gently over and around her ears, down her cheek and back to the base of her neck. Then he changed his movement, altered his position symmetrically. His right hand pushed deeply into the right side of her back while his left caressed her face and neck.

At first the change of pace went almost unnoticed, could have been her imagination. Then it was unmistakable. He was slowing down, softening his touch, until he finally stopped. He hesitated a moment, then moved off of her.

"Time for work," he said. He picked up the teacup.

Her heart was pounding in her throat. She held her breath as he started out the door and watched him descend the steps, teacup in hand. She heard him dump the contents on the ground outside.

⋏

"Hey," Zuka yelled across the yard. "I thought you were going to get more firewood."

Japera, on his way up the porch steps to his hut for a badly needed nap, stopped and said, "We—I did. Look next to the stove." The door slammed behind him.

Zuka kicked the remaining few logs. He looked back at Japera's hut.

"I'll get it." Michael hopped down from the picnic table. "I used a lot more than usual—had to keep boiling water for my brother."

"You must've had a bonfire." Zuka glanced between the buildings.

All of the nearby wood appeared to have been used. He made sure Zuka couldn't see behind the huts from this angle. Zuka shook his head, denying Michael permission to go for the wood.

"Suit yourself." Michael sat back down. He didn't want to seem anxious to get away.

Just then Paul came clumping down the steps from his hut. He moved fairly quickly and very oddly, putting his weight on his right leg with his left held in a stiff angle out from the side until he'd touch it down for a couple of seconds to propel himself forward. He headed straight for the picnic table.

Zuka glanced over at Michael and nodded for him to go for wood.

He didn't need anything more by way of an invitation. Whatever trouble Paul was going to cause was his problem. As soon as Michael rounded the corner behind the lodge, he took off running. He wanted as much time as possible in the woods. He crossed the stream without difficulty, then approached the area where Lorenzo's body had been. Now it all looked the same. For as far back as he could see, the vegetation was consistent, no landmarks, no body. He searched moving in concentric circles until he could barely see the edge of the woods.

Nothing.

He headed straight back to the stream to start over. He rubbed his face, then looked around, tried to remember exactly where he and Japera had parted. He recognized a large boulder that had been on the north end of the stream just after Japera had gone the other way. It was from here that Michael had entered the forest to collect firewood. What was the exact direction he had taken once he left the stream? He'd walked several minutes into the heavily forested area when he had seen Lorenzo's body—a small mistake in the angle he chose now could lead to a big distance fifty or a hundred yards in. He combed the area a second time. Still nothing.

He sat on a nearby boulder, still looking for landmarks. The rock he was sitting on looked vaguely familiar. No wonder—he'd almost run into it right after he saw the body, when he jumped back in horror. The corpse had to be close by. He searched the immediate area, then groaned. Ten yards away there was another large rock just like it. He scanned the wider area. In fact, they were everywhere.

"Michael."

His head jerked.

"Michael, over here." He knew that voice. He couldn't be hearing that voice.

Fifty yards away a tall, thin figure was moving quickly toward him. There was no way it could be Rick. Michael jumped down from the boulder and saw the smile on the man's face. He'd never seen Rick when he wasn't clean-shaven and well groomed. And Rick was dead.

Michael started running—they both were running. They stood holding each other for several minutes before Rick spoke.

"It'll be okay, Michael."

He hadn't been aware that he was crying. He pulled away and wiped his face, then quickly looked at Rick.

Rick laughed. "Still here." His eyes were wet too.

"We thought you were dead."

Rick nodded. "I turned back after the first shot. I thought whoever was shooting would expect me to try to cross so I doubled back to this side of the river, just beyond the jetty. Baruti knew where he was going. He didn't need me."

"But we searched that whole area."

"I know! That guy who came looking with you almost saw me. I buried myself in some rocks on the far side of the jetty.

When you guys came over the top he almost crushed me with the rubble he sent down."

"Zuka."

"What?"

"That guy, it was Zuka." It seemed odd that these Africans were now part of his life and Rick didn't even know their names. He didn't know that Paul was injured, that Jake was sick. So much had happened since that day on the beach. "He killed Baruti. Shot him as he tried to cross the river."

Rick winced. Michael waited while it sank in—no one had gone for help. Rick put his arm around Michael and motioned toward a fallen tree where they could sit.

"I knew you'd recognize the bandana, your mother's. I just knew it."

"Where is he?"

"I buried him—didn't want you to find him again. Once was more than enough. And the hyenas..." Rick shook his head. "You didn't need to see that."

Michael closed his eyes for a couple of seconds. The image of Lorenzo's body was impossible to erase—half buried in the vegetation with his mother's blood-stained cloth over his face. What would happen to him, to any of them, if they were left in this wilderness? He got up and started to pace, he needed to make the visuals go away.

"How's your mother holding up?"

"She's doing okay."

Rick stared at Michael for a few minutes, then nodded. "She'll do anything she can to get her boys out of there."

"She doesn't know you're alive." He tried to swallow through the lump in his throat. "She thought, we all thought...there was blood in the river. I knew it could have been the crocodile, but then I thought it was just wishful thinking." He covered his face with his hands.

Rick grabbed his arms. He pulled them down, forcing Michael to look at him. "She can't know."

"What? But she's—"

"Doesn't matter. What matters is that she continues to do whatever she can to get out. Whatever she's doing, I know she has to. Do you get that, Michael?"

Whatever she's doing? Michael couldn't look at him.

"But what about you?" He raised his voice. "Aren't you going to—"

"Of course, when I can." Rick got up. He took a few steps away. He wasn't a large man but he'd always been fit, muscular. Now he looked weak, his skin pale.

"What have you been eating?"

Rick laughed. "Anything I can, which means not much. I was able to sneak into the lodge through the back at first. Stole some food and stuff. Not now, though. Too risky."

He stared at Michael in silence for a moment.

"I look that bad, eh? No wonder Lorenzo decided to go it alone." He glanced across the stream. "I mean before he got shot by the stocky one. Zuka? I was very lucky he never saw me."

Michael nodded.

"Look, Michael, even at my best I couldn't just run in there like Rambo. I have to watch from the outside and make my move when it makes sense."

Michael picked up a rock and threw it squarely at a tree thirty yards away. A flock of small birds took flight.

"I meant we, Michael. I didn't mean to leave you out. We'll make our move once I have a bit more strength."

"I'm not staying out here."

"You're not going back in there, Michael. You—"

"I have to go." He took a few steps toward the stream. "If I'm not back soon, they'll kill Mom and Jake. Zuka can't know you're alive or that anything has changed."

"Michael, you're out now." Rick had never raised his voice to him before. "I'm not losing all of you." He grabbed Michael's wrist. "She'd want me to—"

"I'm not leaving them there." He twisted his arm and broke free.

Rick looked down at Michael's hands, then back up at his face.

Michael relaxed his fists. "I'm sorry, I—"

"It's okay. You're probably right, it's safer for now, for everyone." His eyes seemed to lose focus. "It's just hard to get you back and let you go almost in the same breath."

"You know how glad I am you're okay?"

"I know."

"I can't show up empty-handed." Michael quickly gathered an armful of wood. "Jake's a little sick, he's not coming out for meals. I'll leave extra food behind our hut. Can you get to it before the animals do?"

"Not a problem. Can you keep our secret?"

"Not a problem."

CHAPTER 27

Jane slammed the food down in front of Zuka.

Zuka didn't flinch. He looked down at the table and gathered together the small pile of rice that had leapt off his plate. He formed it into a round ball with his right hand and tossed it far from the picnic area. Then he picked up his utensils, examined them as if judging her cleaning skills. Jane leaned down within an inch of his ear.

"Leave. Her. Alone."

Zuka took a bite of the meat, some part of a chicken that Jane couldn't identify. She'd just braised it over the open flame and dumped it on top of a pile of rice.

"I said—"

"I heard what you said." He continued to chew his food.

Jane stood motionless behind him. She'd seen Zuka emerge from Shelly's hut in the early hours that morning, before anyone was usually up. The only reason she was up herself was because she wanted to make a special breakfast for Jake, who was finally keeping food down. But when she saw Zuka, she felt the energy suddenly drain out of her. She hated the thought of Zuka taking advantage of the young Australian guide. *Raping* the young Australian guide.

"Zuka." She took in a long breath. "She's young. None of this is her fault, there's no reason to hurt her. If it's sex you want, you've got me, any time, just leave her alone. She's going to be damaged enough being locked up in there for days."

"Damaged?" He laughed.

"You arrogant bastard." Her hands were trembling.

"What makes you think she wants to be left alone?"

Zuka's head jerked slightly to the right as the palm of Jane's hand came across his face. Her hand stung—his cheek must be burning. He stared straight ahead, not moving.

Jane took a step back.

Zuka picked up his plate and walked over to his hut. He sat on the top step and resumed eating.

"That's an interesting tactic." Jane hadn't seen Paul come out of his hut, but there he was, leaning heavily on the branch he used as a crutch.

"What tactic?" Michael came bounding down the steps. He grabbed two plates and nodded for more after she'd put a fairly large pile of food on each. He nodded again when she hesitated. "Jake's really hungry, Mom."

Jane put a second mound on one of the plates, then turned to Paul. "I just don't want the girl hurt."

Paul's hands were trembling, he looked pale and weak.

Paul laughed. "Yeah, right." He sat down and started picking at the food, not much making it to his mouth. "Who're you kidding?"

"Excuse me?" Jane glanced over at Zuka. He wasn't within earshot as long as she didn't raise her voice. But Michael—he'd paused before walking slowly back up to their hut with the plates, and now he was avoiding eye contact with her. She turned and glared at Paul.

He shook his head. "One thing's for sure, he certainly reacts differently to you than to me."

His breathing was labored. She watched him for a few minutes, wondered why he'd even ventured out. He should be in bed. She'd have Michael take him food from now on. He turned his head slightly and she gasped.

"What happened?" There was a large bruise covering his right temple. His eye was swollen almost shut. There were shiny blotches where areas of skin were missing.

He glanced over at Zuka. "I seem to have run into the butt of his rifle."

"Let me see that." She leaned over to have a closer look. "You need some antibiotic ointment on the open wounds."

Paul flinched as she reached toward his face. "No, that's okay. I've got it. Wouldn't want to incite the wrath of your... friend." He glanced over at Zuka, then picked up his plate and limped back to his hut, leaving Jane to eat alone.

⊀

Michael walked up the steps slowly. The best time to leave Rick food would be early evening he decided. He'd been mulling over the options after last night's near fiasco. He'd gone out late, when it was pitch black, so no one would be able see him. But then he became acutely aware of the silence. While everyone slept, any noise would easily be heard by Zuka who was keeping watch. Michael had barely slept all night, leaving Rick hungry like that. But it wasn't safe—better to wait until there was more activity in camp.

In the early evening the light would be low and there'd be noise as they prepared and ate dinner. Zuka and Japera would be focused on their hostages gathered at the picnic area, not paying attention to the areas behind the huts. He just hoped it'd be dark enough for Rick to approach the back of the hut without being seen. It wasn't good to bring Rick into camp while it was still light, but it was the only way.

Jake stirred as Michael walked in, then turned over and fell back to sleep. Michael hid Rick's plate in the corner of the hut. He took half of the large helping on Jake's plate and sat on his cot to dig in.

What could Rick be thinking out there by himself? He tried to imagine whether *he* could survive the elements, the hunger, the loneliness. At least Rick was alive. But it had to be awful, getting weaker and weaker and not being able to help. Michael sat back. He bit the inside of his cheek. There was something disturbing about their conversation. What did he know?

He set the plate down and shook Jake. "Food's here. I'll eat whatever you can't finish." He picked up his book and stared at the page.

It was hard not to think about his mother and Zuka. It sickened him. Michael's eyes wandered from the page. He had to get his mind off his mom.

Who was that guy in the park? He couldn't remember his name, he didn't go to his school. The guy knew Caitlin had a boyfriend, knew she'd even called him that night. But the jerk got her drunk and by the time Michael showed up, she was half dressed, lying on the grass in the park with that guy all over her. She'd passed out, but he didn't seem to care, she could've been asleep or dead as far as he was concerned.

By the time Dylan pulled Michael off the guy there was blood everywhere. He'd figured it was his nose. It wasn't until days later that he learned he'd broken the guy's jaw.

"Why are you so quiet?" Jake stood over him, holding the half-eaten plate of food. It was the first time he'd been up in several days. "Here, I can keep food down now but still can't eat much. The rest is yours."

"What are you doing?" Shelly's voice was barely audible as Jane crept closer toward the window.

She didn't expect Zuka to leave the girl alone just because she'd told him to, but why was he sneaking in? After all, he was the one with the gun. He'd headed for Shelly's hut right after Jane went in for the night—probably thought she wouldn't be back out until the wee hours of the morning as usual.

Jane had turned out her light and watched him from the window. He was lit by moonlight and when he disappeared into Shelly's hut, Jane slipped out of her doorway.

She inched closer. She crouched directly under the window, next to steps that led to the door. If there was any struggle, she'd burst right in. She wasn't sure what she'd do, but whatever happened, it wouldn't be what Zuka had planned for the girl.

"You put it in the lodge," Shelly said. "I don't understand."

Jane could hear sniffles between Shelly's heavy breaths. She walked softly up the steps of the porch, put her hand on the door handle.

"Don't you?" He sounded distracted, unengaged. "If not, then you're even less useful than I thought."

Useful? Jane froze. Had her involvement with Zuka put Shelly in even more danger? There were worse things than rape. Suddenly there was a loud noise she couldn't identify—some sort of scraping on the floor, furniture was being moved, things tossed around.

"I can help you." Shelly's voice, louder now, seemed to come from the corner where her cot had been the other night. Was she tied up again? "I want to help."

"Then where is it?"

Jane gripped the handle tighter. Zuka's voice came from a different part of the hut every time he spoke. If she were going to burst in, she needed to know where to expect him.

"I told you, I don't know." Her voice was soft again. "Please, Zuka, you know you've got everything under control."

That's right—appeal to his narcissism, seduce him. Better than being seen as useless to his mission.

"You probably took it out and put it in your hut, you just forgot," she said. "Sit down, talk to me. We're a good team, always have been."

Always? What's the timeline? How long has Shelly known these men? Jane pulled her hand back from the door.

Something was thrown across the room.

"Forgot?"

"There's nothing in there. Just some of Lorenzo's supplies."

"What supplies?"

"Clothes, medical supplies. I've ripped up the maps, disassembled the flares, just like we planned months ago. We assumed there'd be some hitches, now we just go with them. We're on track."

Months ago? Jane backed up slowly, felt the ledge with the heel of her foot, and lowered herself to the first step. Suddenly the porch creaked, and she froze. Zuka's heavy boots moved across the floor toward the corner of the hut.

"When's she coming back?"

Jane lowered herself down to the second step.

"I don't know," Shelly said.

"I need to know what they're thinking, their next plan."

"I'll get it. Are you giving her enough space to sneak in? Maybe Japera's the problem."

"She'll figure it out if she wants to. She still worried about you?"

"Of course." Shelly laughed.

There was movement toward the door. "Zuka, don't leave. Can't you stay longer?"

Jane reached the edge of the porch.

"Just stick with the plan, I need to know what they're thinking."

Shelly sighed. "Sure."

He swung the door open and looked around before he bounded down the stairs. Jane held her breath. Zuka's steps in his heavy boots had been loud enough to cover hers when she leapt off the stairs. She crouched under the porch, trembling, as she watched Zuka walk away, his rifle slung over one shoulder.

Chapter 28

It was all she could do not to take off running. Wherever Changa was going, it would be hours before he realized she wasn't coming back. She cut through the lots behind the school to follow side streets to Zuka's house. It was important to stay off the main roads, where Changa could be driving.

As she dashed down alleyways and through backyards, she ran through various scenarios in her head. If she could make him understand, Zuka's father was sure to be of help. He hadn't seemed much different from her own father—concerned about his son and mainly interested in making sure he was safe.

A car rounding the corner sent her darting between two houses to hide behind some trashcans. It was a dark green sedan, but she couldn't be too careful. She was close now.

If both Zuka and Japera were in trouble, then Mr. Sibanda and she would be on the same side. But she had to be prepared for other alternatives—hadn't her mother said something about him losing his teaching job for refusing to join the ruling party? Maybe Zuka and his father were using Japera and Thabani for some political reason. Maybe he'd know where they were but refuse to help her. She increased her pace. Mr. Sibanda was her only hope. Whatever happened, she was bound to find out more than she knew right now.

She approached the high wall covered with razor wire that surrounded Zuka's house. The gate in the back was slightly ajar, just like it had been the night she and Japera were there.

She hadn't thought about it at the time, but now it struck her as odd to make sure someone can't climb over your wall, yet leave the gate open. She glanced around quickly before slipping into the yard—

Her knees went wobbly as soon as she saw the house. The doors and windows were boarded up, every one of them. She had just been here a few nights ago, and now if she didn't know better she'd have thought the house had been vacant for years.

"It's always the details," Japera had instructed her since she was a little girl. "If you notice the details, knowledge will follow."

She went back over her visit. She'd gone into the kitchen, had picked up a glass but not opened a cupboard. It hadn't been necessary. The glassware was sitting out as if it had just been washed. Then there was the furniture, which had all seemed comfortable and permanent. Was this a stage? Had there been pictures on the walls? What were the implications?

Katura turned and left the way she had come. Nothing here for her.

Changa was now her only connection to her brother. Friend or foe, he was all she had. She dashed out the gate—she had to get back to Thabani's house before Changa did.

Chapter 29

It was a relief when Japera broke the silence.

"Your brother doing any better?"

Michael knew his mother was right, knew how he needed to act with Japera, but he still hadn't let go of all his anger. He figured a lot of the anger was at himself, for his naiveté—what had he expected? He glanced over at the young black man who sat a few feet away on the edge of the picnic table. There was something about Japera that made him expect the unreasonable.

"A little." Michael looked down. "Hey, I'm sorry about—"

"No need." Japera waved his hand to stop him. "I understand. You're worried about Jake."

It was jarring to hear Japera mention his brother by name. It sounded so familiar. "No, I mean yes, but still I shouldn't have been such a jerk. You were just trying to help."

Japera looked over at Michael. He stared at him for several minutes before he spoke. "You're a good man, Michael."

Man? Was it a translation problem? He'd rarely been referred to as anything but a boy or a kid, or maybe young man when some adult was pissed off. Of course, kids grew up quicker here.

He heard the distant but unmistakable sound of an engine—Changa's supply truck. It would be a minute before they'd actually be able to see the dust cloud it would throw up, another five before they could make out the truck itself. Sound traveled easily in this hot, arid climate. He scanned the perimeter of their encampment. No one was going to sneak up on them without being heard in plenty of time.

"Nothing to apologize for, Michael. Nothing's more important than family."

Michael knew Japera was trying to make him feel better, but he didn't. Family was complicated. What did it mean that he was lying to his mother, that he didn't tell her about Rick? Every time he saw her, he wanted to blurt out that Rick was out there. Of course, it wasn't like it was the first time he'd lied to his mother about something big.

"Oh, I don't know. Sometimes I can be pretty selfish and impulsive when it comes to my family."

Japera laughed. "We have one of those in our family, too—impulsive, but loyal.

Japera could have been referring to anyone. But all Michael could think about was the way Katura had walked right up to him at the airport—so bold, so sure of herself, much cockier than this older brother of hers.

"I bet she's proud of you."

Japera stared off into the distance. "She doesn't know about this."

"How. . .she doesn't know? But you said family's more important than anything. What about honesty?"

"Sometimes loyalty and honesty are the same. Sometimes not."

"Come on, that's bullshit. Isn't that just a way to rationalize doing whatever you want and still feeling okay about it?"

"No, it doesn't feel okay. Just the opposite. But it's the right thing to do." He turned to look directly into Michael's eyes. "I'm sure you can imagine why it's important for my little sister not to know. It's because of loyalty to her that I didn't tell her."

Michael sat back. Did Japera's rationale apply to his situation with his mother?

"What happens if you change your mind? What if you realize down the road that it was just easier to lie, that it was selfish, not really in anyone's best interest but your own?" He was no longer thinking about Rick. His mind had wandered to a cloud that had hung over him for years.

"Then eventually you have to come clean." Japera hopped off the table as the truck drove up the entrance. "Guilt drives a wedge between people. Come on, might have a heavier load this time. Zuka ordered extra, said Lorenzo and Shelly are eating more than he expected."

Michael laughed. "Yeah, right."

Japera turned around. "What do you mean?"

"He said Lorenzo?" Michael's thoughts were racing. Hadn't Japera been in their hut? Come to think of it, Zuka always went in, kept Japera on watch when they were brought food. It wouldn't surprise him that Zuka wouldn't tell Japera that Lorenzo was dead, but why would he keep his escape a secret?

Japera stared at him. "He's not in there?"

Michael was silent.

Japera then turned back, not to look at Shelly's hut, but at Zuka's. "Come on, we'll empty the food."

Michael followed after him. He knew the routine—unload the truck, don't look directly at the driver, behave like Japera's quiet, obedient servant. He stood back while the two men talked. Until that moment he hadn't realized how important it was to him that the girl not be a part of the plan—that her playfulness with him not have been a set-up, making him the fool.

"Hey, what are you waiting for?" Changa said. "It's open." Michael passed by them to start unloading. "I've got to get back before dark, there's more police on the streets these days and they like to stop cars at night."

The heavy van doors separated Michael from the men. He couldn't hear Japera's quieter voice. The back was full of bags. It looked like Changa didn't intend to deliver again for several days. He slowly lifted a bag into each arm, taking his time, listening as he passed by.

"Oh, she's fine, clueless. I've got a guy watching the house while I'm gone, making sure no one tries to go in."

"Doesn't she get antsy to get out?"

"I let her play futbol with some local kids when I'm there, but I watch the papers. If anything shows up, I'll keep her inside."

Michael tried to keep his pace exactly as it had been before, just taking the two bags inside the dining lodge.

He's got Katura staying with this thug? Unbelievable. Michael let his right hand slide up the side of the bag, then released it. He swept his hand down quickly, made a clumsy grab for a potato—it hit the dirt.

"Idiot!" Changa yelled. "Don't put those dirty things back in the bag. Rinse them off, you fool!" He looked at Japera, who nodded at Michael.

Michael ran over to the table to get his water bottle, then up onto the porch to grab his windbreaker jacket, the same one he'd worn at the airport. He rinsed the vegetables that had hit the dirt, dried them with the lining of the jacket, and replaced them in the bag. He looked over at Japera, who wasn't paying him any attention.

Michael swung the jacket over his shoulder and continued unloading. When he entered the lodge he grabbed two small cucumbers, a green banana, and some unidentifiable greens. He stuffed them down his pants, making sure his oversized T-shirt covered all evidence. He held up a ripe tomato, then put it back in the bag. Rick could probably benefit from the fresh juice, but it might get smashed as he walked.

He heard the back doors of the van slam shut as he headed out. Changa carried the last two bags and passed him on the steps without a word.

"Anything in the front seat?" he asked Japera as soon as Changa was inside the lodge.

Japera looked over at the van. "Go see."

Michael circled around the van to the passenger side, out of Japera's view.

"No, looks like we got it all." He quickly tucked his jacket just below the seat, noticeable only to anyone who might enter on the passenger side. Katura's three small rubbing stones still nestled in the right front pocket.

入

Jane rapped lightly on the door. She didn't want to wake Paul if he was finally getting some sleep. He'd complained about being up and down with leg pain over the past several nights and Michael had mentioned seeing him walk around camp near midnight getting water.

Tommy had come by earlier this morning to see if Jake was well enough to kick the soccer ball around. But Jake only had the energy for cards, and they played a couple of games of gin rummy. Jane figured Paul could use the reprieve. She knocked again, then opened the door and peeked in.

"Paul?" She stepped across the threshold and pulled the door closed behind her. She moved to the bathroom door. "Paul? You in there?"

That was odd. She'd just come from her own hut and no one had been in the central camp area. Where would he go? It was then that she realized how different the room looked.

Over the past week she'd noticed that both their huts had become increasingly messy. She'd been too busy to keep things picked up, and Michael and Jake were not inclined even in the best of times. Paul and Tommy's place had been just as bad, but today it was jarringly neat. The bathroom counter that had been strewn with toiletries was now empty. Paul and Tommy's clothes were neatly folded and piled along one wall. In the corner at the foot of Paul's bed rested his large olive green backpack and Tommy's smaller navy blue one. She couldn't remember seeing them out since the day they'd arrived. Space was at such a premium in these small rooms that the packs had been kept under the cots.

She glanced over at the bathroom window. The screen was still gone, but now the window was slightly open, letting in a soft, cool breeze. Paul must have jumped out the back so as not to be seen by whoever was keeping guard at the time. She looked out toward the picnic area. It was empty. Japera had taken his usual walk around the periphery, and if she wasn't mistaken, Michael had gone with him.

Jane leaned over the pack, keeping her eyes on the bathroom window. She unzipped the front pouch and rummaged through the contents. From this angle she'd be able to see Paul slip his fingers in the crack, and by the time it was open wide enough for him to fit through, she could be out the front door.

She closed up the pouch and noted the usual overnight toiletries and some pills she didn't recognize. Her hands moved to the main pouch and felt the outside. She fingered several liter-size canisters, opened the pack quickly, and removed one. A clear liquid sloshed back and forth. She unscrewed the lid and smelled. Nothing. She dipped a finger inside and tasted—just water. She counted eight bottles before replacing the one she'd inspected. She moved quickly over to Tommy's pack and felt the contents through the outside. Six more bottles.

Jane sat down on Paul's cot, keeping her eyes on the window. She could feel her pounding heart return to normal speed. So Paul planned to escape, to take Tommy. She glanced down again at the backpacks weighted down with water. If Paul could alert the authorities, let them know how to find them—

"Can I help you?"

She stood up quickly. Paul leaned against the door jamb, his arms crossed.

"I came to see how you were feeling, how your leg was doing." She glanced down at his thigh. Paul didn't follow her gaze. He just stared at her. "I didn't mean to intrude—"

"Really?"

She moved toward the door, but his body blocked her exit.

"What were you doing in here, Jane?"

"I told you, I came to check on your leg."

"You're worried about my leg?" He shifted his weight to lean primarily on the side without the bandage. "Really, Jane? And when you saw my leg wasn't here you thought you'd just snoop around?"

She glanced out the window. Japera and Michael weren't back yet. She had no idea how far they'd wandered.

"Were you going to tell me you're leaving?"

He smiled. "Good work, detective."

"I don't think you can make it, Paul. Your leg's too bad for a long trek and you can't follow the road or they'll find you. You'd have to take an indirect route and it's likely you'd get lost."

"I'm still supposed to believe it's me you're worried about." He laughed.

"Paul, listen. Lorenzo could have made it out by now. He's probably already contacted the embassy. They're likely working on getting us out right now."

"Right. Sure. Because the Zimbabwe National Army operates on just the same kind of precision as the Israelis in Entebbe, right? They're just going to sweep in here and save us all."

Jane sat back down. "You're convinced they'll just screw it up."

"Yep."

"And you were going to leave me and the boys here to take our chances." She looked up at Paul's silhouette in the doorway. Why had she nursed this man's wounds?

"Look, Jane, we all have to take care of our own. I can't have Jake slowing us down. Tommy says he's pretty sick."

"Michael and I can get him out." She started to pace around the hut.

"And if you're carrying him, you're not carrying water. Face it, Jane—it doesn't work."

"*If* you actually make it out without getting shot, then once you're gone they'll watch us even closer—we'd never get out." She rubbed the back of her neck. "Okay, so we can't wait for Jake to get better. Fine. Michael and I will get him out and carry our own water. We won't expect anything from you." She glared at him. "But we all have to leave at the same time."

Paul moved aside to allow her by. "Tomorrow night, then. If you're not ready, we're not waiting." He turned and looked straight into her eyes. "And once we've cleared this place, you're on your own."

"Got it."

⁂

Michael shifted from one foot to the other as he stood over the fire pit. How was he going to bring it up? It had been so many years. He put his hands over the boiling water. The steam felt good, so warm. The nights had grown colder and colder. He glanced over at the empty huts. Maybe there were blankets left somewhere in those rooms. He'd have to check on it in the morning.

"Michael, could you get some empty water bottles from inside?" His mother came down the stairs of Paul's hut. "I..." She glanced over at Japera, who was sitting on the picnic table in the shade. "I thought we'd fill up a few more for the night."

"We've got plenty, Mom." He took in a deep breath as she came up. "Mom, do you think we could—"

"Honey, just go get the two empty ones behind my cot and fill them." She started to lay out the ingredients for the evening meal. Sadza, as usual.

"Mom, I want to talk to you about something." It was important not to speak about this in front of Jake. He needed her alone. Japera was irrelevant, he wouldn't understand or care—but it would upset Jake. "Remember when…" Bad start. Of course she'd remember. A person doesn't forget the day she walks in on her husband and another woman. "I need to talk to you about something important."

Jane turned and faced him. "Fine, Michael, we'll talk. But will you go and get those bottles first? I need them filled before I start making the sadza with the rest of the water."

"Mom, I just put two in there, that's plenty for the night." He didn't mean to raise his voice. This was going all wrong.

"Now, Michael."

"Fine." He turned abruptly and headed toward the hut.

Chapter 30

"Temperature's really dropping." Jane walked into the hut holding two steaming bowls of sadza. She was as tired of this porridge as her sons. "Everyone's eating inside tonight."

She set her and Michael's bowls down on the backpack frame they were using as a small table in the middle of the room. Jake lay curled up on his cot. The bowl Michael had brought in an hour earlier sat next to him untouched.

"Michael!"

He put down his book. "Okay, Mom." He reached over and picked up one of the bowls, then put it right back down. "It's got to cool first anyway. How'd you carry that in?" He glanced up at her. "What?"

"I told you to wake him up and make sure he finishes the bowl. I can't do everything around here, Michael." She knew that wasn't fair, but she was tired. She let out a heavy sigh and sat down next to Jake.

"I tried, Mom. He said he wasn't hungry and wanted to sleep."

"It's not optional, he needs to eat. He doesn't have any strength. He was doing better, and now. . ."

She shook his shoulder but Jake just moved away from her.

"Jake, honey, you need to get this whole bowl down, then you can sleep through the night. Come on, wake up. It's important." She shook him again.

Jake let out a groan and looked at her through half-open lids.

Michael grabbed his spoon and stirred the sadza. "You said it'd take a week before he'd be back to normal anyway—you said he just needed to sleep it off and drink water." He watched the steam escape in swirls above the bowl.

"He has to get some energy back." She was whispering now.

She moved to the head of the cot, grabbed Jake under his arms, and pulled him into a sitting position.

"Lord, he's hot." She reached around and felt his forehead. "Michael, he's burning up again. Get me some Tylenol." She felt Jake's cheeks—hot and moist. "Here, take some water."

He let her pour water slowly between his lips, then opened his eyes all the way and took the bottle from her. He plopped the two pills Michael handed him into his mouth and took another big swig. He looked over at the sadza.

"I'll eat it all, Mom. I promise." He slid back down and curled up around the jacket he was using as a pillow. "In the morning."

"No, Jake." She pulled the jacket from him and propped it against the wall. "Sit back up and eat this now."

"Mom, why are you torturing him? Let him sleep." Michael blew on a spoonful before taking a small sample. "It's not like this stuff goes bad, it's already bad. Disgusting would be a good word for it."

"Michael, he needs his strength. We have to get out of here. You and I can't carry him and enough water to get very far."

"What? When did this get decided?" He sat straight up. "How come I'm out of the loop? Mom, I've been out there, you don't know, it's—"

"Keep your voice down, Michael."

She felt Jake again. The illness was cycling up again. There was no way he was going to be much better by tomorrow night. She looked over at their daypacks against the far wall, then back at Michael.

"How much water do you think you can carry? If I carry Jake by myself—"

"Mom, you can't carry Jake by yourself. You haven't been able to do that for two years, where've you been? We'll have to wait until his fever's down and he—"

"We can't wait." She looked at her youngest's thin, lanky body. Maybe if she hoisted him on her back, or if he were able to use the strength he had to hold on tight, they could—

"Why?" Michael said. "Nothing's changed with Japera. What's Zuka planning?"

"It's not Zuka. We need to get out before the police get here. Paul doesn't trust that—"

"Paul? This is one of Paul's plans? Mom, come on, the guy's an idiot."

"Michael."

He stared at her without blinking.

"When the police come in they'll kill Zuka and nobody will care." Better not mention what would happen to Japera. "But Zuka only gets the world's attention if we die too. So we have to get out before they get here. We can't give Zuka a chance to take us out as soon as he sees them coming."

She looked back at the packs. Maybe if she could carry the water out first, drop it somewhere far from the perimeter, then come back. She and Michael could get Jake out together much faster.

"How do you know the police are coming?"

No good. Getting out once would be enough of a long shot. Expecting to pull it off twice was crazy. She got up and looked out the bathroom window.

"Mom?"

It would be too obvious to leave from straight behind their hut. They'd need to go at a diagonal, but that would mean crossing the stream carrying Jake. The rocks would be slippery, dangerous even for somebody not carrying anything. If—

"Mom? The police?"

"Lorenzo. He must have made it to Harare by now. They'll be here any day now. We have to get out before—"

"Lorenzo hasn't gotten to the police." Michael looked down. "I found him out there."

"He's dead?" But she didn't need an answer. She knew from the way he put it. From the look on his face.

⋏

Michael walked in carrying three bowls. He brought them over to where Jane stood crushing the pills into a fine powder.

"Did Japera see you?"

"No, he's making rounds and will probably circle by in about fifteen minutes."

"It's about ready." She glanced over and saw that his bowl was half full. "Good, I want you to eat with them. And make sure Tommy doesn't eat any of Paul's."

She poured half of the white powder into a bowl, mixed it in, and handed it to Michael. "Remember, Paul's is in your right hand. Give it to him first. Maybe you should put some of yours into Tommy's bowl so you're sure he has enough and he doesn't take any of his dad's."

"Mom, I got it. Don't worry. You just take care of Zuka. This only works if they're both out."

"We can't use enough to put them out completely, it'll just make them sick and really sluggish. We have to keep some back to use later." She looked over at Jake, who seemed to be sleeping soundly.

"Too bad we can't just get more at the local drugstore."

She laughed, then stopped. More? Why hadn't she thought of it before?

Michael waited at the door. "Mom? If Zuka figures out he's being drugged—"

"I know, Michael. That's why we're doing this slowly. And having two get sick will make it more plausible." She certainly couldn't count on getting to Lorenzo's medical kit, and there was no guarantee he'd have anything useful anyway. Yet—

"Mom." He put down both bowls and sat to face her. "Things could go very bad, very fast, and I need to talk to you about something."

Jane glanced over at the two bowls. Paul's was still on the right. "What is it?"

"Mom, if you hadn't walked in on Dad that day…if you hadn't seen him. Do you think you could have gotten over it, stayed with him?"

What? They hadn't talked about this in years. She glanced out the window. She needed to make sure she took Zuka's bowl to him before he came out of his hut so he wouldn't see her bringing it from hers.

"I don't know, honey, that was a long time ago. Maybe. Possibly. People get over these things." Was this about him and Caitlin?

"So if you'd just heard about it? Maybe it would have ended or you wouldn't even know for sure?" His voice was trembling now. "Mom, I'm so sorry."

She looked at him intently, trying to read him. They'd had the usual discussions years ago about how kids often feel responsible for divorce. This was something else.

"Sorry?"

He looked down at the floor of the hut. "Mom, it's my fault you saw them, that you went home."

"You were at school, you'd forgotten your lunch."

"I went home. I saw them first—"

"No." But even as she talked, she knew he had. "You weren't allowed to leave school, that's why you called me."

"I walked home, okay? I wanted to get it myself. But when I heard them..." He got up, rubbed the sides of his cheeks. "I could've just grabbed my lunch and left." He sat down next to her "I'm so sorry."

Jane looked at the pain on her son's face. Torment was more like it. For a long time, apparently.

"Look at me, Michael. It's not as if it was the first time. And I had no fantasy that it would be the last. It was inevitable, no matter how it came down. What I saw caused me pain, but looked at from another angle, saved me pain."

"But, Mom, it was selfish. He was always so angry with me— I'm never good enough. I wanted to show him he wasn't so perfect." His eyes began to tear. "It was selfish."

"You were *eight,* Michael."

"I'd probably do it today."

She smiled. "I have no doubt that you'll eventually figure out your relationship with your dad. He's a pretty powerful guy, but so are you. And selfish? We're all selfish. We all have impulses, sometimes act on them and regret it later, maybe even learn something, but only maybe—and then struggle with forgiving ourselves." She made sure she held his eyes. "I never expected anything different from you, Michael."

He got up, collected the bowls. Without turning he stopped at the door.

"Thanks."

⅄

Jane took a deep breath and hoisted herself through the hole in the canvas. Shelly grabbed her arm and steadied her.

"What a relief to see you." Shelly hugged her, then sat back down on her cot.

Jane smiled. "How're you holding up?"

She sighed and kept her eyes fixed on Jane. "I knew it wasn't you—the shot, I heard you scream and Michael's voice—but still, it's good to see you in person."

Jane looked out the side window. "Can't see much from here."

"I raced to the window as soon as I heard them arguing, but it was just out of view."

"That must've been scary."

"The noise was deafening. I hid in the corner, afraid he might go on a rampage—like I could hide from that."

Jane continued to scan the grounds. Shelly's back window faced into the jungle but had long been overgrown by brush. Through this side window she could see the lodge, Changa carrying bags to the kitchen, and part of Japera and Thabani's porch. But Zuka's hut was totally obstructed from Shelly's view and the guest quarters were on the other side of camp. It wasn't clear what Shelly knew, but she couldn't have observed anything directly.

"At least they only killed one of their own," Shelly said.

"I'm afraid they killed our best chance."

"What do you mean? What about Japera? Jane, I'm sure you could—"

"Not a chance. His reasons for doing this are solid, and nothing's going to change that."

"You think? When Zuka killed his cousin—"

"This issue with his brother, actually a promise to his father back in Botswana, seems more important to him than anything else."

"So what's next?" Shelly picked up the rope still on her cot and started untwisting it into three separate strings of twine.

Jane watched a great flock of birds circle over the lodge roof and land in the large acacia on the other side. There were so many, they blackened the tree.

"Zuka?" Shelly started braiding the twine.

Jane shrugged. "His politics drive him, seem core to his being."

Shelly put down the braid and stared at Jane. Then she nodded. "That's probably true. So?"

Jane ran her fingers through her hair and looked out at the sky for a few seconds. She could feel Shelly's eyes on her. She shook her head and turned away from the window.

"What is it, Jane?"

"It doesn't matter. We're not getting out of here."

"What do you mean? You can't give up hope—what about the boys?"

"That's just it, Jake's not going to make it. He's getting worse and I don't have enough antibiotics, especially for all of us."

"What's he got? It's contagious?"

Jane just stared at her, unfocused.

"Oh, God, this is terrible." Shelly got up and started to pace. "But Jane, just tell Zuka what you need, he'll send Changa. He doesn't want anyone else to die, he needs us all as hostages."

"Too late. Changa was just here, he won't be back for another day or two. So even if Zuka wanted to help, even if he ordered exactly what we need and Changa was able to get it, nothing would get here for several days." She glanced out the window again. "I just stopped in to make sure you were okay. I've got to get back to Jake. His fever's rising fast."

Shelly stopped pacing. "Maybe it's just a simple virus, maybe it'll pass on its own."

Jane sighed. "You know the problem with a medical degree, Shelly? It doesn't allow you to enjoy naïve optimism. Without medication... I've got go. I'm glad you're doing better, I really am."

"Wait, I—"

"Sorry, Shelly, Jake needs me right now." She turned to go.

"Jane, I just remembered. What about Lorenzo's emergency medical bag? He's so anal, I'm sure he carries anything you need." She dug through the closet, found the waterproof bag, and took out a dozen or so bottles of medicine.

"Hurry, someone's coming," Jane said.

"I don't hear anything."

"Quick." Jane peered through the opening. "Someone's circling behind Paul's hut, they're headed this way. I've got to go now. Forget the medicine, chances are it wouldn't help. I don't have time to go through them."

Shelly threw all the bottles back into the bag. She turned her body sideways, but not fast enough that Jane didn't catch her tucking the scalpel and packet of blades in her pants pocket. Jane hadn't expected to get them, but it would have been a nice bonus.

Shelly thrust the bag into Jane's hand. "Take it—what you need could be in there. And Jane, good luck." Shelly leaned down and kissed her on the cheek. "Give Jake a hug for me."

CHAPTER 31

"You ought to ask Changa to check his sources for the food he's bringing in." It was the second night she'd stayed up to monitor Zuka's symptoms. "I'm cleaning everything with boiled water. I don't know what else I can do."

Zuka continued to take his shifts despite the vomiting, but he wasn't making the perimeter rounds as often and when he stood, he'd grab the table for a few seconds before taking any steps. He'd entered her hut twice, rummaged through their things, and nearly found the morphine. He even picked up the container with the white powder but just pushed it aside—he seemed to be looking for something larger, then moved on to Paul's hut.

Jane watched him closely. As soon as he started to perk up, she'd add small amounts of the morphine to his food, careful not to give him too much. She'd need a lot of it to use the minute Jake was stronger.

She looked at her watch. "Time for Japera's shift, you letting him sleep late?"

"I'm taking a couple extra hours." He put a hand over his mouth.

"Are you sure?" She watched him fighting the bout of nausea.

He waved her away. She picked up the large aluminum bowl she'd found in the lodge kitchen and handed it to him.

"Then you're on your own." She rose and headed for the huts. "I'm going to check on Paul, then I seriously need some sleep." As she mounted the steps to Paul's hut, she heard the last of Zuka's dinner hit the bottom of the bowl.

Jane sat on the edge of Paul's bed, counting respirations—slowed but not labored. Was his skin yellowed? Hard to tell in this light. She held his wrist and felt for a pulse. Strong and regular.

"Wake up. Time to eat." Michael came through the door bearing a large portion of sadza with tomatoes on the side.

She glanced up at him before taking the food. He nodded.

Paul sat up slowly and leaned his back against the wall.

As she started to hand him his meal, she saw his eyes. Pinpoint pupils, an unmistakable sign. She put her other hand up to her nose and sneezed into the food.

"I'm so sorry—look what I've done. Michael, get Paul another serving. Be sure to clean this out well. I can't believe I did that."

Michael stared at her. "But—"

"I said, get him a clean bowlful. He's not feeling well as it is, the last thing he needs is my germs."

Michael looked over at Paul for a moment, then nodded. "Back in a few."

Maybe it was the hepatitis. Maybe his liver wasn't breaking down the morphine and it had built up to toxic levels. Whatever the cause, he was taking this much harder than Zuka. He let out a big yawn and stretched his arms. Then he reached under his shirt and scratched violently at his belly.

"Paul, stop." She pulled up his shirt and saw scratch marks at various stages of healing. She reached into the bag at the side of his bed and pulled out a tube of Cortisone cream. "May I?"

He shrugged.

She dabbed the cool cream onto his skin and began to rub it in. "Have you considered Interferon?" She felt his stomach muscles tighten.

"No, and I don't plan to."

She squeezed out another small amount on his chest. "I hear they're getting better and better results—"

"You tried that stuff yourself, Doctor Jane?" He moved her hand off his chest. "You're not the first doc to try and push it on me. But I've talked to people in the waiting rooms who say they've felt like shit for a whole year when they felt just fine before they started taking it. Weak. Not able to work. Not able to play ball with their kid. Vomiting. Looking like they just got out of a concentration camp. No thanks."

He rubbed in the rest of the cream and pulled his shirt back down.

"Anyway, we've all got to die sometime of something—car accident, heart attack, cancer, or two-bit terrorists waving rifles in some god-forsaken place in the jungles of Africa. We'll all die sometime, Jane. I just want to get Tommy out of here." He glanced out the window. "If something happens to me, I want you to get him out. As for me, I don't really care much. This was supposed to be the trip of a lifetime for him to remember me by." Paul let out a deep sigh. "To counter everything else he'll figure out about me."

She stared at him for a few minutes. "There's no good way to get it, is there?"

"What?"

"Hepatitis. There's no good way to catch it. No way a dad wouldn't feel humiliated when his kid looks it up on the internet or hears about it in school. You'd prefer to be shot out here and let your secret die with you than have to face Tommy's questions."

"I couldn't have predicted this."

"No, you couldn't have." She got up and started to pace around the room. "You had another plan. Probably for soon after you returned."

He looked away.

"That's what I thought. But now that these cards have been dealt, you might as well play them. To die a hero for your boy. It all makes sense now."

"Jane, Tommy doesn't need to know any—"

"Of course not." She watched him slide back down onto the bed and pull the sheet over his shoulders. "You should eat all you can when Michael comes back with your food."

"Then leave a bag next to the bed."

She started to head for the door when he called out to her.

"Jane, wait."

She moved closer, his voice sounded weak.

"We need to get out as soon as possible. Let's plan on tomorrow night.

"You know, I was thinking, Paul. Zuka's getting weak, and there might be another way. If—"

"It doesn't take much strength to pull a trigger, and they're holding all the guns. If we're going to get out, we can't wait."

"What did you just say?"

"I said if we're going—"

"That's all right, I heard you."

Why hadn't she thought of it before? All the guns? She leaned against the doorjamb. Her mind was racing. That must have been what Zuka was searching for in Shelly's hut, then in theirs, not for medications—for Thabani's rifle. Where was it? If it had been in Zuka's hut, she'd have seen it. She'd searched the room several times. He never would have trusted Japera with it. Wherever he put it, it must have disappeared.

"What?"

No wonder he was taking extra shifts, staying up as much as possible.

"Jane?"

"You're right, we'll leave tomorrow night." She opened the door, then stopped and turned back to him. "You know, Paul, I have more faith in your son than you do. I think he has the capacity to be proud of a dad who's brave enough to face the darkest parts of his past and do whatever it takes to keep on being his father."

⅄

"Feeling better?" It was the first day in five that Jake had ventured out onto the porch. He sat in one of the chairs with his feet propped on a stool, reading science fiction.

"A little. Japera said I should come out and get some sunlight."

"Did he tell you anything else?" She glanced over at the young African, who now sat on the central picnic table.

"You know he's actually read this book?" Jane glanced down at the paperback in her son's hand. *Ender's Game.*

"Some coming-of-age stories transcend cultures, I guess. Third reading?" He nodded. She sat in the chair next to him and scanned the campsite. It was then that she noticed Zuka. He was slouched in the lounge chair on his porch. Asleep? She couldn't tell from this angle. She moved her chair over a few feet to get a better view. There was a bowl sitting on the floor next to him. She smiled—Michael must have given him Paul's first bowl.

Just then Michael emerged from Paul's hut with Tommy. As they descended the stairs, a soccer ball came bouncing through the air and landed at Michael's feet. Japera was on his feet ready for the pass back. It was an odd sight, rifle slung over his shoulder as he alternated between Michael and Tommy. She watched for several minutes, until Zuka sat up and looked at them.

Jane stood up. Something was wrong. Zuka wasn't following the ball, he was staring at Michael. Zuka started to stand up, faltered, then regained his balance, all without taking his eyes off Michael. The ball took an odd bounce. Michael went after it, moved away from the other two and closer to Zuka's hut. Zuka's right hand reached down to his rifle.

"Hey!" Jane yelled. She flew down the steps and stood facing Japera. "You stay away from my son." She turned toward him. "Michael, get into our hut, right now."

"But Mom, what are you—"

"Now!" She could see out of the corner of her eye that Zuka had sat back down. Michael stormed past her as she turned back to Japera.

"I'm tired of you playing up to my boys. You think I haven't noticed what you're doing? Stay away from them." Before Japera could respond, she turned and followed Michael back to her hut.

⋏

"Mom, Shelly's gone." Michael sounded out of breath.

"What?"

"Yeah, Changa dragged her out kicking and screaming. It was awful."

Jake sat up. "Maybe they're planning on separating us—taking us to different places." He grabbed Jane's arm. "Mom—"

"No, not like that," Michael said. "Changa acted like he knew her. Mom, I think she's MDC."

"Shelly?" Jake swung his legs over the side and sat on his hands. "But she was so nice, such a good rafter—you can't trust anybody. Maybe Paul's in on this too."

Michael laughed. "Unfortunately, the idiot's on our side. Anyway, Jake, not everybody in MDC is a bad guy, they actually have a point, you know. Mugabe's been destroying—"

"Michael, I need you to focus." She'd ask him about the political rhetoric later. "What was *said*?"

"I didn't really get it all."

"How did you know Changa knew her?"

"He was trying to calm her down. Trying to tell her she needed to be moved for the good of the operation, they'd keep her safe at the hideout."

"She didn't buy it?"

"How can you say the MDC isn't bad?" Jake had stood and was glaring at his big brother. "They killed Rick and Baruti."

Michael stood speechless for a minute. "Zuka fired those shots, it's not the MDC way to—"

"Apparently it is now. " He sat back down.

"Michael, what did Shelly say to Zuka?"

"It didn't make sense. She was yelling at him, something about how he wasn't listening, it was only antibiotics, she'd separated stuff."

"What'd he say?"

"He's a man of few words and didn't waste any on her. All he said was, she'd acted on her own and they don't tolerate that, and she started scratching at him. So he threw her in the back of the van and they were gone. Mom, what's in that bag? Where'd you get it?" She hadn't realized that she was staring at the bag Shelly had given her.

"It's Lorenzo's medical kit."

"Antibiotics?"

She smiled.

"Not just antibiotics?"

She nodded.

Michael did a silent victory dance around the hut.

"Michael, are you sure about what Shelly told Zuka?"

He sat back down, put his head in his hands for several minutes. He looked up and smiled. "I remember exactly. She said she checked every bottle, they were just antibiotics. Why would she lie to him?"

Jake laughed. "Why would she tell him she screwed up?"

CHAPTER 32

Odd. It seemed like there was actually less food than the last time she was in the kitchen, yet Changa had just gone to the market. It was going to be hard to throw something together. Katura looked at the clock—already late, and she was famished.

She chopped up what vegetables she could find and put them on to simmer, heavily spiced to flavor all that water. Not much of a stew, but it would thicken some while she waited. She carved out the small areas of mold on the last loaf of bread, cut thick slices, and toasted them in the oven. She sat down at the table with a cup of tea and leafed through the newspaper, or what was left of it, after Changa had separated out the best parts for himself. She wanted to eat with him, see what information she might glean from casual conversation over a meal, but as the time ticked on, she couldn't wait. Here she'd spent the morning trying to figure out how to lose this guy and now she was anxious for him to return. She paced around the small living room. Maybe he wasn't coming back at all, maybe something had happened and she'd lost her one last connection with Japera. She ate her supper, such as it was, then flopped on the couch and closed her eyes.

She had no idea how long she'd been asleep when she heard the front door unlock. She jumped up.

"Where the hell have you been?" Her nerves were shot. She was tired of playing his game. It was time to get some answers. She glanced out the window and realized it was morning. "You've been gone all night."

"Nice to know you're worried about me." He walked into the kitchen and opened the refrigerator. She followed him in.

"Look, I don't know who you really are or what you want with me, but you better start talking."

He poured himself a beer, skimmed the top off the cold stew into a bowl, and sat down at the table. He picked up the day-old newspaper that lay open in front of him.

Katura put her head in her hands and began to cry. She didn't mean to, but once it started, she couldn't stop. "I can't stand this," she finally got out. "I don't know what's happened to my brother or my cousin. I don't know why you're here, or where you go, or if you're coming back." She was wailing now. "And that's after you've been guarding me like I'm a prisoner. It doesn't make sense." She knew she was out of control but she had nothing to lose at this point.

Changa sipped the stew and read the paper. Katura escalated to yelling. "And didn't you notice that there was nothing to eat in this house? You're eating cold stew, which is terminally weird, but did you realize there's no meat in it? What if you hadn't come back? I starve to death, no problem, I'm just a prisoner?"

At that Changa set down his paper and got up unhurriedly. He reached into his front pocket, took out his keys, and walked out the door. Katura heard the click of the lock.

Great, that went really well. She wiped the tears from her face. Now she was locked in, no food, and probably no Changa. Ever. But before she could get up she heard the door again. Changa walked in carrying two bags of groceries he must have had in his van.

"I ran into your friends at the market." He began unloading food into the refrigerator. "Seems there's no game today."

"Oh? I guess I misunderstood—"

"I'm going to take a quick shower." He held up a fresh loaf of bread. "Mind making me a sandwich for the road?"

She glanced over at the lock on the door—her mind was racing.

"Katura?"

She took the bread from him. "Coming right up."

He put a bag of grain in the cupboard above the counter. "This should tide you over for a while."

She moved closer, grabbed a can of cooking oil and set it next to the grain. "Yeah, I'll be fine."

He left the kitchen. She heard him walk down the hall and shut the bathroom door.

She laid out two slices of bread, but once she heard the water running, she tiptoed down the hall. Within a minute came the familiar loud hissing of the pipes.

"Changa?"

No response. She heard the shower running.

"What kind of sandwich?" She was yelling now.

She opened the door to the bathroom very slowly—just enough to get her arm in. She felt around the floor until she could feel his pants and drag them toward her. She slipped the keys out of his pocket, holding them tightly bunched so they wouldn't make any noise. She dashed out to the van. He'd said a quick shower.

She wasn't looking for anything in particular—just something that would give her some idea of what was going on or where Japera was. She opened the driver's side of the van. Maps— maps of the surrounding area, maps of the national parks, maps of the whole of Zimbabwe. But there were no highlights, no pen marks, and no map noticeably more worn than the others. She came around the van and opened the back to see it stuffed full of bags of food. For a sick mother? Not likely.

She closed up the back and opened the passenger side of the van. No sign of a struggle, upholstery intact, trash strewn on the floor, the usual papers stuffed in the glove compartment. She felt around the sides and under the seat. She pulled out a dark blue windbreaker, nothing else. She was just about to stick the jacket back under the seat when she stopped and took a good look at it. She felt inside the right pocket and sure enough, there they were— her rubbing stones. She stared at them in disbelief. In wonder.

She looked down the empty residential street. She could run now—while Changa showered—but run where? She had no money and she couldn't follow his truck on foot to her brother, if it went to her brother, which was a big if. She turned toward the house. She could still hear the water running, the pipes squealing.

She quickly stuffed the jacket under the seat, unlocked the back of the van, and ran back into Thabani's house. She got the keys into Changa's pants just before the water turned off. When he emerged from the bathroom she stood just down the hall, her own towel flung over her shoulder.

"My turn," she said and walked past him into the bathroom. She shut the door and waited.

"Hey!" he yelled from the kitchen. "Where's my sandwich!"

She ran down the hall, fully clothed but barefoot. "I'm sorry, I didn't know what kind you wanted." She grabbed the jar of mustard out of the refrigerator. "It'll just take me a minute."

"Hurry up, it's getting late."

"I asked, yelled really loud, but you couldn't hear with those pipes—"

She dropped the jar. The glass shattered, sending shards of glass everywhere—surrounding her feet and his heavy boots.

"Sorry! I'll get the broom." She lifted her right foot and searched for a place to put it down.

"Don't move." He grabbed her under her arms and lifted her out of the kitchen, then pushed her toward the hallway leading to the bathroom. "Just take care of yourself, I'll be gone by the time you get out."

Katura turned on the water. As soon as the pipes started to screech, she grabbed her shoes and headed into the hall, locking the bathroom door behind her. She could hear glass crunch beneath Changa's boots as she rounded the corner to the front door. She shut the door softly, ran down the driveway, and climbed into the back of the van.

As she pulled the doors closed, she saw Changa on the front porch, locking the two deadbolts.

Chapter 33

"Just wait, something's bound to shift," Rick had told Michael. "When it does, you'll know."

Much too vague. How would he know?

He stood on the porch and looked out over the horizon. He knew the routine. Ten minutes after the low, distant engine noise, Changa's truck would pull up next to the main lodge and he'd be expected to empty it. When Japera was on duty, he and Changa would help. But with Zuka in charge, it was all up to Michael. The two Africans would whisper off to the side with occasional outbursts of laughter that made him self-conscious.

He glanced over at the central table and saw Zuka glaring at him, daring him to buck the system.

When it does, you'll know.

Michael kicked the dust as he walked toward the loading dock. What if he misinterpreted things? What if he thought things had shifted when it was nothing? Or missed the perfect major opportunity? With his dad it would have been different. He'd have told Michael exactly what to do, when, how. He might not always be right, but he was always sure, always confident. He'd always resented his dad for that, but right now...

Changa got out of the cab and went to Zuka. Michael un-hitched the latch to start unloading. He pulled the doors open—

And jumped back. He had to, he was in her way.

The girl from the airport darted past him so fast he doubted she even saw him and headed straight for Zuka.

"I locked her in the house!" Changa was looking at Zuka's hand on his rifle. "I had no idea."

"That's right, fool. You had no idea." Zuka's words were slurred, sweat poured down his face, but his right hand gripped his weapon. "Your only job was to get food here and keep her—"

Katura slapped him across his face.

Michael's eyes widened. *This girl's nuts.*

"These people have nothing to do with my family's troubles." She stood tall, squarely in front of him. "What right do you have to drag them into this? You're no better than the scum who're holding Tafadzwa. Wrongfully. Shamefully!"

Zuka pushed her away from him, but...nothing changed, she didn't budge. Katura was young and strong—Michael was beginning to admire her tenacity.

"My family has been afraid my brother would be tortured, maybe killed by this regime. So now you use our situation to show the world that Mugabe is right to use such force against his lawless people—people who take the innocent hostage, people who—"

"That's enough!" He shoved her harder this time and raised his rifle to his shoulder. He aimed toward the tall vegetation on the far side of Jane's hut.

Despite the glaring sun, Michael could just make out the two figures some fifty yards away.

"No!" Katura screamed out.

Paul grabbed Tommy's hand and took two more steps.

Zuka cocked the hammer. "You two stop right there."

Katura stepped in front of him. "No, Zuka, you have to stop this craziness." She backed up slowly toward Paul and Tommy.

Michael lunged, caught her arm, and pulled Katura out of the line of fire. She struggled against him but couldn't break loose.

"Katura," he whispered. "You don't get it—he's already killed Thabani and Lorenzo. You know that's not the end of it. You're nothing to him, none of us are."

"But he can't do this." She started to cry. "That's a little boy, he can't shoot at a little boy..."

He pulled her closer. Her body collapsed against him. He relaxed his hold ever so slightly, and suddenly she was gone.

"I won't let this happen." She ran across the grounds and stood in front of Tommy and Paul.

Michael turned to Zuka to find the rifle aimed squarely at his own chest. A smile spread slowly across Zuka's face. He lowered his head to take aim.

"You've been trouble from the start. Should have done this long ago."

Michael felt his heart throbbing in his throat when two shots echoed through the canyon.

⅄

Jane's eyes were squeezed shut and she fell to her knees.

"Mom." It was Michael's voice, strong and clear. "Mom!"

She opened her eyes to see Zuka's body slumped on the ground. Blood flowed from his right shoulder and chest.

Japera stood on the porch of the far hut, his head down, his rifle held loosely at his side. A wisp of smoke emerged from the muzzle.

"You did the right thing, Japera." Katura ran up the steps to join him. "They'll know how you turned this mess around. You'll make them proud again."

Japera lifted his head, but it wasn't Katura he faced. He looked up at Rick, who stood on the lodge landing. Thabani's rifle in his right hand was also still smoking. It was now aimed at Japera.

"Dad will understand, Japera. He'll forgive you."

Japera walked down the steps past his sister and laid his rifle at Rick's feet.

Katura called after him, tears wetting her face. "You have to forgive yourself."

Chapter 34

"Looking for these?" Michael held up the keys to the van. Changa had sneaked into the cab after the shots were fired and was frantically searching his pockets.

"I think you'll be riding in the back this time," Rick said. He winked at Michael, then turned to Jane. "So, when'd you figure it out?"

"I always knew. Of course, I knew." She couldn't look straight at him as she said it. Her eyes swelled with tears. "Anyway, I always hoped."

He put his arms around her and pulled her in. "You can't believe how much I dreamed of being able to do this."

Paul walked up to them, his limp barely noticeable, his eyes scanning Rick.

"Where the hell did you come from? And not a second too soon." He reached out to shake his hand, hesitated for a moment, then pulled Rick in and hugged him. "Hey, don't mind me. You save my life and I still have complaints. Ask your wife, it's who I am."

Rick laughed. "Good to see you too, Paul." He looked up at the sky. "We need to get on the road before dark. I don't want to spend one more night out here."

Paul nodded. "I'll ride in the back with Japera, Changa, and the girl."

"And kids in the middle. Jane up front with me." Rick turned back to Paul. "Are you sure? It'll be crowded in the back."

"Actually, I wanted to talk to you about that." Jane put her arm around Rick's waist and led him a few feet away from the others. "I want to leave Japera."

"Here?" Rick looked around camp. Zuka's body was still lying near the picnic table.

"If we take him back, they'll kill him."

"But…" He looked into her eyes and let out a sigh. "You're right."

"I'm afraid so."

"Japera, come over here." Rick leaned down and whispered in Jane's ear. "I love you, you know."

"I know. Me too."

Japera stood facing Rick with his hands clasped behind his back.

"Can you make it back to the river?" Rick asked.

Japera's face was a blank. "Of course."

"Cross the river into Zambia and head west. Don't stop for at least three days before you drop back down into Botswana."

Japera nodded.

Jane picked up Paul's backpack weighted heavily with water bottles. "You'll need this."

"Hey, that's—"

Jane threw Paul a look that stopped him cold. He waved his free hand at her.

"Whatever."

Japera fastened on the backpack, then turned to face his sister. Katura hugged him tight.

"Hey." He pulled her away, forced her to look straight at him. "I'll beat you home."

She smiled through her tears, then turned and headed for the van. Michael stuck his hand out to Japera.

"We'll make sure she gets back safe," he said. "If her mother's anything like mine, she's probably going nuts."

"You'd be surprised." Japera glanced at Jane. He took Michael's hand, shook it once, then pulled him in for a hug.

"And maybe I'll see you over there," Michael said.

"What?" Jane broke away from Rick. "No, we're going straight—"

"Mom, the clinic isn't far from where Katura's family is, just two villages over."

"But we're not still—"

"Of course we are, Mom. There's still work to do, and they're expecting us. We're only a few days late. We can take Katura back to her family, then go straight to the clinic. Maybe she could even help."

Jane looked up at the afternoon sky and shook her head. Michael's determination had become so solid, so familiar.

Rick turned to Japera. "Better get going. Those shots might attract some attention and you want to be long gone before anyone shows up here."

Japera nodded and turned toward the path from the river they had walked in on just ten days ago.

"And by the way, I think I'll make a stop at the embassy to see what's going on with your brother. I may only be a state senator, but decades in politics have given me some negotiating skills and a few important connections. No promises, but I can be pretty tenacious."

"Clearly," Jane said. She put her arm through his and they headed to the van.

ACKNOWLEDGEMENTS

I'd like to thank The Editorial Department for working with me tirelessly over the many years this took to come to fruition— Ross Browne for his enthusiastic support, encouragement, and ever-present optimism in a difficult trade and Renni Browne for her careful attention to detail and her extraordinary ability to dissect difficulties while pushing for solutions. In fact, without Renni Browne's wonderful book, Self-Editing for Fiction Writers, with its clear explanations and fabulous examples, which I read no fewer than five times, I could never have written this book.

The help I received from Beth Jusino was thorough, detailed, and focused—exactly what someone new to this process needs and I thank her for her patience.

And especially I thank Peter Gelfan, whose editorial skills are a wonder to behold, whom I thought quite possibly delusional in his faith in my potential, but mostly I felt honored to have him push me to be a better writer than I thought possible.

I very much appreciate the detailed editing and commentary provided by my friend and step-son, David.

Thanks also to my sons, Eric and Brett, whose early lives were templates for my characters (with lots of literary license). And importantly, they showed me a brilliance in youth that is often overlooked as they became men that I now admire.

There are not words to describe the gratitude I feel to my husband, Mark, who pored over every chapter and revision with patience, care, and devotion. Again, no words to describe my appreciation.

NOTE FROM THE AUTHOR

Dear Reader,

Thank you for investing your heart and time with me and this story. I hope very much that you have enjoyed it. Your opinion and feedback is very important, not only to me, but also to future potential readers and I encourage you to go to Amazon or Goodreads, or wherever you like to browse for books, and write a review to share your thoughts.

Are you in a book club or discussion group? Would you like to talk about Rubbing Stones with your friends and fellow readers? These characters, and the difficult decisions they must face, can lead to deep, challenging conversations. I've provided a list of discussion questions on my website, www.nancyburkey.com to help round out your meeting.

And I'd love to join you! I am available to visit book clubs, either in person or via video chat, to talk about the book and the writing process. Please use the Contact form on my website to tell me about your group.

Thank you,

Nancy Burkey

About the Author

Nancy Burkey is a practicing psychiatrist who closed her private practice in Northern California and now travels the country for several months every year providing temporary services to clinics and hospitals from coast to coast. She turned to fiction as the perfect escape from spending much of her time inside the minds of very real people, and she particularly likes the split between what people think and what they say out loud.

Rubbing Stones is her first novel, and it evolved from an adventurous trip she took to Africa with her sons in 2004.

To find out more, or to sign up for her newsletter, visit her at www.nancyburkey.com.

Made in the USA
Middletown, DE
09 June 2021

41674152R00161